RIVER OF INNOCENTS

<u>Note:</u>

If you encounter slavery or suspect its presence,
please contact the National Trafficking Hotline
as indicated on page 186.

RIVER OF INNOCENTS

by

TERRY LEE WRIGHT

RIVER OF INNOCENTS

A novel of modern-day slavery.

http://www.riverofinnocents.com

This book is a work of fiction.

But slavery is real, and very much alive today.

ISBN 978-0-9801990-0-0
ISBN-10 0-9801990-0-X

A Written Leaves publication (http://www.writtenleaves.com)

1st Edition
2008 10 09 08 07 06 05 04 03 02 01

Because it was there;

and there but for the grace of God go we.

Chapter 1

Before She Was a Slave

"All Human beings are born free and equal in dignity and
rights...

No one shall be held in slavery or servitude; slavery and
the slave trade shall be prohibited in all their forms."

–Universal Declaration of Human Rights, United Nations,
10 December 1948.

AFTER SHE PUT HIM TO BED, Majlinda walked quietly through
the little house and into the shop, where dim moonlight shone
through the glass door. She sat in an aisle with her back to an old,
ribbed washboard, and she felt tears wanting to spring into her eyes.
"But tears will not come," she told herself quietly, firmly. "I will not
let them come. He will be fine in the daylight. It's only in the night:
two nights of drinking. Two nights for her and for how hard it is,
and maybe for himself. I won't begrudge him missing her. I won't
begrudge him being poor."

When morning came he made no mention of the night before. He
haggled cheerfully with customers over home-made bread and pot-
ted plants and old, used clothes; he turned a tidy profit on boxed
soap and even sold one of the books that lived in the back corner. If
Majlinda had not known him so well, she would not have spotted the
new darkness under her father's eyes or the tiny lines aslant above
them. "They will fade," she told herself.

But that night he drank again.

"Like her," he mumbled, reaching out with one hand to touch
Majlinda's cheek. "You're like your mother. Such beautiful dark hair."

He shuddered and looked at her face carefully, pulling his hand away and waving it clumsily to either side. "It all falls apart. Like dust. Your mother and the store. Pinch it and it's gone. Can you feel it?"

Majlinda took his clammy hand and hugged him gently. "It will turn round, father." His other hand floundered at her back. "Business will turn around, you'll see. And I'm still here–I'm not dust. I'm not gone." The sickly, wet sensation of his tongue on her earlobe made her push him away. She bit her lip gently, but not fearfully; and she took his arm and led him back to his room, where she left him in his bed with a picture of his wife.

"Three nights," Majlinda told herself. "Three nights for her and for how hard it is, and maybe for himself."

During the week that followed, the nights and the days grew separate in Majlinda's mind. At night her father drank and she soothed him to bed, she refused to cry and she refused to condemn him. She never feared for herself, but she feared for him. In the day her father haggled, and she tutored or she worked in the store; the sun shone brightly and her father was sober, and she let herself believe he would stay that way.

But as the days and the nights passed, and the week turned into two weeks and into three, and then to four, and five, the darkness of the night seemed to creep slowly into the features of her father in the day, as if he bore the night like a banner of despair that even day could not cast down.

Business grew worse. Late one afternoon in July, only three people had come into the store, and one failed to buy anything. Majlinda's father left to go to the liquor store as he did several times a week; it was then that the strange young man in the smooth shirt came into the store again.

"You remember me," he said firmly, his sure eyes smiling when he saw her. "I came through two months ago–"

"–passing through, on business from Vlorë," remembered Majlinda. She returned his smile slightly. He seemed impressive, what with his pressed pants and his smooth, silk shirt. "You were wearing the same blue shirt. You bought towels from my father."

The man laughed; Majlinda blushed. "I only remember because it's a nice shirt."

"I remembered you, too," answered the broad-shouldered stranger. "That's why I came back."

Majlinda found two butterflies fluttering in her chest, and she determinedly pulled them out. Her eyes narrowed. "You came for me?"

He shook his head in an Albanian *yes*, his soft smile calling to her, sending the butterflies right back in. "I remembered you telling me how much there wasn't to do here," he explained. "I work for a recruiting agency in Vlorë with clients in Florence, Venice, and Rome."

Majlinda blinked unbelievingly, her thoughts not daring to anticipate him. One of the romances she'd read had been set in Florence, and the heroine of the novel–a prominent artist who'd been a daughter of poverty–came to her mind. It could not happen to her. She was only Majlinda.

When Majlinda didn't say anything, the stranger added, "I'm Murat."

"Majlinda," she answered, thinking Murat was never a name she would have put to this strange man, with his sure, soft smile and his fine clothes. No, his name would have been something exotic, something... more butterflies had flown into her breast, she realized, and she pulled them out again. "How can I help you?"

"We have a number of well-to-do clients–good families who pay their housekeepers well, and we're always on the lookout for young, talented, new hands for them." The smile he wore suddenly grew softer, even more earnest, and more friendly. "And if I didn't work for them, I'd still enjoy talking to the prettiest girl in town."

The butterflies came back a hundredfold. Majlinda blushed wildly, even as her eyes narrowed in the sort of delighted mock-suspicion that sometimes answers wanted praise. Softly, Majlinda asked, "What is it like?"

"Good, honest work," explained Murat. He had stepped closer to her over the course of the conversation, and now he stood right across the counter from her; she could have reached out and touched his hand, which rested on the countertop, and she was tempted to. "Nine, ten hours a day, some of it when the family is there. Enough money to send some home."

To send some home, Majlinda thought. She could help her father.

"I didn't mean that," she said. "The cities, tell me about the cities." She had seen Tirana when she was very young, and she remembered it dimly. It had seemed exciting, though not so exciting as the cities she'd read about or as some of the ones on television.

Murat kept on his earnest, easy smile, and she found her own hand had crept slowly forward to rest near the middle of the counter. The man was shaking his head gently, the way her father would when he was haggling, before he closed a particularly pleasant trade. "Beautiful," he said, "like the cool after a gentle rain in summer, and well-built. Italian cities—" he cocked his head pleasantly to one side. "The cities of Italia are like none other on earth: millennia of craftsmen built beauty to last, and it's still there. But they're young, too. Filled with accomplished men and middle-aged heiresses and strong young men and women, the sort who build futures and work every day at something—" he looked around her father's store, over the tired wooden floor and the old shelves littered with curiosities, and Majlinda felt woefully inadequate, felt like she was surrounded by darkness and dust and failure and Murat was the only bright thing in the room. "Something that's more than a store in a mountain town."

Her hand touched his now—his still near him, hers reaching across the counter—and the tingling of her fingers at the touch frightened her, that he might pull away; but he didn't. No longer smiling, he ran his eyes appraisingly over her face, and she wondered if he liked what he saw. She hoped he liked what he saw. These might be the eyes of a rescuer, she thought: of the hard, strong, independent man who swept the heroine off her feet. Majlinda was not a heroine, yet; he would make her one. She swallowed at the thought.

"You're insulting my home," she said quietly.

"No," he said, nearly as softly as she, but more firmly. "Your home is beautiful, with the mountains, and the sea, and you. But there are things more beautiful still, and more exciting: city lights and dancing, the theater and the quick pulse of opportunity. Beautiful new friends who will understand you like no one here does. Places where anyone—even a young girl from Albania—can make a good life. If she is brave enough to try."

"My father," Majlinda whispered hoarsely. She took a deep breath, summoned her resolve, and spoke more clearly: "My father would worry for me. He needs me here."

But Murat only tilted his head gently, raising his eyebrows ever-so-slightly. "You'll help him more by being there," he said with perfect assurance. "And it will be safe enough for even his approval." He rubbed his thumb along the back of her hand softly.

"He won't trust you," she said.

Murat smiled. "If you say yes, a woman will come—Odeta. She'll explain how everything works, and he will trust her."

Majlinda sucked in her lips thoughtfully, bringing to her cheeks dimples that were usually hidden. She pulled her hand from Murat's and ran it gently through her long hair, wondering if anyone could convince her father to let her go, wondering if she could really be so lucky, if this amazing thing could be happening to her. Her eyes came to rest on the old glass door at the front of the shop.

Her father would be back soon, returning from the liquor store. Tonight he would be the same as he'd been every night for the past two months. She knew that, now–she could no longer lie to herself about what would happen come nightfall, about how he would stumble into her room and say she was like her mother, say he was sorry and maybe try to nibble on her ear, or run an arm down her side. For the first time in her memory, it felt that the night had escaped into the day through more than her father's eyes, and she was surrounded by it. Murat was the only bright thing in this nightmare of a store, the only thing undimmed by her father's drinking and the now-unbearable smallness of a mountain town. Murat was offering her a way to escape the night and to save her father, and how could she say no?

She swallowed, and she answered him, "I think that I should like that very much."

Chapter 2

A Way Out

THE DAYS PASSED SLOWLY. The dry, clear Albanian summer was beautiful in a way the rest of the world might have envied, and Majlinda spent what spare time she had on the shores of the river Besim, hiding from the thought of her father. If you followed the river far enough its tiny twinkling waters would feed into the Seman, and that would run westward down to the small coastal plain and to the sea. Majlinda would think of that, sometimes, wondering what she would find when she crossed the sea to Italy.

Better men than Valdrin, she thought, with his broad shoulders and his soft kisses and his leaving town a year ago–men like the nice stranger with the smooth shirt. Valdrin was the only boy Majlinda had ever kissed, but the stranger washed her old thoughts of him away. "Murat," she would say, playing with the name loosely on her tongue.

Sometimes she would read from the few books her father sold in his store–gardening books, some of them, or Western romances. The latter were fairly new: her father had ordered one by accident a few months ago, and to his surprise it had sold quickly. The heroines were stubborn, powerful women in great cities, and the men were rich, strong heroes who inevitably fell in love with the women and took them off to exotic places for weeks on end. Majlinda didn't understand why the women would leave the cities, but she liked the men.

•   •   •

It was raining when Odeta came. She walked into the store like a flower grows amid weeds: bright and bold and meticulous. Her silver-lined pendant and small, studded earrings were elegant but not gaudy, and the light blue fabric of her shawl seemed the same. She was tall but not too tall, fair-spoken but not pretentious, and cosmopolitan, but with an unassuming smile that charmed even Majlinda's father.

Charmed him, that is, until she explained why she had come: "It's a wonderful career for a young woman," Odeta was saying, holding papers in front of her and tapping them reassuringly, when Majlinda's father realized what she meant. His eyes darted suddenly, fearfully to Majlinda. "The money is good," Odeta added, "and the work isn't too hard–it's a little repetitive at times, but the money makes up for that and she can vary her routine a bit."

Majlinda had known her father would look at her, so she was hard at work cleaning the store's shelves, seemingly oblivious to the woman who came seeking her. Slowly, the fear on her father's face was replaced: a resignation seemed to grow downwards from the worry-lines written above his eyes, a resignation mixed with suspicion and maybe– just maybe–the slightest of hopes.

"Would she be safe?" he asked Odeta.

She shook her head *yes*, her hair–longer and smoother than Majlinda's–sweeping gently behind her. "These are good families in safe neighborhoods. Sometimes there will be a maid's quarters, but more commonly the girls stay in an apartment held by our company." She smiled soothingly–it seemed Murat's friend was very good at smiling, and Majlinda felt a stab of jealousy.

"Someone looks after them?" asked Majlinda's father.

Odeta cocked her head. "We're very careful. The company keeps a chaperone in residence–I've done that job myself. It's expensive, but the girls are worth it. I've never heard of a significant problem in the apartments."

"Significant? Are there insignificant ones?"

Odeta regarded him evenly. She hesitated, then shook her head slightly. "Some," she admitted quietly. "You're a man of the world," she added, lowering her voice as if to share a confidence, "and you know girls that age can be... trouble."

Majlinda's father shook his head in agreement, and Majlinda wondered what he had to do that about. She, certainly, had always been *wonderfully* well-behaved. "Not my daughter, though," he said.

Odeta held up a hand defensively. "No, I did not say so. We're careful about whom we select for our clients: many girls would want the money, but wouldn't be industrious, wouldn't work hard to send money home. If a girl becomes a problem we send her to our apartment in Rome. In time, her contract expires and we send her home, but until then it's best to keep the troublemakers together like that–it prevents them from being a bad influence on the other girls."

He frowned worriedly. "Majlinda would not go to Rome?"

"If you'd like," said Odeta confidentially, "I could see she gets a good job in Florence or in Brindisi. It would keep her kilometers away from the Roman house, and our girls hardly ever choose to move between cities." She smiled. "The Brindisi office handles our financial arrangements–that's where your checks will be cut, and of course it provides a nice community for the girls."

"Brindisi," echoed Majlinda's father. "She will–she would–be safer in Brindisi." His eyes widened as he realized what he'd said, and they darted swiftly back to his daughter. She ran a cloth over old pewter dashboard-ornaments he had bought several years ago that still hadn't sold.

"And you'll be better off," said Odeta, tapping a line on the contract. "It pays well, for her and for you." He looked down at the black text under her blue-polished fingernails, where a number was written–enough to pay the mortgage for half a season.

"Her work is worth twice that," he answered without thought. Haggling to him was as natural as breathing, even when it was over his own daughter. "Three times, at least, or you'll beggar us both. She's"–his voice grew oddly strained, as he realized the truth of what he said–"She's all I have."

"Her work is worth much more," agreed Odeta. "This is the amount she sends home to you."

He glanced to her face to see if she was toying with him, his well-schooled eyelids moving not at all as his eyes tracked to her: she seemed serious. He fought the urge to swallow–swallowing would have shown his surprise too clearly, and it never paid to let the other side know how much you wanted something. He glanced back down to the contract and brushed aside the finger of hers that pointed to the number. "How often would she send it?" he asked with a practiced mild curiosity. Once a season would keep him from sinking into greater debt. Once a month, and that many lek would let him build his shop slowly into the best in town.

"Every other week," answered Odeta.

Majlinda's father couldn't help it: he inhaled sharply. Majlinda herself, listening quietly, imagined herself with a small fortune to spend, though she had not yet seen the number on the paper. It would not be enough, she thought, to live like the heroines did at the end of the romance novels; but it would be enough to become the heroine at the beginning. She could even send money home to her father, whose drinking would disappear with his debt.

Now, quietly, he pored over the contract, reading it carefully, looking for any loophole or detail he might be meant to miss. He knew how contracts worked: sign the wrong one and you'd regret it for the rest of your life. "A lot of money is taken from her paycheck for housing," he said dubiously. "That's not my only problem with it."

Majlinda tensed. What was he saying?

Majlinda's father looked up to study Odeta carefully. "Not many years ago," he said, "a man asked me to invest my savings in a mine, and to borrow money to invest more. The interest on the investment? Better than forty percent a year. I said no. My friend said yes. He doesn't own the gas station any more." He cocked his head thoughtfully to one side. "When numbers are so large, it's a warning. It was a pyramid scheme, like all the others. When it failed, my friend lost his gas station. No one ever found the mine."

Odeta bobbed her head sadly. "I am sorry for your friend, but this isn't a scheme. Would housing cost so much if it were? Things are more expensive in Italy. Even without the price of housing, costs in Italy are higher than costs here. That's why she'll make so much money: there's more of it there." Odeta half-turned, as if to face out the door, as if she could see over the mountains and over the plain and over the sea, out to Italy. "We're rebuilding from an economic failure a few years gone—the collapse of the pyramid schemes you remember. We haven't recovered, though we're getting better. Italy had no such failure." Odeta turned back to Majlinda's father. "That's why so many of our young people work abroad and send money home: thousands upon thousands of them. Majlinda won't be alone, and she'll be safe, just like the others. And one day, our country will be like Italy—rich—but it will still be Albania. Your daughter will be one who helps to make that possible."

Pride trickled into his breast: not pride for Albania, but pride for his daughter. "She *may*," he said reluctantly. "But if she works with you, she does it for one third again what you are offering." Majlinda's breath caught in her throat when she heard her father's demand.

Odeta's lips pursed in amusement. "No. I can give two percent above this."

"Ten."

"Four."

"Five."

"Four percent," said Odeta. "That is all I will give. There are other girls who would do it for less."

Majlinda's father smiled. "Four percent, and only if she agrees to it." His eyes, almost sharp again for the first time in months, gazed across the room to his daughter, who now watched him openly. Still speaking to Odeta, he added, "I will discuss it with her tonight. When must you know her answer?"

"I will come through in ten days," explained Odeta, "bringing the final contracts–this one is a sample–and picking up the girls who are ready to begin work. Ask her to be packed already when I arrive, if she is going." Odeta pulled a manila envelope from under the contract on the counter. "Here are instructions for what she'll need: a passport photo is the most important."

●   ●   ●

That night was the first in over a month when Majlinda's father did not drink. Instead, he scrutinized the contract as if its words were scorpions of ink, each waiting deadly and silent to strike at his daughter.

Early in the morning he came to her room and shook her awake. For a moment, she did not recognize him: he had not turned on the light, and it was a dark shape above her who told her again of the life Murat had offered her. She pulled her familiar sheets up about her, as fearful now to think of leaving as she was hopeful to think of going.

Chapter 3

Across the Sea

"Europe is for Albanians the land of aspirations, the incarnation of civilisation, power, the dream of wellbeing, the shelter in which to feel secure and protected. Yet there are contrasting images of 'Europe the faithless', Europe the inimical cause of many wrongs... Europe the immoral."

–Piro Misha, Invention of a Nationalism: Myth and Amnesia [17][1]

IT RAINED AGAIN the day Odeta returned. Wind and rain that were rare in Albania's dry summers batted at the walls of the shop as a new, blue minivan rolled quietly out of the mist and stopped near the door. Odeta emerged from it in an off-white dress, and it seemed to Majlinda, who saw her through the open door, that the rain failed to touch her. It was only when Odeta approached and entered the shop itself that the black umbrella which shaded her from the rain became visible, as she left it to dry by the door of the shop. Raindrops like tears rolled off its new nylon and onto the old wooden floor.

"I'm coming with you," said Majlinda as soon as Odeta entered. "It's decided: I'm coming with you." Majlinda smiled. "I've been packed for a week. I'm a hard worker, and I'll be good at this." She looked forward to the work, but she also wondered if she'd see Murat again: she had thought of him often in the last few weeks.

"Welcome, Odeta," said Majlinda's father politely. "Is your family well?"

---

[1]Numbers in the form [#] cite a specific entry in the bibliography at the end of the book.

"Of course," said Odeta simply. "I'm glad to see you in good health." She turned away from him to smile at Majlinda. "Can I see your passport photo?"

Majlinda shook her head *yes,* holding out the little envelope she'd been given. Inside were two identical prints of her face, their mouths unsmiling, their eyes excited and hopeful. Odeta glanced at them approvingly, then slid them into a grey folder she carried under one arm. "Excellent, Majlinda. Why don't you take your things to the car?"

Majlinda's father coughed pointedly. "I must see the contract, but first, will you join us for coffee?" It ought to have been Majlinda offering coffee, but her father had not been born Albanian; when his wife had died, he had taken over her part in the ritual, and nobody had had the heart to correct him.

Odeta shook her head. "Two girls wait in the car already, so a small cup only." She smiled brightly at Majlinda. "And then you're off to Vlorë! And to Italy after. You'll love it, Majlinda."

Majlinda's father poured three small mugs of Turkish coffee, adding a dash of cold water to help the grounds settle quickly. He pushed two of the mugs across the table: Majlinda stood nearer to Odeta than to him, and perhaps more than the contract would be, this simple drink was a symbol of the hope he gave–in trust for his daughter–to this woman, who seemed to him so earnest in her offerings.

Odeta drank courteously, professed her thanks, and pushed a contract across the table.

"Are there any changes?" he asked, quickly scanning the paper.

"Only the numbers. Four percent higher, as agreed."

He had memorized the contract over the last two weeks, pored over it diligently time and time again, considered everything its words might mean. He was convinced by now that there was no scorpion hiding in the ink to steal his daughter: the recruiting agency spoke plainly, though with the formality expected of a legal document.

"Can I sign it, father?"

Reluctantly, he shook his head *yes.* He lifted his head from the paper then, to study his daughter's eager face. She was sucking on her lower lip in the way that brought out her dimples, and he was reminded how much like her mother she looked, and he realized again that she would be leaving him. "Majlinda, are you sure you want to go? You don't have to."

She swallowed once, and then shook her head *yes*. She smiled softly at him, and his heart was moved to sorrow that she had to leave; but he knew it was better for her to go than it was for her to stay with a father who could no longer support her in a town where she had no prospects. Worse by far than that admission was his knowledge that he might drink again: in the most generous part of his fear and the darkest part of his heart, he believed that if she stayed, one night he would sin in a way that would make him no longer her father, but ever afterwards only a bottle in the shape of a man.

Odeta provided a pen–a good, round, black pen which wrote beautifully–and Majlinda signed her name carefully, elegantly, in the spot reserved for her. She wrote out her father's address so the company would know where to send his money, and she passed the contract to her father, who signed his name in consent. The procedure was repeated for a second copy, and a third that her father would keep.

After he signed the last of them, he looked one more time at the line that told of the money, and then he looked at his daughter. "You'll call home? And you'll write to me?"

Majlinda shook her head. She hugged her father, and he seemed suddenly especially familiar to her: he smelled of home, and she was safe here, in a way. A part of her wanted very much to stay with him; but by leaving him, she knew, she could save them both.

Firmly and resolutely, Majlinda pulled away from her father's embrace and smiled at him. Then she pulled on her faded blue raincoat, picked up her only suitcase, and–with Odeta–walked into the rain.

●　　　　●　　　　●

Odeta stopped three times that day to pick up more girls, and Majlinda learned their names: Miriam, from Berat; Zana, who was more tearful than excited; and Arlinda, who smiled beautifully. The two who'd been in the car already were Lule and Kaltrina: Lule was very young–fifteen or sixteen–but Kaltrina seemed nearer Majlinda's age, seventeen. Each girl had a different tale, and all had met Murat. Majlinda found herself jealous.

It's silly to be jealous, she thought.

The girls spent the night in a small, blue-painted apartment in Vlorë. They hadn't seen much of the city on the trip–it was busier than Majlinda would have thought, but aside from that all she could tell was that there were more people and fewer animals than there had been in the countryside.

The apartment didn't have enough beds and it smelled like long-damp biscuits, but it would do for one night. The girls opened its little windows to let in the warm summer breeze and stayed up late into the morning hours talking about their new lives. Lule hoped the family she worked for would have a garden. Arlinda wondered if the family she worked for would have reliable electricity. Zana cried, because she'd never been away from home.

In the morning Odeta drove them to the docks and helped them carry their bags to a one-room cruiser whose name they never learned. Murat was there, waiting, and Majlinda hardly noticed when Odeta said goodbye.

Murat showed them their new passports and led them below.

The cramped cabin was actually rather nice: there was a little bar with water and juice, and padded chairs in the middle of the room were more comfortable than the benches on either side of the hull. Small, round windows looked out onto the water of the sea.

Majlinda was the only girl who looked out one of the windows for more than a few moments. Holding a hand against the wall to steady herself, she watched the docks as the boat pulled away, and then she smiled softly and uncertainly at each wave upon the surface of the water.

Goodbye, Albania, she thought.

A hand tapped her shoulder. "The sea is very beautiful," Murat said.

She had been thinking of Albania, not of the sea; how could he not know that? Turning away from the little portside window, Majlinda saw Murat's handsome face smiling surely down at her. A blush burned quickly across her cheeks, half-pursed her lips in amusement and tricked her dimples into a smile. She glanced away from him, back towards the sea. "Yes," she agreed. "I suppose it is."

"It's dangerous, too," he said.

"It's only water," said one of the other girls–Lule, if Majlinda's ear was right. Majlinda didn't yet know their voices well, and she didn't wish to look away from the sea.

"Water that carries us away from home," said Majlinda softly.

Murat's hand, which had only tapped her shoulder before, now came softly to rest upon it. Murat himself stood behind her and, she thought, looked out at the sea. Or did he look at her? For the first time, she did not know if she wanted him to look at her. There were butterflies in her stomach for him still, but somehow, she felt the butterflies wished to fly away over the sea.

"Do not fear the sea," said Murat softly, almost whispering into her ear. "Albania will still be here when you return."

●   ●   ●

They never saw the Italian customs officials. When they reached the docks Murat went above and spoke to some men, and Majlinda couldn't quite hear, from the cabin below, what they said. She wondered why he'd asked the girls to stay down here.

"Do you think we'll have to wait long?" asked Zana.

Majlinda nodded her head. "No. He'll be back."

"Why does he like you?"

Majlinda blinked. She looked around and realized the other girls were looking at her enviously. "Do you really think he does?"

"He must. Why else would he–"

Murat appeared suddenly in the doorway to the cabin. "Come up, then. There's a van waiting for me to take you to your apartments. You're going to like them, I know, and you'll thank me for them soon enough." He disappeared as quickly, and the girls gathered their things and climbed up onto the deck. Majlinda was the first to leave the boat, stepping past its gunnels and carrying her bag low over the old wooden dock. Murat stood a few paces off, with Italy behind him! But Majlinda turned away to look out over the mid-afternoon sea. She felt a powerful urge to run to the dock's end and dive into the wild blue waters, and to swim towards Albania; but Murat was waiting for her, and she had no time to play the dolphin. Reluctantly, she turned towards him and towards the girls she'd travelled with, who'd slipped past her already.

ITALY

1999: "Parsec estimates that 1,000 to 1,500 [Italy-based prostitutes] were trafficked forcibly. In December 1997, police broke up a Milan ring that was holding auctions in which women abducted from the countries of the former Soviet Union were put on blocks, partially naked, and sold at an average price of just under $1,000."

2006: "Approximately 2,500 new victims were trafficked to and within the country in 2005, the latest year for which data was available. Eight to 10 percent were believed to be underage."

Human Rights Reports, Italy, 1999 and 2006
US Department of State [23][24]

Chapter 4

Blood Christening

"Trafficked victims of all types often are held by psychological threats to their families or to themselves and are
subjected to all manner of abuses. I heard the first-hand
story of a domestic help who was physically, emotionally,
spiritually, and sexually abused on a daily basis. After one
particularly brutal beating, she was given a spade and told
to dig her own grave. When she said that the police would
find her body, her captor told her that he would use a special liquid to dissolve her bones so that no one could tell
she'd existed. It's not what you expect when you dream of
coming to California."

–Julia Ormond, 14 June 2006
UNODC Goodwill Ambassador for the Abolition of Slavery
and Human Trafficking [18]

MAJLINDA'S EYES GLANCED RESTLESSLY through the windows
and over the parked cars lining the street. Cars here shone
more brightly than cars at home, perhaps because all seemed a few
years younger; some were even new. The roads were better, too: the
van didn't have to swerve around old potholes or drainage ruts, and
it never had to pass goats or horses. Majlinda suddenly realized she
hadn't seen any animal larger than a bird since leaving Vlorë.

She longed to explore–what little open land the van had passed
had been pretty, if not so pretty as the Albanian mountains. *Soon
enough,* she thought.

She glanced forward, to where Murat and a man she didn't know sat in the van's bucket seats. Majlinda was a little surprised, after Odeta's talk of chaperones, that no woman had been with them since Vlorë. It hardly mattered, she admitted to herself. What mattered was that she was in Italy. A little rush of excitement ran through her.

Again she turned her eyes to the side. The van was passing a black, metal-fenced courtyard with square, stone pillars marking either side of a small gate. Countless tiny white flower buds speckled a shrubbery along the fence's base, each bud bright and seeming ready to burst open at any moment. Majlinda smiled in kinship, thinking the flowers like her life: ready to explode into something new and vibrant and beautiful.

She was a little afraid.

"I can do this," she whispered.

Miriam, sitting next to her, smiled and squeezed her hand reassuringly. "We all can."

Murat stopped the van under a short tree that shaded it from the afternoon sun. He turned to look at the girls, grinning confidently. "You'll love the house. Leave your bags here; I'll get them for you after you've seen your rooms."

When Majlinda stepped out onto the sidewalk, she felt dizzy; she'd been fine in the boat and in the van, but the sudden absence of motion here was unsettling. Murat came to her side and led her quickly over a brick walkway towards a two-and-a-half story white building.

From the inside the building seemed old, and neither clean nor well-maintained. The living room held a low coffee table, a few chairs, and a couch. Light yellow curtains blocked daylight at the windows and lent an unnatural color to the air. Majlinda wrinkled her nose at the smell of cigarette smoke and at the stained white carpet.

"Upstairs is better," said Murat, still smiling. "Come along." Sparing a glance for the other girls, Majlinda followed him to the second floor, where the stairwell opened on a wide hallway. A blue-tinted window at the far end caught Majlinda's eye, but Murat spoke again: "These are your rooms. One person per door. Go ahead, it's all right." Three closed doors stood on each side of the hall, with a seventh, smaller one at the end on the right. "Majlinda, over here," he pointed. "I'll show you."

Majlinda followed him into the first room on the right, the room Murat had picked for her. *My Room,* she thought, her dizziness fading.

Windowless with off-white walls and cracked plaster, it was devoid of furniture save for a single bed–she hoped her father had not been swindled out of the money they would spend on housing.

She turned towards Murat: he stood not a meter from her, looking down at her, smiling. She felt the butterflies she'd felt before, and she swallowed lightly and uncertainly; she felt intensely aware of him, in a way that almost washed the white walls away. He was familiar, here where nothing was familiar.

"We can get my things now," Majlinda said. She should move, she thought–her eyes felt trapped by Murat's, but she should move. She began to turn–

Murat stepped forward and kissed her.

His lips probed hers softly, gently, sucking at her lower lip and then moving up slowly and methodically as his hands stroked her back. For a moment, she was still; but then she responded eagerly, caressing the young man who had chosen her over all of the others, answering the warmth of his lips with her own, lost beyond thought in the blissful, mindless joy of touch.

His kiss lingered delicately; and then, when Majlinda thought he would pull away, he forced his lips between hers as a lever forces open a hinge. Startled at the sudden incompetence, she pushed against him.

He did not fall away; rather he clove to her by the strength of his arms around her, arms which trapped her like flames might trap a cube of ice: already they had melted her, and now she cracked and crackled in their grasp. Again she pushed against him, and again he did not fall away. Joy died, and now fear and the echo of longing warred within her.

He threw her; the back of her leg caught on the bed and she fell to its mattress. Her eyes grew wide–terrified in disbelief–and she started to stand, but Murat's hand slammed into the side of her face.

Still not crying, still thinking that somehow Murat had made a mistake, that it was all an accident, Majlinda turned her head back to look at him–this time without trying to rise from the bed–and found his hands pulling open the buckle of his belt, and the same easy, confident grin on his face he'd worn when she'd first met him. Now a corner of his lip was curled in lust.

A bitter taste came to her mouth, a fear which still she wanted to deny. His cleanliness did not seem any less; his short, perfect hair mocked her with its almost saintly air.

"Stop, Murat," she said, struggling to keep the quiver from her voice. Had she done something wrong? *I shouldn't have let him kiss me.*

He pursed his smiling lips slightly and shook his head, while his hands did something she did not watch. Her eyes darted past him, to the door. Could she make it to the door? She looked up to Murat's face. *Probably not.* Could Odeta help? No, she hadn't seen Odeta since Vlorë. She was alone. Majlinda shuddered.

If she had to–if she really had to–it might not be so bad, she thought; it was never bad in the stories. She swallowed, her eyes darting down to where his trousers–the finely pressed trousers that had impressed her in her little mountain village–had been. Then she looked up to the leer of his face again. "If I do," she asked, her lips quivering, "will you see I work in a good home? The best home?"

A raucous laugh escaped his throat, and in fear she rolled to one side, off the bed. The white floor rushed upwards. She caught it and Murat's hands closed on her shoulder and her skirt even as she tried to scramble away. He threw her to the bed again, but held her skirt and pulled it off in the throw; and down he came, and now he was on top of her. The warm flesh of his cheek pressed against hers, and he whispered in her ear, "*You are home.*"

Majlinda bit at his ear and tried to kick. He slapped her and held her down, and then, with a smooth, practiced way, moving close above her wearing only the blue silk shirt she'd liked so much, the blue silk shirt that would haunt her while she lived, he pierced her.

She cried out: a plaintive cry of rage and disbelief. Through the walls, it seemed she heard an echo of her cry, and then another and another. She whipped her arms and flailed her body; but she could not flail away from her confinement, or from what her body, betraying her, confined. She felt a pressure close around her neck, pushing against her throat and up into her jaw: Murat's fingers, his clean hands choking against her flesh.

Her cry became a whimper, and she was lost.

Sensation chewed at her and her eyes seized on the ceiling, on the cracks in the old plaster and the joint where it met the wall, on its off-white and shadow and on the cheap, bright plastic of the light fixture. Nothing was real, but these whites and light shadows were all she would see. Murat moved inside her; she wailed again, and his hand tightened on her throat. Her whimpering had a terrible, mottled rhythm to it, a dull thing where an edge would chime and fade and break.

Time stretched on.

Years or minutes later, when new sensation finally stopped and the hand pulled from her throat and the warm body above her withdrew, the sore echo of betrayal and violation racked at her insides. Majlinda half-curled to the side, her mouth fallen open and her eyes glazed; tears crept in them, though worse by far was the torpid dullness of her face, which sat as if a wave had crept upwards over her body and torn her will away. Somewhere both remote and immediate to that dullness, her mind grasped at meaning.

Hands grabbed her legs and twisted to face her up. She kicked but could not get free. The man standing over her wore no silk shirt, but a rough, grey cotton; above it, the curves of his face were chiseled Italian. For a moment Majlinda did not understand: she thought this was Murat, that this had always been Murat, that somehow he had changed in the moment before, when everything around her and inside her had changed. Then the veil of ignorance fell from her eyes; she moaned, a soft, mournful moan that ought to have cracked the little world to pieces all around her and summoned help from far beyond the earth.

But no angel flew to her. No reader came through the ink of the page of the world to save her. Again her whimpering took on its terrible, breaking rhythm, to chime and fade, and to catch at sobs, and then to churn once more. The hands pushed at her throat, pulled roughly at her hair, forced down her shoulders and ran along her arms, and raked towards her bosom. Her blouse bunched under his fingers as they traced over her breast.

In a renewed panic Majlinda pulled her arms tightly over her chest, slipping them in between his hands and her blouse; he barked a laugh and continued his riding within her. What did her breasts matter, next to that? Majlinda moaned. What did any of it matter? She held her arms clenched over her chest, until he caught them both in one massive hand and forced them aside. He tore the blouse open. Just one more tear, just one more tear like the tear of his every motion.

She tried to beat at him, but he had her pinned too well, and he pushed at her throat again, and he made it more painful as she fought him. Hours passed in seconds, every pain and thrust and slap was a new insult and a new shame, but worse than and melded with the shame, she could *feel* every touch.

After a time the man stopped. She thought she cried, then. Her eyes closed, but she could not keep them closed, could not close them against the naked physicality of truth. She tried, but she felt the bed depress under her; her eyes fluttered open, and a new face, a hard but leering face, was above her.

Majlinda could never remember, afterwards, how many men came to her that day. At first each face and every motion was a terror, and would bring with it a slight rise to her cries, an edge to her whimpers; but then the edges would fade, and the whimpers would retreat, though even in her numbness she could never escape. She remembered, in moments, who she was: those moments were the most difficult, when she cried out or tried desperately to hold on to some fragment of her life–Valdrin, or the river Besim, or her father, or his store. No fragment could save her, and it was in these dim glimpses of consciousness that she most felt the men–the beasts above her, and recognized the few cries that still made it through the walls as what they were: the fading whimpers of the other girls. Majlinda had no heart left to mourn for them.

Sometime in the night, she was left alone. When no new man came, she waited limp and numb; and when still no man came, she turned and lay on her side. The painful echoes of the interminable night ran through her body, as if she'd been working a long day, but more: bruises joined her exhaustion, and pain in places she had not known. She moaned as she had not moaned in hours. She had no more tears to give the moaning, but she thought of her father, of what he would say and how he would look at her.

Soon the pain called her back from her half-lucid thoughts–the pain and the dryness of her throat. She reached up and wiped at what ought to have been tears; but her face was as parched as her throat, and her own touch frightened her.

•   •   •

Murat closed his trousers over the smooth, blue tails of his shirt. He didn't think Majlinda aware of him: she lay on her side on the bed, and the dimples he'd liked so much seemed emptier now, and dry. Her eyes were half-open, and for a fleeting moment he wondered what she'd thought of him. She would thank him before the end, he knew: they always did. He turned from her and left the room.

Two men–Armand and Peppino–sat quietly in chairs at either end of the hall. Armand smoked an unfiltered cigarette in front of the small, blue-tinted window; a scattering of blue sunlight grasped at his neck. Peppino scanned the day's newspaper, probably looking at the movie reviews.

Murat slipped past Peppino and headed downstairs. A small crowd was laughing and joking in the living room at the bottom, sitting in ancient, stained brown chairs and on a matching couch, gambling over a worn coffee table. Murat scowled at the chairs as he passed them; he could not abide filth.

In the kitchen, he sprinkled cool water on his face and wiped it away with a soft white handkerchief which absorbed not only the sprinkled, chill tap water, but also the salted grime of his recent exertion, the tears and sweat that had been stolen from the girls upstairs.

He half filled a short, wide glass with water and returned to the living room, where the men had opened cheap wine and started a new game of cards. They beckoned to him, but Murat walked silently to the front windows, slipping past their closed curtains. His gaze wandered over the street of densely packed off-white houses, their terra cotta roofs sloping downward over straight concrete walls. The eaves and window-works were slightly different on each building, being little expressions of individuality imparted by craftsmen of another age.

"How much more?" asked Roberto. Murat turned his eyes to meet those of the short Italian who had approached him. It was Roberto's first time working a first night, a *prima notte*. His eyes were wide in eagerness, Murat thought, but with a tinge of fear.

"Perhaps ten days," Murat explained. He took a sip from his glass. "Repeat it all three times a day for two days and then four for three, and down to two for a while. Never predictably–at different times each day, so they never feel in control. Then only once a day while we let any wounds heal. It is better if they are unblemished when it begins."

Roberto nodded. Behind his back, the others were putting vodka in his wine. Murat noticed and nodded slightly. Roberto would be welcomed to the group, and more so if he lost some money at their card game.

Murat continued, "The time alone, locked up, helps–it lets them think about us. Once or maybe twice a day, we let them use a bathroom and give them food. Only with permission, and only as reward for doing what we say. Every few days a shower without soap. They'll want to be clean, but they have to understand that they're not. They'll never be. So we take them in the shower, too."

"The first one," said Roberto, "Kaltrina was her name–she was new." He licked his lips. "Would she have brought us more money new?"

Murat nodded. "More money, but harder to control. If the girls are younger, sometimes we sell them unbroken." He frowned; he ought not to be so loose-lipped. Murat nodded towards the others. "You did good work tonight, and more will follow. Go back to the game, though."

Roberto squinted slightly, as if he thought to say something else; but then he nodded and turned away. Murat followed him back to the table, put his glass down amid the open wine bottles, and touched one of the men there–Fitim–on the shoulder. Fitim rose and followed him silently out the front door.

The colored eaves of dim white houses leered at them disapprovingly as they walked over the brick walkway to the curb, where their old white van was waiting. Murat walked around the hood to the driver's side, suddenly stopping when he saw the door handle. A hint of rust above it made him curse lightly in Albanian–it was always important to check for rust on used cars bought near the sea, and someone had failed here. The van had cost little, but the imperfection bothered Murat, as if he himself were somehow tied to the tiny, particulate orange that chewed outward from the handle of the door.

Murat glanced through the windows to the girls' luggage, thinking. He still needed to get rid of the luggage, and to pull batteries from and throw out any cell-phones the girls had owned. Tonight he would tell those at the Factory how many girls he'd brought. Madame Vaccaro, too, would like to know a new crop was in. Uncle Angelo might be interested, but Angelo preferred younger girls than this lot–twelve and thirteen-year-olds brought the best money from him; Murat would try to get some from Egypt next month.

•   •   •

The sound of footsteps, followed by a harsh cry, brought Majlinda's eyes up from her just-fastened skirt. She'd folded her blouse together where it had been torn, too, and tried to collect herself. But now the wailing from the corridor–a wailing followed by a sudden near-silence and a chortle–filled her with renewed dread, and the echo of Murat's hands and his skin and his sweat seemed to sweep over her body in a shudder. For a moment, she cringed away from the door and shrank against the wall.

But then she swallowed. They would never accept her at home again, she thought. The town would condemn her, and her father would look at her with shame for what she had become, and with an anger he would try to deny and she would not be able to bear. She had nowhere to go, but that did not mean she had nowhere to run from.

She moved away from the wall, slowly stepping towards the doorway. Movement past the edge of the door frame made her stop; she did not want them to see her. A black pit formed in her stomach–a stomach she had thought already numb–on seeing the sickening tableaux before her, the forceful, jerking motion of the man in the middle of the hallway. One of the other girls–the ones she had heard cry out, the ones she had travelled with–lay under him. His back was to Majlinda.

The pain in her stomach cycled, waxing and waning with the sloppy rape before her. In a burst of rage, Majlinda ran into the hall and jumped onto Peppino's back, reaching around his neck and digging her fingers into his throat. He bucked up under her. A hand yanked at Majlinda's hair from behind: she hadn't seen Armand. Desperately, she held onto the throat before her.

Armand reached under her chest and threw her across the hall. The corner of the door frame jammed into her back, and she cried out. The cry faded to a whimper as a hand closed tightly around her neck–a single, large hand that held her as easily as she might hold a doll. Majlinda tried to pull her head away, but the hand only tightened; its owner–Armand, with the rank scent of cigarette smoke lying about him like a cloud of oil–exchanged a glance with Peppino, who had stood as soon as Majlinda's hands had left his throat.

Lule–the girl Majlinda had saved too late from Peppino–did not move from the floor, but lay as if dead. Almost Majlinda cried for help, but who would come? There was no help here: there was only the hand around her throat. Armand moved his face nearer hers, and to her horror she did not pull away, but only turned her head; if she'd pulled away, the hand at her throat would have tightened, and already she could barely breathe: pin-pricks radiated upwards from her neck, up along her jaw and onto her lips, and breath leaked wheezing from her throat. Armand's other hand brushed back her hair, and his tongue slathered across her cheek. Instinctively she jerked away and cried out; but the hand tightened.

"Tsk, tsk," said Armand, lowering his head beside hers. The hard line of his teeth nipped at her neck.

Out of the corner of her eye, Majlinda saw Peppino pull Lule to her feet, saw him take her dishevelled clothes from her, and push her, naked, back through one of the doors on the side of the hall.

Chapter 5

A Cage of Need

THE FIRST NIGHT, they took Majlinda's clothes away. She did not know how long it was until they gave her new ones: time did not exist in the white building on the white street where they took her virginity from her. Time belonged in that house no more than did hope, rage, or desperation.

Time, hope, rage, and desperation had all belonged to Majlinda even after her body had been stolen from her, but it seemed hundreds or thousands of thieves came to her and took them all away piece by lonely piece. In the aftermath of each violation, of each taste or scent or touch, and of them all together–in the aftermath of each sensation she could not close her eyes against–she became a numbness; and some small part of her remained in each numbness, and could neither return from it nor retreat to someplace deeper within her soul; and she was lost.

It would have been more poetic if numbness had been all that she felt, if the malignant abuse of what ought to have been beautiful had brought only darkness that might somehow have cried out to the masses about what might and should have been: about a world where Murat and his men had never learned to rape, or to break or to bend what was beautiful, or where their crimes would not have been allowed. But Majlinda's life was not a poem. A human girl lay upon the sheets, and she learned, terribly, to adapt.

Majlinda learned from Armand, first–learned his hand could close, and she could not breathe if it did, and not to turn her head too far. She learned from Murat that he would slap her if she touched his shirt.

She learned from Roberto that he liked it when she fought him; he said they all did, but he seemed embarrassed to admit it, and for a moment she felt pity for him. Uncle Angelo and Dirty Gian came once, with three strangers, and they together taught her that she would be not just for Murat and his men, but would be for whomever they said.

Somewhere in the middle of it all, she stopped struggling. In the interminable string of violations, she could not remember when it was, and she did not care. It was gone. It was gone like the life she'd had before, and now her life had this in store. She might remember that there was a world outside this room and beyond the always-guarded corridor; but that world was around the corner, and out of the house, and far away—how could it possibly be real?

One time, as Murat was re-buckling his belt, he told her, "Rise."

With a wince, Majlinda stood. He hadn't hit her this time—no one had hit her in a long while now—and she wondered if he wanted her to stand only so he could knock her down again.

"Get your clothes on. We're going."

She blinked. "Going?" The thought was strange to her. She walked to the side of the bed and bent down to pick up her clothes from the floor—a tight-fitting black t-shirt and short cotton skirt, also black. They weren't really her clothes—the clothes belonged to the men, who switched them every so often for others of the same make and color.

Dimly, Majlinda knew that if Murat had told her to rise a week ago, she would have asked him a question. Its shadow tripped into her mind, and she asked, "Where are we going?"

His hand slid over her naked hip, and she had no reaction—it was only touch. "Where I say, Majlinda." He remembered her name. She shuddered slightly at the sound of it, for she hadn't heard it in what seemed like forever. Almost she had forgotten it. She lowered her shirt over her head.

Murat pulled his hand like a fearful adder away from the descending blackness. "We have your papers," he added. "Without your passport and without a job, you'd be arrested. They are not nice to whores in jail."

Majlinda wasn't sure if she believed him, but his words didn't matter—the men would never let her escape, she thought. She pulled her skirt on and then stretched slightly to work the soreness from her muscles. "I'm ready," she said to Murat. Her eyes did not meet his—

she had been swept away by his eyes once, she remembered dimly, and now she could not meet them.

"Ready for what?"

"Ready to go."

"To go where?" There was an edge in his voice, an edge Majlinda now recognized as the timbre of a man who sought control, who needed to feel he'd fought and won, and who needed to hear submission.

"To go where you want me to go."

He took her hand–an oddly intimate gesture, for him–and led her into the hall. Roberto was there, bent over and scratching at an insect bite on his leg. Peppino came out of a door on the left, and his arm was wrapped gently around Miriam's torso. Miriam was dressed in the same black t-shirt and black cotton skirt that had become the norm for Majlinda, and she walked unsteadily, as if just now remembering how to put one foot before the other.

Seeing the other girl, Majlinda realized that neither Miriam nor she wore shoes; would they get sandals before they left the house? Were they leaving the house, or only going downstairs? Would the men be waiting in the living room to teach her another lesson? The thought held neither fear nor revulsion for her, but only brute possibility.

Murat led her down the stairs and through the living room. Nobody was waiting there to rape her. The narrow front door stood open, and after Majlinda passed through it her bare feet burned on the brick walkway. Sunlight–the first natural light she'd seen in days–played down over her arms. She thought the arms looked lighter than they'd been, but she found she couldn't quite remember what they'd been like before. She wondered, if she found a mirror, what she'd see in it; the thought frightened her more than Murat's arm on hers.

Armand was waiting at the end of the walk, standing by the rear door of a featureless grey van. He opened the door for her, and Murat pushed her in.

Zana and Arlinda were already there, sitting on the floor in opposite corners of a wire cage that filled the back of the van. A soft hand–a girl's hand–landed on Majlinda's back, and she stepped further into the cage and turned to see Miriam had joined them. The taller girl kept her eyes on the cage floor, and lowered herself to sit in its third corner, alone.

Armand latched the cage shut with a *click* and closed the back door.

Majlinda, still standing, looked at Miriam dimly. An idea–a real idea, rather than a reaction to a man or a moment–was making its way into Majlinda's consciousness, but she couldn't quite bring the idea into focus. She knew they had no home–that wasn't the idea, but it was a thread of the idea: none of the girls had a home any longer. They had nowhere to go. The entire world had been stolen from them. Everyone would condemn them and no one would understand them, and they were utterly alone.

Majlinda squinted, catching hold of the idea that nagged at her: they were alone in the world, but they were not alone *here*.

She looked around thoughtfully. The other three girls sat in the corners of a cage, separated from the world by the cage and the men outside and what they had become, but separated from each other only by shame and fear. There was no need for that here.

Majlinda lowered herself gently onto the floor between Miriam and Zana. She reached out with both hands, her fingers just touching the girls' shoulders. "Come here. Miriam, Zana, come here. I'm here. We're all here. It's all right." It would never be all right again, she thought. But if no one else would ever understand these girls and what they'd been through, at least they could understand each other.

They didn't say anything. Miriam didn't even look at her–she was too ashamed of what they were, of what they had become. Zana did look at her, but Zana's eyes were bereft of emotion, were as empty as a hollow stone. Majlinda's touch was soft on their shoulders: it asked them to come to her, but did not demand.

After a moment, both girls shuffled slightly closer, and they leaned against Majlinda. She reached her arms around them gently–gently, but not confiningly. That was important, she knew–it would have been important for her. Already she felt confined, with a girl leaning against each of her sides. Yet the warmth of their touch, and their genuine–no matter how remote–need for understanding, these things touched Majlinda in an honest way that no touch of Murat's could ever have done.

It wasn't much, she thought–these girls whom she could not help, save to keep them from being alone–but it was all she had.

The girls didn't cry, though a sorrow inscribed wrinkles around Miriam's eyes, hinting at mourning. Arlinda still sat in one of the corners on the other side of the cage, buried somewhere in the shell of her body.

"Arlinda," called Majlinda quietly. "That's your name. Nobody's taken that from you. Arlinda, come here. We know you. You don't have to hide from us. You never have to hide from us." The words rung hollow in Majlinda's ears, even though she knew them to be true: any words might ring hollow to her now, but these felt especially hollow because she knew they ought not to be.

Arlinda came. She sat beside Zana and reached an arm–gingerly–around them.

It was strange, Majlinda thought: Majlinda had never hugged much, and now she hugged not for herself, but because she thought these girls might need her, hollow words and all. "It's all right," she whispered again.

Light flooded in as the rear door to the van opened. The red end of Armand's cigarette glowed at the boundary between the sunlight and the darkness. He took it from his mouth and tapped it, letting ash fall to the road as he studied the huddled girls. For a reason he did not understand, he was filled suddenly–not with shame–but with fear. A brief shudder went through him. He tapped his cigarette again, and with its falling ash shook off his fear.

He unlatched the cage to let Kaltrina and Lule enter, and then closed and locked it behind them. He slammed the van door shut. A flake of rust on the metal handle caught his attention. Groaning, he glanced over to Peppino, who stood quietly next to him.

"He doesn't need to know," suggested Peppino. He opened a pocketknife and scraped a few specks of the rust away, until it was almost invisible amid the good paint around it.

Armand nodded silently. He locked the rear door–he didn't really need to, what with the locked cage within, but you were always careful with new girls. He and Peppino walked to the front of the van and slipped inside. Murat would follow after–he rarely travelled with the girls once they knew what they were.

In the rear-view mirror, Armand saw the six girls huddled together on one side in the back. He frowned–he'd never seen a new group together like that, and it bothered him. The first ride in the van, for them, was always a solitary one, no matter how many might be on board. New girls usually wouldn't even look at each other.

Armand dropped his cigarette in the ashtray and started the van. The air conditioning began streaming in through the vents, fighting off the warmth of the midday sun. He slipped the shift into gear and began the drive to the Factory.

•   •   •

Majlinda was the first to leave the van–she had to be, she thought, after what had happened inside. Barefoot she walked over the grey cement floor, and barefoot the girls–her girls–followed her. She looked around slowly and cautiously. Armand, Peppino, and Murat were the only men she knew here, though a dozen others lounged in chairs or stood about the huge room. Two, she saw, wore guns in holsters under their arms; but her eyes slipped from them and darted back to the men she knew.

Murat sat down beside a large Italian man, behind a long, wood-veneered table. Opposite the table, across a large, open floor, lay a few dozen old white mattresses, each perpendicular to the wall and against it, and each with perhaps a meter of space on either side.

Fifty or sixty girls were scattered about the mattresses, sleeping or sitting or standing, some whispering quietly to one another. Most watched the newcomers with a sort of easy disinterest. All were dressed in the same black and black that Majlinda had been forced to wear, that the girls with her had all been forced to wear, since being touched by the vileness of Murat and his men. Some girls wore bright earrings, but these gauded girls seemed somehow uglier than those bedecked only in honest, unadorned blackness.

"You are in debt."

Majlinda blinked.

"You are in debt," Murat said again, peering at them over the table. "We brought you here from Albania at great cost to us. We provide housing, food, and clothing, and all of them are expensive here. You can earn your way out of debt. The lives you came to find–they still exist, but you have to earn them. It takes time, it takes effort, and it takes hard work, but it's possible." There was a frankness to his voice–it was not the easy, promising voice he had used in Majlinda's village, nor the domineering, lecherous voice he had used in the bedroom, but was coarse in a way that almost Majlinda believed. She wanted very much to believe–it had been so long, it seemed, since she had believed in anything.

"But you have little of value to us," continued Murat. "And no way to earn back what you owe, save one. Gians will arrive. We count how many you serve and what they pay, and we count it against your expenses, and towards the debt you owe. Do well, and maybe we'll arrange a better job for you." Murat frowned. "If you run away," he said skeptically, as if no one could be foolish enough to try, "the authorities will arrest you for whoring. That's if you could run away, and you can't–the doors are locked and guarded." He frowned. "If you try to run, your families and your neighbors will be told what you've become. They won't want to hear that.

Murat held up the six Albanian passports that belonged to the girls; a quiver went through Majlinda at the sight of them, one symbol of hope in this place that seemed devoid of it. "Your passports will be in care of Diovanni, here." He nodded to the tall man sitting beside him. "He runs the Factory, but your debt is to me. Listen to him as you would me, for he is not as... tolerant... of your missteps as I have been." A chill went down Majlinda's back.

Her girls, she thought: they had become her girls in the van, and she had, somehow, to take care of them. She barely had enough energy in her to care–but that absence of caring bothered her slightly, despite all that had been done to stamp out her spirit. She couldn't do much, but maybe she could do a little, for them. Show submission, she thought, and make them seem submissive. They were, in truth, but the more compliant they were, the easier it would be, for a little while. Tomorrow... tomorrow was tomorrow.

"Parlate Italiano?" asked Diovanni. His voice was thick and heavy, like the bristles of an old wire brush scratching at plastic. "Rispondami."

Majlinda shook her head *yes.* "Sì." Italian was a common second language in her part of Albania because so much of the television programming came from Italy. Two of the other girls echoed her *Sì,* and three frowned in confusion.

"And English? Do you speak English?"

Majlinda winced at the sound of the harsher language on his already rough tongue. An unharmonized chorus of "yes" came from the girls, and then silence.

"If you work hard," continued Diovanni, "you will be rewarded and one day might leave. If you work poorly, then you will only hurt yourself: you will be given to the worst of the Gians, to those with a taste for beatings and knives and bruises." He stood, and the six feet or more of his bulk seemed to extend forever above the table, even though in such a large room he ought to have seemed very small.

His dark blue clothes–a button-down collared shirt and slacks–seemed somehow darker to Majlinda than did the black she wore.

Diovanni clasped his hands together behind his back and walked round the table casually to stop in front of Majlinda. *Submissive*, she thought, and she glued her eyes to the floor.

"You do not want to get diseases," Diovanni said.

She hadn't thought of diseases in some time–she'd worried briefly about them during a few of her lucid moments in the white room, but what little she knew of them hadn't seemed real or important in the face of what was happening to her.

"And you do not want to get pregnant," added Diovanni. "There are some Gians who like it, but they are sick, perverted men. You do not wish to know the fate of a pregnant whore." Majlinda felt as if her belly were being squeezed–to be pregnant by men like these might be worse than death. What child could come from here? He could not be born here, hidden from the sun within these walls, and hidden from hope within this life.

Diovanni must have approved of the sickly cast to her downturned face, for he moved on, to stand in front of Miriam. "If a man comes to you without a condom," he added, "you tell us. But if he brings one, he has bought it from us, and you *will* do whatever he wants."

He stepped past Miriam to study Lule. She was the shortest of the lot, and Diovanni towered over her in a way that would have been comical had it not been deadly. "If you fight when a Gian wants you to be soft, nothing you have done that night will count towards your debt, and you'll have to service two of my men. *And*," he added harshly, "if you fight *them*, you will have to service *me*. And you will not like that." His hand shot up suddenly to hold Lule's arm; she did not flinch–she had lived through too much too recently for her to flinch at his vice-like grip. Diovanni's other hand he raised to her jaw, where his fingers dug into her flesh and impressed her cheek into the side of her teeth.

Diovanni pushed Lule suddenly; she slammed to the floor. Majlinda almost moved to help her, but she realized that if she helped Lule now, Diovanni would only hurt them both. She half-swallowed, not letting the swallow sound for fear of attracting attention. Diovanni moved on to stand before Arlinda. "You satisfy lust. You do not fight. You allow anything we want. You allow and you embrace. Do you understand?" he asked.

"Yes," said Arlinda weakly.

"*All* of you," said Diovanni gruffly. "Do you understand?"

"Yes," came the meek chorus, even from Lule on the floor. "Sì," answered Majlinda. Her mind was still caught in the Italian he had spoken briefly–perhaps because the language seemed so unsuited to his temperament, being softer and more lyrical than the unkempt sounds of Diovanni's English.

Uncertainly and slowly, Lule rose from the floor; Diovanni ignored her. "Work hard," he said to Arlinda. "If you work hard, you will be well-treated." He ran the back of two fingers gently over Arlinda's cheek, and smiled. It was not like Murat's smiles–neither the smile of a man who needs to dominate, nor the charming smile Murat had given Majlinda in her father's shop–but was just the plain, coarse smile of practicality. Here was a man who bore his property no particular ill will, but who was as ruthless as his business demanded he be.

He turned away from them and walked back to the table. "Go," he said dismissively as he walked. "Go join the others–the ones by the wall."

Majlinda stood in silence for a moment; then she turned and walked towards the wall, tapping Lule and Arlinda gently on the shoulder as she passed them. They fell into step behind her, and the others into step behind them, shuffling barefoot across the cement floor with their bowed necks and their black skirts.

Chapter 6

Bukura E Dheut

"I believe one of the finest documents in existence is the UN Declaration on Human Rights, and modern day slavery is one of the most egregious violations of that document; that we all agree on. Trafficking is a form of modern-day slavery; a violation that globalization has ripped open and flung to every corner of our planet. This is not a new phenomenon. It is the surviving and thriving mutation of one of the oldest issues in the world, one we have never conquered; but humanity has now surely reached the point where we are far better placed to do so."

–Julia Ormond
UNODC Goodwill Ambassador [18]

"Only in one sense have the Albanians been rich. Their traditional folk culture, which evolved over the centuries in relative isolation, offers a surprising wealth of elements. Yet this culture, without a knowledge of which the Balkans cannot be fathomed at all, remains little known to the Western world, even among ethnographers and anthropologists specialising in the Balkans."

–Dr. Robert Elsie
A Dictionary of Albanian Religion, Mythology, and Folk Culture [3]

THEY WERE PROFESSIONALS. They were accountants and carpenters and lawyers and schoolteachers. They came in jeans and in suits, in slacks and in shorts, some with hairy backs and some shaven all over their body, some thin and some fat, some old and some young. They came alone, and they came with friends. They spoke English or Italian, or languages from upcontinent–but never Albanian.

A young man with smooth legs was uncertain. A dark-faced man with a wide mustache was vicious, and the mustache smelled of olive oil. A man with callouses on his hands made Majlinda bite into them, and from the taste he'd been working with dirt. A blond German kept talking and talking and talking, and Majlinda preferred his talk to the talk she could understand: 'whore' and 'slut' and worse had little effect on her any longer, no more than did the narratives some men gave or the harsh sensation of their slipping bodies or their grunting; but hearing the language she did not know, she could pretend he was reading her a story or talking about the weather or speaking words of any thing that was not here.

The men were short or tall, pimply or clean, sometimes well-spoken but more often crude–but it was a licentious crudeness, the sort that spewed from their mouths because here there was no rule save their rule. They came with their condom–their ticket to a body they could buy and a girl they let themselves believe desired them to buy her–and they became the demon in the night that society could not let them be in the day.

The Gians came. And they came again, and new ones came. And when they were done, they would leave and return to where they could not be so crude, to their jobs and wives and children. Some bore a secret shame, but more knew the rationalization of the criminal, and deceived themselves to believe the scripting of the popular underworld to which they had descended. The descent of the Gians was more transitory than that of the whores: the Gians chose this underworld for a night or for a habit, while Majlinda and the whores who were her friends–or as near to friends as she thought she'd ever have again–had been forced to live here.

Here they had nothing. There was not even the most rudimentary of privacies: there was a room with a few sinks and toilets and some lipstick and hairbrushes, so they could clean themselves between one Gian and the next; but there were not even stalls around the toilets. It was a walk-through bathroom, one that connected the Factory Floor to the blue lounge where girls would meet their Gians.

From the lounge, the girls would go with Gians into corridors lined by little bedrooms. The bedrooms reminded Majlinda very much of the white room in which she had first been raped, and at first each trip into them seemed like a trip into hell; but before long she grew accustomed to the journey, even as she'd become accustomed already to things far worse.

When the hour grew late enough and almost towards morning, the number of Gians coming would slow to a trickle and fade. When no more came, the girls at last would be alone. Majlinda's girls–Miriam, Arlinda, Zana, Kaltrina, and Lule–stayed with her, and though they learned the names of some of those who had been at the Factory for a time, they seemed a clique apart. The terrible intimacy of their hug in the van had brought them together and set them apart.

On the very first day, in those early morning-after hours, after they'd each met a score or more of Gians, Majlinda and her girls crowded together on a small mattress at the edge of the Factory as the girls around them drifted off to sleep. Majlinda lay on her back in the middle of the flat mattress, with her body sore and her heart numb. She had been used to the empty feeling that would follow Murat's men– that would follow the men whom she had begun to know, if only on a visceral, terrible level–but so many new men made her feel something slightly, like a memory of revulsion creeping through her numbness. It was only that memory that made her raise her head slightly and look at those who crowded around her on the mattress.

Arlinda, Kaltrina, Zana and Lule nestled close against her, but there wasn't quite enough room for Miriam: she lay half on the floor, her torso resting gently on the mattress and her cotton-clad shoulder just barely touching Majlinda's limp hand. She had chosen the hard cement floor and what little company she had over finding a soft bed elsewhere for a battered body that was no longer hers.

Majlinda lowered her head gently back to the mattress. Through the soreness of her body, she tried to feel–tried to force away the emptiness that had become her home, and to feel the warmth of those who surrounded her: the touch of a cotton shirt here, of splayed hair or heavy head or warm skin there.

"Once upon a time," said Majlinda, speaking softly so her voice would not carry beyond her bed or the girls who lay around her, "a young hunter was exploring. He was a young man–a boy, really–but he was a good one, and they still exist somewhere in the world.

"In the mountains near Korab, he was carrying his small bow and looking for game when he caught sight of a great eagle flying low above him. It was coming in gently to land upon an outcropping of rock near the summit of a mountain, and it carried a large snake in its beak." Majlinda didn't know how long it had been since she'd used words like 'summit' or 'outcropping,' and an eagle seemed a thing from a different world, a world far from the Factory and the white room. It seemed to her a thing that could never exist outside of a fairy tale; but it was a fairy tale—a legend—that she told now, and so she went on.

"He hurried up the mountain, for the eagle was beyond range of the shot of his bow. When he saw the eagle fly away, he felt sad at his slowness and wished he could have come close enough to strike it down, or at least to see it better. He had never before seen such a large eagle.

"Though the eagle was gone, the boy climbed to the outcropping. As he peered over the ledge, he found the eagle's nest. There an eaglet played with the dead snake that had been in the great eagle's beak.

"But as the young eagle pushed at the long tail of the snake, the boy saw the snake's head twitch; the snake's eyes came alive, its jaws parted, and deadly venom dripped from its fangs. Swift as thought, the young hunter pulled his bowstring and let fly his arrow, striking and killing the deadly snake."

Did Arlinda's eyes lose a part of their emptiness? Was there a twinkle in them Majlinda had not seen before? Majlinda dared not look more closely, for fear her own voice would break in sorrow or pity and she would be unable to complete the story; but she took a light breath and kept talking. "He held out his hand to the eaglet. Curious about the youth who had climbed into its nest, the eaglet plucked at his hand, and a friendship was born. As the youth had climbed into the nest of the eaglet, so did the eaglet climb into the hand of the youth. Amazed by the beauty of the delicate eaglet that would become the greatest of birds, the hunter took it from its nest."

Majlinda closed her eyes, and in her mind she saw the green hues of low mountains, the trees that would decorate them and the rivers running in their valleys, and the boy who walked across them carrying a tiny eagle. He would pet the eagle, she thought—but the girls would not like to hear talk of petting. "The boy set out towards his home. He crooned to the eaglet, and he sang to it in his beautiful young voice. It was too young to speak to him, but it crooned to him as it could, and it liked his eyes. It even tried to sing with him.

"A great wind swished through the trees above his head, and worriedly the young hunter looked towards the sky. A moment later, in a flash of feathers through the leaves, the great eagle he had seen before landed on a branch above his head. Its eyes studied him, and in them burned a fiery rage checked by contemplation and wonderment.

"In a thunderous voice that shook the trees, the great eagle asked, 'Why have you stolen my child?'

"The youth eyed the great eagle's talons and thought of the little eagle who was beginning to be his friend. Then he raised his eyes to meet those of the great eagle. To its wild, unblinking eyes he said, 'I have not stolen your child.'

"'My child is in your hand,' snapped the eagle swiftly, its patience tried. 'You have stolen my child.'

"'My child is in my hand,' replied the boy. 'He became mine when I saved him from the snake. You dropped a snake in your nest for him to play with, but the snake wasn't dead. It tried to eat your child, but I saved him and he became mine. When you save a child, you become the child's parent, in a way. When you bring a snake to kill him, can you call yourself a parent any longer?'" *When you save a child, you become the child's parent, in a way.* Majlinda wished, somehow, that she could save the children all about her, the girls who should be children still. She wished that she could save herself.

"The eagle studied the youth in silence. The wind was still and the moment seemed to stretch out forever. The eagle was proud, so it would not admit the boy was right; but in its heart it knew shame, that it had thought the snake dead and so had nearly killed its own son. This young hunter impressed the eagle, for not only had he saved its son, but also did he stand now unafraid before the great eagle which had come in wrath to reclaim its child.

"'Thank you for saving my son,' said the eagle. 'Return him to me now, and soon I will give you the sharpness of my eyes and the great strength of my wings. You will be unrivalled among men, and you will be called by my great name!'

"And so the youth handed over the eaglet to the eagle, who had promised a great gift and had thanked him for saving its son.

"In the years that followed, the eaglet grew into an eagle. Playful at first, and powerful as it grew, it spent much time with the youth who had long ago saved it from a snake and carried it far from its nest. By the time the youth became a man—a good man—the fully grown eagle soared always in the skies above him. The youth grew to be a great hunter and warrior, who slew many beasts of the forest and defeated many evil men in combat. Always, he was watched from high above, and the eagle who was his friend helped and guided him all the days of his life.

"Amazed by his deeds as a young man and by his prowess as a hunter and fighter, the people elected him to be their chief and their king, and they called him *Shqipëtar*, 'son of the eagle.' He was called 'son of the eagle' because, when he had looked over the eaglet, he had become its parent and its guide; now that the eagle looked over him, it had become his parent and his guide. And so he was *Shqipëtar*. The people called his kingdom *Shqipëria*, 'The Land of the Eagles,' which is Albania."

Majlinda's voice had been quiet and soft, and little more than a whisper–but it had also been constant and real, and a voice that was other than cruel. The story was over now, and Majlinda wondered if it had mattered and if the other girls had been listening to her. Or was she just talking into a void, into the ravaged nothingness they all must feel? Behind her still-closed eyes, the pictures of the youth in the mountains and in the forest echoed in her mind, with their wild blues and greens showing her something more than the life she now knew.

Opening her eyes, Majlinda saw the others.

"Thank you," said Miriam quietly. Still spilled over the side of the mattress, lying half on the floor, she smiled very softly. It was the first smile Majlinda had seen in weeks that had been neither lecherous nor false. In Majlinda's breast a butterfly shook its wings swiftly, as if shrugging off a mountain of dust, and Majlinda remembered what it was to be happy even for something so small. A smile came to her own lips: a slightly broader smile in answer to Miriam's, in answer to the knowledge that Majlinda could still know happiness, and could still bring it to others. Murat had not taken joy from her forever, and she reveled in that knowledge and in the smile of Miriam before her.

Miriam's hand sought out Majlinda's arm and tightened on it lightly and thankfully. "Thank you, Majlinda," she said again.

"Thank you," echoed Lule.

"Thank you, Majlinda," said Arlinda.

Zana shook her head slowly. "Thank you."

"Thank you, Majlinda," said Kaltrina, echoing the others as if in ritual. Kaltrina blinked then, as if the sound of her own words had startled her; and she said more firmly, "*Thank you.*"

Majlinda, thought Majlinda. *Names matter.*

"Kaltrina," whispered Majlinda. "Lule. Arlinda. Zana. Miriam. Majlinda." She looked over them with her smile, tenderly and sadly and gladly and with belonging, over their tiny, tiny half-smiles and their unkempt hair, and their black shirts and black skirts.

"Tomorrow I will tell you a story of *Bukura e Dheut*, the Beauty of the Earth, and her sister *Bukura e Detit*, the Beauty of the Sea." It was odd to think of beauty in the Factory, where so much false beauty lay, and so much of beauty was corrupted–but perhaps in recalling true beauty, the girls could hold on to something of the world beyond the Factory's walls. It mattered little, perhaps–but it was all Majlinda knew to do.

●   ●   ●

The next morning, after the girls were counted, groups were taken in turn into a tiled room on the far side of the building: a group shower. They left their clothes with one of the men before they entered, and another watched them as they scrubbed and cleaned. There was no shampoo, but there was soap–the first soap Majlinda had seen in some time. She'd almost forgotten what it felt like to have clean skin, and she wondered why they hadn't showered last night, before the first Gians came.

"Is there any shampoo?" she asked the girl next to her, quietly, in Albanian. The girl stared at her blankly. She tried again in Italian, gesturing to her hair with the soap.

"Tomorrow," explained the girl, pushing some locks of her own long, wet hair back past her shoulders, turning towards the shower to soap up her arms. "There's soap every day, and shampoo every other day. It's not bad, really, unless the Gians get something in your hair."

Majlinda winced–almost miraculously, she hadn't experienced that particular unpleasantness yet. "I'm Majlinda," she offered.

"Anna," said the other. "You're one of the new girls."

Majlinda shook her head.

Anna frowned. "That's strange. I was sure you were."

Majlinda blinked. "Oh. Sorry, things are different at home–you usually shake your head for yes, there. You nod for no. At least traditionally."

"How odd."

"Different, not odd. Everyone here does things backwards."

Anna smiled. "That language you spoke first–what was it?"

"Albanian."

The lights flickered. Anna nodded towards the entrance, where the man who watched them had a hand on the switch. "Finish up," she said. "They'll close off the pipes in a moment."

Majlinda tossed her hair to one side and turned to let the water course down her back for a few more seconds, and then it sputtered and died above her as the man at the door turned a large valve. Cool water dripping from her body, Majlinda fell into line behind Anna and filed out the door with the other girls. Led by the man who'd watched them shower, they walked into the corridor, past the room where they'd left their clothes, and on towards the main floor.

"Where are the towels?" asked Majlinda quietly. She was almost enjoying the feel of the cool water air-drying from her warm body, for she had little modesty left to guard; but washing had been a habit, once, and that habit remembered towelling dry.

"No towels," said Anna quietly. "They'll give us clothes again when everyone's done and dried–we dry naked, in front of the big, grey fan on the Factory floor. Stay off the mattresses till you're dry–better for mildew." She shrugged. "Mornings are like this. It's not so bad."

Majlinda thought that perhaps Anna was right, and it was not so bad. Her skin was clean for the first time in she didn't know how long, and if the price of that was to dry in front of others, it was a price she'd pay. The realization that she would have once shuddered at the idea made her feel oddly self-conscious. When they passed onto the main floor, she saw new guards, men who hadn't been there last night. Perhaps they worked in shifts. Majlinda moved her arms to cover herself, but pulled them away as quickly again, knowing that covering herself would only make the men look all the more. If the men thought of her as a beast then they might treat her as a beast; but if they thought of her as a person then they would treat her as a person, and that could be far worse.

•   •   •

The Gians came again that night, and they brought their teeth and their hair and their legs, their backs and their scars and their fat, their leanness and their muscle, their lechery and their stink, their perfume and their panting and the slurping of their tongues. None brought tears to Majlinda's eyes, but only dull routine to her form. Several times that night she wished there could have been tears, but she'd almost forgotten how to cry them; and some part of her felt she needed to hoard them, to save them for a day when they were truly needed, or else she'd find she had none left to give.

When the night was almost over and her work was done, and time was creeping towards the morning, she lay on a mattress surrounded by her girls.

"Once upon a time," said Majlinda, speaking softly so that her voice would not carry beyond her bed, "*Bukura e Dheut*, the Beauty of the Earth, stood on a mountain by the sea, speaking to her sister, *Bukura e Detit*, the Beauty of the Sea."

Majlinda went on to speak of how *Bukura e Dheut* met Tomor the supreme, who commanded the winds, and of their courtship and their love. It felt odd to speak of courtship and love in this building that knew neither, dozens of feet from men who would rape her on a whim. Most of her mind lashed out at her as she spoke: chanted "It does not matter, it does not matter, it does not matter" in her ear as she struggled to keep her desperation from her tone. Yet in some small corner of her mind, some token neither of protest nor of resistance but of unschooled stubbornness told her that love and courtship and hope mattered most here, where they did not belong and could not be, in a world as alien to them as midnight was to the sun.

And so, that night and in the nights that followed, Majlinda told her girls what legends she knew of ancient Albania, mostly the ones she'd learned from Old Man Koti. She was sure she got some details of them wrong, but that mattered less than that she told them to the girls who needed to hear them.

Thoughts of their homes–in her case, of her father or town, of school or the river, of the shop or her few friends or her neighbors– thoughts of their homes were perilous, for such thoughts spoke of what the girls had lost and what they could never return to. But legends and myths were reminders that spoke of something other than their loss, so Majlinda could find refuge in them and give refuge there too to the girls who needed her.

At the end of each storytime, Miriam would say, "Thank you, Majlinda." The other girls would follow after her in one order or another, but Miriam was always first. These would be the first words the girls had spoken since work ended for the night, and some days they were the only earnest words Majlinda heard.

"Kaltrina," Majlinda would whisper. "Lule. Arlinda. Zana. Miriam. Majlinda." She would smile at them—an honest tiny smile if she could summon it, or a forced wider one if she could not—and say, "Tomorrow I will tell you a story of the dragon Stihí, and how she got her treasure." "Tomorrow I will tell you of Ljubi, and the first blood-price of river's water." "Tomorrow I will tell you how Perendi met Prende, and of the great thunderclouds that came over the mountains when they fought, and of the beautiful storms that danced across the sea when they made love."

As long ago she had made the day and the night separate in the house of her father, in the wake of his drinking, so now were these stories the snippets of daylight she found in a world of eternal night. In the night there was only one moment and the next, one sensation and the next, and the reality of living what was no life.

But in the little daylight of her stories, in the little daylight of the girls around her, there was something almost more than unwilling whores reaching for what they could not have, and there was something almost human.

Chapter 7

Scrolling Downward

FULVIA'S LEFT HAND rested on the keyboard, and with her right she clicked an icon to access the records she would need. A window popped up asking for her password. She had to change it once every three months. This quarter it was *222222*. Last quarter it had been *111111*. Why did they make her change it?

"You say she left in August?"

"Very early in August," answered the man on the phone. "I haven't been able to reach her. No one answers at the agency's phone, and last night it stopped working: an Internet voice mail company answers."

"Majlinda?" asked Fulvia. "Em Aay Ell Eye–"

"Em Aay Jay Ell Eye En Dee Aay," said the man. "Majlinda."

Fulvia entered the name; the computer began its record search. "Nobody named Majlinda received a work visa in August, but one was issued in July. Is your daughter in agribusiness?"

"No." The voice was tightly controlled, as if to choke back grief or fear. "She was looking for domestic work through the First Star Employment Agency. A woman named Odeta chaperoned her. Majlinda should have called home, but she hasn't; someone from the company should have called me back, but they haven't. Their voice mail account expired. Money from Majlinda's first paycheck should have arrived a week ago, but it didn't. I was worried, but the voice mail worries me more. I can't reach my daughter."

Fulvia frowned. Why did *she* always get these calls? When would parents learn that Italy was a big place? "Sir, do you have the name and address of the place she was staying in Italy?"

She opened a new database, this one belonging to the *Ispettorato del Lavoro's* office. Listening to the tight voice on the phone, she entered the name and address as he read it from a contract: First Star Employment, Via Persa 19A, 72100 Brindisi, Italia. She repeated it to him to be sure she'd gotten it right.

But the computer couldn't find anything. She frowned, wondering if the Embassy's link to Rome was down. But if it were, she thought, she wouldn't have seen the other work visa. Was the company operating illegally? She should make a note and forward it to the Labor Department. For now, though, she still had the girl's father on the phone.

"I don't see a reference to the company, but perhaps the address is slightly off or there is a problem with the database. Does your daughter have a phone?"

"If she'd had a phone, I would not need to call you," answered the man. "I should have bought her a phone, or I should have given her this one. I was a fool, and now I can't reach her."

"Maybe she isn't working," suggested Fulvia. She sat back in her chair, letting her eyes wander down to the clock in the corner of the computer monitor. Her lunch break would be starting soon. "If she went to Italy to work, but then the job fell through, she might not want to admit it." There might be a simple reason—a miscommunication or a daughter who wanted to get away from her parents. "You might file a missing person's report. It hasn't been very long, but I know how a few weeks can seem like forever." Noemi stood at her desk across the room and glanced towards Fulvia. Fulvia raised two fingers in a vee. *Two minutes.*

"Majlinda would have called," insisted the voice. "Another girl might not have, but Majlinda would. She is a good daughter."

"I'm sure she is, sir. Would you like to file a missing person's report? I can find you the right phone number." Hurrying lest she cut too severely into her and Noemi's lunch hour, she made her computer display a directory of services and began scrolling downward.

Chapter 8

The Stolen Child

"Most customers come into a massage parlor thinking nothing is wrong; that it's a job we choose," she said. "It doesn't occur to them that we are slaves."

–You Mi
Diary of a Sex Slave, SFGate.com [15]

SOME TIME AFTER they arrived at the Factory, Lule became the first to say "No."

The fifteen-year-old girl was on a bed in one of the back rooms, under the bulk of a large accountant–a man who had paid for her each of the last three nights, who insisted on calling her Donnatella–and suddenly something in his rounded face reminded her of her brother. In an instant she remembered who she'd been. She bucked sideways, and she slapped at him and knocked him away and kicked him, and she scratched at his eyes. Her nails dug deeply into the side of his face.

He screamed and fell backwards off the bed. With a *clunk* he landed on the floor; then he stood, feeling at the scratch across his cheek. Filled with disbelief, he watched Lule as she retreated to stand in a corner of the room. Her head tilted downwards and her eyes watched him like a mad animal watches its predator, looking out from her slightly lowered head to track his motions.

Sepeño's disbelief yielded into a quiet anger. "I've paid," he said. "I've paid already, Donnatella. What's wrong?"

"*My. Name. Is. Lule.*" Lule growled each word wrathfully, barely able to breathe at the upset and the anger and the shame she suddenly felt. She raised her head in stages with each tortured breath, each one feeling like the rasp of a great sob, though she had no tears. "You can't buy me. You can't buy us." He could, she knew, and he had. But he had reminded her so much of her brother, in that moment above her. "I'm not–" she raised her head, closing her eyes and retreating further into the corner, arms stretched out to feel the heavy white walls. "This isn't me." She thought of her home, of the village she'd come from, of her brother and her sisters and her mother, of climbing mountains in the fall and loitering amid the olive trees in spring. She raised her head further, plaintively, painfully, and if her eyes had been open she could only have seen the ceiling, but because they were closed she could see the sky, and not-quite-sobs wracked her voice as she said again, "*This isn't me.* No walls. No pain. Every day hurts too much to be me. It can't be real. *Please.*"

She wouldn't open her eyes–not when she could see the sky and the mountains of her home. Only, she could not feel the coolness of the autumn–her body knew she was in the sweltering heat of the Factory in summer, just as it knew what she'd been doing all night: it knew the soreness she'd grown used to.

Why had he not forced her? Why had this man–Sepeño–not leaped across the bed and pushed her eyelids open, or not cared that they were closed and forced her legs apart, and forced her down? In her shock, she opened her eyes, letting the fine blue sky fade into memory.

Sepeño's rage had dissipated: he guiltily looked away from her and fingered a small ring upon his finger. A wedding ring, perhaps. Blood came lightly from the scratch on his face, painting him a vicious shade of guilt. Without a word, he turned and left the room.

Suddenly Lule moaned–moaned to think what Diovanni might do to her. Why had she said no, she wondered? Why had Sepeño reminded her of her brother? She shuddered.

Quaking in fear over what might happen next, she took her clothes from the floor beside the bed and put them on. The mattresses in the back rooms–unlike the ones on the Factory floor–were for Gians, not just for the girls, and so these mattresses had box springs and frames beneath them; and Lule slipped to the floor and crawled under the bed frame, back as far as she could into the darkness there that was her only refuge. Men watched the halls, men watched the Factory floor and the blue lounge and even the bathroom, and if she returned to any of them she'd only be sent back to work and raped again, and maybe she'd be beaten first. But if she was under the bed, they might not find her for a little while. She'd never seen a man go under a bed.

Silently, she thought of the sky she could not see, and she thought of home. She remembered it fondly, and as a thing far more beautiful than it had been to her while she'd lived there, and as a thing more beautiful still because it was now forbidden to her: she would never return to her home. Murat's promise of a better job and a better life was a lie, and all of the girls knew it—they only pretended otherwise, lying to themselves because the lie was better than the naked truth and the truth of their nakedness.

She didn't know how long she lay under the bed. After a time she heard a noise and opened her eyes, and saw legs coming in through the open door from the hallway. Two sets of legs—a man and a woman. Lule crawled forward to the edge of the bed, to where she could see a short man—a short Greek—kissing Majlinda. Majlinda seemed neither happy nor sad, but simply there, simply catching his kisses and responding gently.

Lule knew that gentleness—it was an almost robotic thing, a thing she'd grown used to. In its own terrible way, it was an art: a question of responding just enough that the man would not hate you for not responding, and would not be rougher to get that response. And worse than that roughness, if a man was unsatisfied he could report you to Diovanni.

The Greek pulled Majlinda's black shirt over her head in the same way Lule's had been raised from her she knew not how many times. Lule was afraid of the light, afraid to be seen here, hovering in the half-shadows at the edge of the bed. If she were seen by the men who walked down the hallway from time to time, she'd be beaten or sent to work again. But though she was afraid, she stayed to watch Majlinda, called by this vision of Majlinda performing an act which Lule performed a dozen times a day.

The Greek ran his hands caressingly down Majlinda's uncaring side, and Lule knew the feel of it, of the fingers—clean or rough, strong or weak—upon the warm flesh there. Here that feeling was a terrible thing that did not seem terrible, a learned numbness within what appeared to be a sensual caress, though there was no sensuality in Majlinda's eyes. Lule did not feel sick to see the touch, but neither did she feel the emptiness she felt when she experienced its like: instead, it occurred to her how, had things been different, it might have been beautiful. Here the caress was awful; but between the great loves of the Albanian folklore Majlinda taught to her, or between husbands who were better than the husbands who walked into this shop and their better wives, might such a touch be beautiful?

The man swung Majlinda around and pushed her onto the bed, and his hairy legs stood inches from Lule's face. The bed sagged above her, though it didn't come low enough to press against her back. The legs before her were strong, darkly-tanned legs in dirty white socks and grey sneakers.

He pushed his trousers down and they clumped over his legs, and he pulled himself onto the bed. Above Lule, the bed was nearly still for an awkward moment, and then it began to shake, slowly at first, with a clumsy bouncing motion she knew too well. "I am Lule," Lule whispered fiercely to herself. "She is Majlinda, and I am Lule."

She did not know how long she spent in the darkness. When the Greek finished with Majlinda, they lay on the bed above her. That, too, was an art–how long could you keep a man there when he was done, creating time in which you didn't have to do worse than lie with him? How many men did you need to service a night if you didn't want to be beaten or raped more harshly by Diovanni's men than you would be by a normal Gian? Like her school had had, this life had its rules, and the fifteen-year-old Lule had tried to learn them well.

After a time, the Greek stood and pulled up his trousers. Majlinda walked across the room and slipped back into her shirt and skirt, and when the Greek left she followed closely behind. Lule snaked quickly out from under the bed and hurried to catch up; she touched Majlinda on the shoulder. They walked down the corridor together, behind the Greek of sated lust and under the watchful eyes of Armand. Armand sat in a chair at the top of the stairs–they were on the second level of rooms–smoking his perpetually lit cigarette.

Lule wrapped her arm around Majlinda's, and together they walked to the head of the stairs. Armand's foot came out to block them before they could descend.

Lule's heart shrank, and her eyes could not meet his. Majlinda, though, looked up to face him.

"From the same room," said Armand quietly. "The Greek, he did not come up with two; and before, a man complained his girl did not seem happy." Armand's eyes narrowed, and he took a drag of his cigarette. Lule's feet quivered and she longed to run; but there was nowhere she could go. "You, dear," he said, looking over to Lule, "you came second from the room. You hid under the bed, or else you waited and she came in and he was Gian to you both without paying, and you hoped we'd forget your earlier transgression. It was you, because you came out second. This Gian's girl would have come out first." He took another drag on his cigarette and swept his foot over to tap Majlinda's bare leg. "You can go. Go be a whore, but this one"– he glanced back to Lule–"this one still needs to learn what she is."

They would take her back to the white building, thought Lule desperately. They would all take her again and again and again, and painfully, and this time they wouldn't stop. She didn't know how to–

"No," said Majlinda firmly.

Armand blinked in startlement. "*What?*"

"It wasn't her," said Majlinda. "It was me. I hid under the bed. I didn't satisfy a Gian earlier. I yelled at him, and when he lowered his pants I mocked him, and I hid under the bed because I thought you'd punish me. Because I was afraid." Her voice, though firm, was also strange–strained and distant, as if she could barely hear herself, though she spoke clearly. "I did it, so you can punish me."

Lule stared at Majlinda in disbelief. Why would Majlinda say that? Why, when it would mean... Majlinda's eyes were locked squarely on Armand's, but Lule could almost feel them wanting to look at her, could feel Majlinda's peripheral vision watching her, urging her to leave, quickly, as soon as she could. *To save me,* thought Lule.

"Go," said Armand, kicking Lule's leg lightly, his eyes still locked on Majlinda's. "This one stays, though."

Swallowing, Lule ran down the steps. She didn't look back. She wasn't strong enough to look back, or to protest, or to insist that it had been her. She only knew she didn't want to suffer. So she forced down her tears, went back to the blue lounge of the Factory, and under the watchful eyes of men she despised, she continued her whoring.

•   •   •

Armand studied Majlinda thoughtfully from his chair. Her eyes met his, and hers seemed unafraid even as she expected her punishment. He suddenly felt the same fear he'd felt a week ago, when he'd seen the girls huddled together on one side of the van. He didn't know why he felt fear, and he squashed it immediately, with the same ruthless efficiency his father had taught him long ago, when his father had still hoped he'd become a banker. Fear was unhelpful in a man, his father had said, save to keep you alive. Save your fear for when your life is in jeopardy.

But it wasn't Armand's life that was in danger, and so he didn't recognize the girl who stood before him, and he didn't understand that the fear he felt was not for his life, but was for his soul. Even as he extinguished it, he reached up to grab Majlinda's hair and pull her head down, and she bent–she did not kneel–to come closer to him, following where he pulled.

He released the hair and gripped again, closer to the scalp, and pulled her until her nose almost touched his; and he puffed out the air of his cigarette. Her eyes watered before him, and she bent very low, but still she did not kneel. There was something odd in her, something Armand did not know how to see.

"Kneel," he said finally, not understanding that the word was an admission of defeat. She knelt silently before him, her coal-black hair bunched in his hand and trailing down her back. He forced her head towards his legs and pulled her hair to one side. "Stay still." He released the hair and brought his hand over to her shoulder. There was sweat there–perhaps sweat from the man she'd serviced, perhaps her own from the servicing–and Armand scratched at the sweaty skin lightly, and then hooked the neck of her t-shirt with his thumb and pushed it aside, away from her neck until it would stretch no more. "You will listen when we talk. You will service whom we say. The Gians we send you, you obey. Do you understand?"

"I understand," she said. There was no defiance in her voice, but neither was it meek. Armand frowned at her–her eyes were looking to one side now, to the wall behind him. Why did girls' eyes so often do that?

Armand took another drag on his cigarette.

Then he took it from his lips and moved it out past her neck, so the burning end sat an inch above the skin he'd bared behind her shoulder. "You will not cry out," he said to Majlinda suddenly. He'd never said that before during a burning; and he felt weak in the saying of it, though he didn't know why. "You will not cry out." He lowered the cigarette.

At the end of the pure off-white of its wrap, the red-burning tube of nicotine and gunk smeared into Majlinda's skin. A tautness shot into her shoulder muscle, outward into all of Majlinda's muscles, and into her face–but she didn't cry out.

Armand pushed the cigarette into the skin more deeply, and twisted it. She only knelt before him, staring at the wall, tension flaring in her face and in her neck and in her body–in everything except for her eyes. Her eyes stared at the wall, and they did not seem empty, but rather full of a wild blue flame: a small but unquenchable fire greater by far than that of the cigarette which dug into her skin. Armand picked up the cigarette and moved it an inch to the left, and pushed down again; but the cigarette broke when he pushed, bent in half from a twist too many.

Frowning, Armand pulled it away from Majlinda's neck. A single edge of its paper wrapper held the remains together. He rolled the limp tube over, the wrapper snapped, and the red end fell. He dropped the rest to the floor and stepped on it all.

Majlinda hadn't moved. She was less tense now that she felt only the pain of afterburning: fire's echo scorched at her skin. Her neck was still bare, the back of it showing the punishment with which Armand had marked her.

He leaned forward over her neck, parted his lips, and brought his teeth down to rub their rough grit against the cigarette burns. He nipped at them each. Her muscles flared again at the pain; he sucked on the burns and darted his tongue out to lick them. And then, placing a hand around Majlinda's throat, he turned his head, slid his teeth half-open along the ridge of her neck, up her cheek, and to her ear. There he pulled an inch away and said quietly, "You wear clothes, but you are naked even now. We can burn you, can tear you apart, can beat you. You are nothing, girl. Say it."

"I am nothing," said Majlinda. She squinted against the pain of the burns on her neck, but her voice was not meek. The cupping of Armand's hands and the impressions of his teeth and the catch of his bite could barely touch her through the shell she'd learned to wear.

"You are always naked," whispered Armand in her ear. "If you were in one of those big black Russian overcoats, you'd still be naked. Clothes can't cover a whore. Say it, puta; say it, mignotta. Kargiola, Hure. Clothes can't cover a whore. You are always naked."

"Clothes cannot cover a whore. I am always naked." Her voice was louder than his, but empty of tone: it was plain and unafraid. A Gian–a fat one–came up the stairs with Anna, whose eyes widened at the sight of Majlinda on her knees before Armand. The Gian paused to study the bare-necked girl on her knees, and lightly he licked his lips at the sight of such beautiful coal-black hair swept to the side, at the sight of a pretty girl like this prepared, he thought, to do–prepared to do what he thought she was prepared to do. He'd heard her say she was always naked, and though she was clothed, he thought of her that way now. Whores, he thought, were such wonderful things. And they so often seemed to like it, and he believed them.

"Here," said Armand, looking past Majlinda's shoulder and up to the Gian. "Have a second girl for free. She will please you." Armand pulled her head up and cupped her jaw. "The lesson isn't over. Be a good little whore. Come back when you're done."

He let go of her.

She rose, turned, and walked down the hall with Anna, back to the first unoccupied room: the one where Lule had hidden under the bed, more afraid of the light beyond its edges than she had been of the dark.

Chapter 9

Why They Loved Her

In Italy, a girl who's paid $40,000 to her captors at $5 per five-minute trick might still owe $15,000. In two more years, she says, she might earn her freedom. That's only a little over four rapes a day for the next two years, if she doesn't have to pay for food, housing, condoms, or doctors. [6]

M ADAME VACCARO CAME TO THE FACTORY early on a Tuesday morning, after the lights had been dimmed for sleeping.

Majlinda lay on her mattress, where she'd just finished telling a story about a tree that grew by a river and how the tree was always thirsty and drank from the river, but it grew all of its leaves away from the riverbank, so the leaves didn't shade the river, and the river dried up. It was a simple story about trying to do well by one another, and it didn't come from Albanian folklore–Majlinda had imagined it. She'd begun making up her own stories and mixing them in with the traditional ones several nights ago, when she realized she'd already told the girls most of the stories she knew.

A great, rolling noise sounded: one of the garage doors on the side of the Factory began to open.

That was rare: the few Gians who came to this room entered through corridors, and so did guards. The garage doors–the only way sunlight ever reached this room–hadn't opened in weeks. Now one rolled up in its track to let a light blue van drive in over the grey Factory floor.

The van stopped. Peppino closed the door behind it–Majlinda hadn't realized Peppino was here–and suddenly a soft, clean, silk shirt beside him caught her eye: Murat's shirt. Majlinda tensed. Murat came once every few days and took two or three of the girls into the back to 'inspect' them. He'd taken Arlinda, and he'd taken Miriam, but mostly he'd taken girls Majlinda didn't know, who'd already been at the Factory when she arrived.

Murat had never come with a van before, and Majlinda wondered if new girls might be inside. Anna said he brought new girls sometimes–she'd seen him bring girls from Egypt who'd been even younger than the fifteen-year-old-Lule. He'd brought girls from Switzerland, too, though Anna thought that rare; and he'd brought other girls from other places.

A moment after the van pulled to a stop, the passenger door opened and out stepped Madame Vaccaro. A large woman, something in her manner made her girth seem a pleasant plumpness rather than a crude fat. Her smile was subordinate to the crispness of her step and to the sharpness of her eyes. A proper grey blouse and a grey skirt below, bounded between by a knotted white sash, seemed out of place here despite the grey of the Factory floors and the white of the mattresses; all of the girls and women here wore black, and to have a woman here who wore other colors–who could, perhaps, wear what she wished–fit with nothing Majlinda knew of this place.

Why was this woman here and why was she unafraid? Who, once she knew them, would not be afraid of Murat and Peppino and their ilk?

Two large men, tall and moderately well-built, emerged from the van–one from the side door and one from the driver's seat. One scanned Murat's men, and the other followed Madame Vaccaro closely; she walked purposefully over to the girls. Peppino dialed the overhead lights up from the dimness in which the girls were accustomed to sleep. Some rubbed their eyes, and others sat up curiously. Majlinda watched and waited.

Madame Vaccaro paused at the first mattress. She traced her eyes thoughtfully down the body of one girl and back to the girl's face, discounted her, and scanned a second girl, and then a third. She moved quickly down the wall from whore to whore until she reached Majlinda's mattress, stopping when Majlinda met her eyes.

Miriam and Zana were nestled in Majlinda's arms, and Lule and

Arlinda and Kaltrina were scattered about the mattress or half-upon the floor, but all were touching Majlinda somehow. Some watched Madame Vaccaro uncertainly or fearfully, and some watched Majlinda. Lule's eyes were closed–she'd fallen asleep early tonight, or perhaps she feared to see what might happen.

"These are the new ones?" asked Madame Vaccaro, though she clearly wasn't speaking to the girl who met her eyes.

"Yes." Murat's voice. Murat and his shirt, Murat had come near. Majlinda's eyes lowered to herself, lowered only to see her bare ankles beneath the hem of her skirt, exposed just below where Lule lay against her thigh. She remembered the first afternoon in the white room, and how Murat had ripped her skirt away; and she felt again a portion of the terror she had known then. Fear climbed into her breast, fear and shame such as she'd thought she could no longer know; she thought of her father looking at her now in her nest of whores, and what would he think of her?

"The one in the middle," said Madame Vaccaro. "And the one on her leg–the left leg, mind. And the one on her shoulder on the opposite side. Those three." *Lule. Miriam.* Majlinda's eyes started upwards in worry–but again she felt Murat's presence, saw the smooth press of his trousers, remembered how he'd kissed her and the kiss had turned to dust, and to terror, and to a thousand kisses more she wished she'd never known. Her eyes tripped back down to her legs.

"They'll be ready tomorrow afternoon." Murat's voice again.

"I'll inspect them then," said Madame Vaccaro. "Good condition only, mind, or I'll go somewhere else." She wore slippers, realized Majlinda: slippers of brown leather which must be soft on the hard floor of the Factory. Maybe whatever this woman wanted, it would be easier than working at the Factory. How could it not be? Once already Majlinda had felt Armand's cigarette, had felt him punish her for Lule's... for Lule's doing the right thing. That punishment had felt a victory, even when the cigarette had burned into her skin and she'd yearned to cry out, and yet she wouldn't have cried out, she thought, even had Armand allowed it.

But she had said no on her own–had said no when two Gians had come to her together, taken her to a room, and tried to turn her over. She had fought and kicked. One Gian had fallen to the floor, she remembered, when she'd kicked him between his legs. The other hit her with his fists and threw her down. She'd had her shirt off when the struggle had begun, she remembered–odd to remember her nakedness so easily. Once upon a time it would have mortified her to wear no shirt in a room with two men. Now she showered under the eyes of a different man every day, and air-dried in front of sixty girls and ten men, and the men had guns.

The two Gians had gone, but Diovanni had punished her dearly. She'd been shackled to a bed for a full day, and the men who ran the Factory, who watched the girls in the showers or sat in the corridors, who burned or bit or scratched or beat the girls, or did worse, these men had had their way with her, alone and in pairs, and all of it had made the Gians seem simple country youths as innocent and pure by comparison as they were uncaringly abusive in truth.

That day Majlinda had screamed and cried out, had been filled with terror and shame, had been reminded that there still was a part of her that cared what happened to her, and had had that caring stolen away by rough rape after rough rape after rough rape, for hours on end. The day had been meant to break her, and it would have succeeded if not for her girls.

Late in the morning the shackles had come off, and Majlinda had limped back to the mattresses, where the girls had been waiting for her. They'd laid her down gently, and then they'd laid around her, barely touching her for fear of what touch might do to her. She'd barely been able to think or do more than whimper; but Miriam had kissed the back of her hand–the back of her hand had never been kissed, not by the Gians or the men or Murat–and had whispered to all of them, gently, the story of the youth who was hunting in the mountains when he saw a great eagle above him, and how he became *Shqipëtar*, 'son of the eagle.'

And yet–though that day had nearly broken her–the sight now of Murat near her, Murat with his clean, pressed trousers and his soft, silk shirt, filled her with pain and shame at a memory of the white room that had been far worse than that day.

Majlinda's eyes could not leave the floor now that he was near; but before long she saw his pressed trousers move away, and she looked up, somewhat angered by her fear. Murat and Madame Vaccaro were striding towards the long table in the middle of the floor. Peppino dimmed the lights again, and the near side of the room fell into shadow.

"Who is she?" asked Arlinda. She was asking Clarissa, one of two girls on the next mattress.

"One of the Madames," responded Clarissa. Her voice was soft and sultry. Perhaps she'd been speaking that way to a Gian, and her voice had gotten stuck. "Like Diovanni, but a woman. I've seen two Madames come before. Sometimes they browse, and sometimes they buy."

"Buy what?" Arlinda asked.

"Buy us, of course. It's what they do. I'm jealous of your friends—that must be a better life than the Factory, here."

"We are not just for here," said Majlinda thoughtfully. "We're bought and sold. We're the towels from Shkodër, the home-made bread, the dashboard-ornaments that don't sell well. We're the romance novels from the West—the pleasant fictions the Gians believe and pay money for, and so Murat will kidnap more of us, and sell us again and again. Until we die; or we grow too old or fat, and he throws us to the street; or he kills us himself. He will sell us until we are like rental mules too old to pull, cut down for sausage or for saving time."

"She's unhappy," said Clarissa, still speaking to Arlinda. "Why do you love her, if she's unhappy?"

Arlinda frowned, turning to look thoughtfully back to Majlinda.

Was it a kind of love, wondered Majlinda? She hadn't thought love could exist here, though she knew these were her girls. A twitch of movement on her lower thigh told her that Lule had looked up to watch Arlinda, and was listening.

"Everything else here," said Arlinda slowly, "is real because of force. It's real because if you clamp your arms closed over your breasts, a man will open them again, and if you put on your skirt a man will make you take it off." She reached up with one hand and touched Majlinda's cheek: a touch more loving and simple than Majlinda thought her cheek had ever felt. "But Majlinda is real by choice. Not by force. We love her because we don't have to."

There was silence for a moment, and then Miriam added, "The Gians can't buy love."

"They buy it every day," said Clarissa, shaking her head.

"No," said Lule uncertainly. Majlinda looked down, and Lule's eyes met hers: the young girl looked up from where her head rested on Majlinda's naked thigh, looked past Majlinda's stained skirt and tight black shirt. And Lule was smiling. She pinched her own cheek lightly. "They buy this. They buy flesh and bodies. But that's not love, is it?"

"It's not," insisted Miriam. "You're right, Lule. That's not love."

"They don't want love," added Kaltrina.

"Yes, they do," said Arlinda. "Some of them. One read me poetry, once." None had read poetry to Majlinda, and she wondered what that would have been like. "It was very old Italian, I think, and I didn't understand it. By someone called Petrarch. The Gian said it was about unrequited love, and that no one had ever really loved him. Loved the Gian, I mean–I don't know about Petrarch." She brought one hand up from the mattress to push back a lock of her hair. "I think he was trying to get over some girl, someone who didn't love him. If he'd said so, it would have seemed cheap. He'd have been no more than another Gian, between one Gian and the next; but he seemed so sad that it was almost beautiful. Not like a boy moping, but something more. Even a broken love can be beautiful. I tried–" She frowned for a moment, and then she smiled slightly. "That was the only time I've ever tried to be good at what we do: I wasn't doing it because I had to, or because they'd hurt me, or out of rote. He was just..." There were a very few tears in her eyes now, though she was not sobbing. "He was so sad. I wanted to help him, and I'm a whore. What else could I do?"

Arlinda shook her head lightly and continued: "I hugged him, and did the rest. And I spoke to him at the end, and I meant what I said. Everyone else–" She frowned. "Everyone else had me because they bought me, or because they stole me. This man paid for me too–and that isn't right–but I wonder, if things had been different, if I might have loved a man like him."

There was silence. A tear rolled down Arlinda's cheek.

"What was his name?" Majlinda asked.

Arlinda smiled. "Would you believe it, his name was Gian?"

Gian, thought Majlinda. Perhaps all the Gians, as they might have been. It was a special man who would read poetry to a whore, even if he was trying to get over some other girl.

"You liked it once," said Clarissa quietly. She'd edged closer to their group during the conversation, and now she sat up against the wall on the edge of her mattress. "It's not a sin to like it, Arlinda. Most Gians you try to forget." She shivered. "It's different in those rooms. It's not really you, it's this other girl. And she has to pretend to like the Gian. If she pretends well enough, maybe one in a few hundred men, she fools herself too. You take what you can get in a life like this."

Arlinda's eyes narrowed—was it shame, or anger? Or something else, some realization that Clarissa did not understand about hope and love and what might have been, and maybe did not want to understand? *Do not let them fight*, thought Majlinda. She didn't know what would happen tonight, or what Murat might do to them before Majlinda and Lule and Miriam were 'ready' for the Madame; but she knew tonight might be their last night as a family.

"Kaltrina," she said, and the soft, steady tone of her storytelling voice cut through the warm Factory air like Gian had cut through Arlinda's stream of Gians. "Kaltrina, Lule, Arlinda, Zana, Miriam, Clarissa, Majlinda." Why had she added Clarissa?

Because Clarissa was there, she thought. Because Majlinda and Miriam and Lule might be gone on the morrow, and the larger the family they could leave, the better it would be for those who stayed behind. Let them learn to bring others into their circle. She spoke in English this night, instead of Albanian. Maybe the girls would switch between the languages when she was gone, so that Clarissa and other girls might understand some of the stories. "Tonight I will tell you two stories: the story of *Gjergj Elez Alia*, who fought against *Bajloz i Zi*, the Black Knight, for the honor of his sister; and a story of Verbti the blind, who could stand in a crowded marketplace in Tirana and from there hear the sound of raindrops falling over the ancient Rozafa castle in Shkodër."

She told the stories quietly, and the girls listened. Clarissa likely did not understand why they listened so intently; but because she listened, she grew a little closer to the family. Perhaps in time she could be more than just another girl to them.

Majlinda wished she'd thought to reach out to others in her time here—it might have left her girls more hope when she was gone—but now there was no more time.

When the stories came to an end, and while Majlinda was wondering how long she had before she'd be taken away, Miriam's hand sought out her arm and tightened on it lightly and thankfully. "Thank you, Majlinda," she said, and her voice meant it as more than ritual.

"Thank you, Majlinda," said Lule.

"Thank you, Majlinda," said Arlinda.

"Thank you, Majlinda," said Zana.

"Thank you, Majlinda," said Kaltrina.

Clarissa did not echo the others, but at least she had listened. "Kaltrina," whispered Majlinda. "Lule. Arlinda. Zana. Miriam. Clarissa. Majlinda." She looked them over with her smile, tenderly and sadly and gladly and with belonging, and with a goodbye. She looked out over their tiny, tiny half-smiles and their dirty hair, and over their black shirts and black skirts. "Tomorrow," she said, "tomorrow Arlinda will tell you the story of *Bukura e Dheut*, the Beauty of the Earth, and her sister *Bukura e Detit*, the Beauty of the Sea." It had been some time since they'd heard that story.

"You're leaving us," said Zana. Her quiet tone was not quite accusatory, but neither was it quiet enough. At the table across the room, one of the guards raised his head from a board game and looked towards the girls. Majlinda saw his head rise, and so she laid a finger to her lips for silence.

When it was his turn to move, the guard looked away. Majlinda released a slight sigh of relief. The guards had beaten them all once, when they'd grown too loud. They hadn't been especially loud that night, and Majlinda still thought the guards had simply wanted to beat them.

"I'm not leaving you," said Majlinda quietly. "I'm being taken. That's what these men do–they take. There are good men in the world, still; but they are not here, and these men take. Never trust them, never believe them, and remember always that you have a choice to defy them." It wasn't much of a choice, Majlinda knew, and the consequences of it could be terrible. If the men heard her say these words to the girls, they might well kill her. She forced away a tightness to her throat at the thought–odd to think mere death could scare her, after what she had become. "There is a price to that defiance–in pain, or blood, or sweat, or screams–but there are times when it is worth the price." She reached down with one hand to take Lule's, which was resting on the mattress near Majlinda's waist. "It was worth it for you," Majlinda said, remembering the cigarette burns on her neck and the lumps of Armand's teeth on her skin. Why did she remember those teeth, among all the teeth she'd felt?

Majlinda looked around to the others. "It would be worth it for any of you."

Chapter 10

Murat's Goodbye

MURAT came before the dawn. Armand and Peppino flanked him–Armand considering his ever-present cigarette, and Peppino's face plastered in a naked leer.

Murat looked down at Majlinda with a knowing expectation in his eyes–an anticipation of some secret thrill, something more than just another rape. Majlinda hadn't slept this night; and though she hadn't been able to meet his eyes earlier, now she forced herself to, so she might know clearly the face of her despoiler.

She stretched her muscles–an act that forced the other girls, sleeping all around her, to wake, and look up, and know what was happening–and then, still on the mattress, she rose to her feet. Eyes meeting Murat's, she touched each of her girls on the shoulder once, though she could not say their names–Kaltrina, Arlinda, Zana, Miriam, Lule. Miriam and Lule she helped to their feet, though her eyes never left Murat's.

She reached down to grab the lower hem of her black t-shirt: her stained black t-shirt that wasn't really hers, that had changed each day with a shower for another of the same size, another with different stains, but always the same blackness and the same cut. She pulled it smoothly over her shoulders and let the cotton fall to the mattress, where Arlinda caught it.

In a quick dip Majlinda bent, pushed her skirt down from her waist, and stepped forward out of it to stand again. Beside her, she saw Lule and Miriam do the same. She hadn't meant for them to echo her.

Peppino barked a laugh. "They want it."

"They always do, before the end," said Murat firmly.

Armand only took a drag on his cigarette and watched Majlinda consideringly. He felt no fear, this time, like the fear she'd caused him twice before–but he sensed that here was something he did not understand, and he was glad that it was Murat, and not he, who would conquer her this morn.

Majlinda took Miriam by one hand and Lule by the other, and the three of them stepped forward off the mattress, away from their skirts and past the silent forms of Kaltrina, Arlinda, and Zana. As she stepped forward, Majlinda raised one arm and lowered the other, and swung them together, guiding Lule to cross under Miriam's arm in front of her, so that Lule would be nearer to Peppino and Miriam would be nearer to Armand. Lule had a great fear of Armand, and Majlinda hoped that Miriam would better survive an encounter with him.

These delicate steps might have been the beginning of a dance when the world was new, 'ere man had learned to wear clothes; it might have been something young and innocent and sweet, something simple and free; but it was only Majlinda, on the harsh grey Factory floor, under the eyes of Murat and Armand and Peppino, trying to see Miriam and Lule through another rape.

•   •   •

"Did you even see the scars on the back of her neck?" asked Madame Vaccaro, standing behind Majlinda's naked body and poking at a cigarette scar.

"They're sold as-is," said Murat. "Do you want them, or not?"

Ignoring him, Madame Vaccaro ran a quick hand down Majlinda's back, searching out any other obvious imperfections. Trapped inside the sort of shamed, fearful numbness that only Murat could inspire so completely, Majlinda barely noticed. Madame Vaccaro pushed at an arm, and Majlinda let it dangle limply.

"Look at how unresponsive she is. Barely worth what we've agreed."

"She'll respond," said Murat. "She responded last night. Majlinda, raise your arm." Still trapped inside her world of nothingness, Murat's words trickled through her shell, through the void that was reality to find... to find another shell, but one that could control her arms. Robotically, she raised her right arm.

"Put it down, dear," said Madame Vaccaro.

Majlinda lowered the arm.

"You've abused her," added Madame Vaccaro. "Good stock isn't abused. You've abused her and cleaned her up, and you've probably hidden scars under makeup."

"We haven't," said Murat. "She's been well-treated."

Well-treated? Majlinda's shells fell in her anger, and suddenly she was naked in the room. Fear lanced through the anger. Her eyebrows furrowed despite her fear.

"You've abused them, Murat. You always do." Madame Vaccaro walked around to the front and looked at Miriam closely. "This one's been bitten recently, see?" She touched a spot on Miriam's chest. An anger far more intense than the one she'd worn for her own mistreatment flashed over Majlinda's face, but she smoothed it away quickly.

"Don't give me excuses," said Murat. "Majlinda, there, she's thanked me for all I've done for her. Would she have done that if I'd abused her?"

Majlinda almost laughed. Why else would she have ever thanked him, save that he'd beaten the words from her? It did not shame her, she knew, to have thanked him, for there was no shame in words forced from lips of a body that had been sold, save the shame of the one who bought it. Murat hadn't paid, but he was a Gian all the same, only a bit worse than all the others.

Murat frowned. "Give me numbers," he said to the Madame. "What do you want?"

"Ten percent off."

Murat rolled his eyes. "We set the prices last night. You agreed to them!"

Madame Vaccaro shook her head. "It was an agreement contingent upon inspection. I am not satisfied."

Murat grunted. "The girls aren't meant to satisfy you. They're meant to satisfy your *wallet*. You'll recoup your investment in–" He cut off, frowning at the girls. He couldn't talk too precisely, Majlinda realized, lest they know when their "debt" was paid off. Murat turned his silent frown back to Madame Vaccaro.

The plump woman met his gaze for a moment, and then her eyes twitched up and to one side. Majlinda thought she was looking at a small vent near the room's ceiling. "This would have been an office once." Madame Vaccaro nodded towards the vent. "No window space, so not an important office, but an office. Funny that you choose an unimportant office to speak in."

"It was here," said Murat dismissively. "The girls, Vaccaro. They're worth what I charge."

"Do you know what this factory was built for?" Madame Vaccaro continued, turning back to face him. "They made the 'Suola del Corridore' here. 'The Sole of The Runner,' for running shoes and other high-impact footwear."

"Your point?" asked Murat tautly.

"The owner was a nice man, but he had no business sense. He paid too much for substandard stock. I won't. His sole never made it off the ground. The year after the factory was built, he went bankrupt. I won't do that either. My point, Murat, is that I want my ten percent. I could buy Nigerian girls for less, and you know it."

Murat snorted. "Ten percent less, and you'd be lucky to get gaptoothed grandmothers. I'll give you five percent off, because you're a good customer; but they're back up to full price tomorrow."

"Done," said the Madame. She turned to Majlinda. "You–Majlinda, was it? Take these two and follow Carmine to the van."

Majlinda silently turned to follow one of the men who stood by the door. He led the three girls down the corridor and onto the main floor.

Majlinda saw the girls who would be staying behind, and she waved goodbye. It was a very human thing to do, a vestigial or resurging remnant of a world not hers. She would miss them. She wondered what she'd find in the world outside, and what sort of a brothel this Madame Vaccaro might run. She knew it would be an extension of the white room and of the Factory, and it wouldn't belong to the world of her stories or to the world of decent men; but she wondered what it might be like, all the same. For the first time, she realized that she might be beyond the reach of Murat. In an odd way, she felt directionless with that knowledge, as if the shame he'd given her had defined a part of her life, and without it she didn't know who she was.

Carmine approached Madame Vaccaro's grey-blue van and opened its side door, gesturing for the girls to enter. Majlinda stepped in; Lule and Miriam came behind her. The interior showed it to be a club van with darkly tinted windows. The girls shuffled in next to each other on the third seat, more naked than they'd been on the days they were born.

"Put on the robes," said Carmine. He closed the side-door and walked around the van to the back. Majlinda saw no robe. After a moment, she looked behind her seat and discovered half a dozen white robes. She felt one of them curiously, and found the fabric softer and fluffier than anything she could have imagined wearing at the Factory.

"They're so pretty," said Lule quietly.

"We'll get them dirty," added Miriam, but she reached for one anyway.

Majlinda passed a robe to Lule silently and took another for herself. She slipped her arms into its sleeves, stood halfway up–up until her head touched the ceiling–and tucked it under her and around her. She sat, closing her eyes, feeling the soft white around her, feeling the clothing that–for the first time in what seemed like forever–was not a tight t-shirt and a tiny skirt.

A slam came from behind her. That would be Carmine closing the rear door, she thought. For now, she was alone with Lule and Miriam. She felt them moving beside her, getting dressed in their own white robes.

Majlinda opened her eyes and looked out over the grey Factory floor, past the guards with their board games and guns, to the old ragged mattress where Arlinda and Kaltrina and Zana still sat. They couldn't see her through the tinted windows, she thought, but still they watched the van.

As Majlinda watched, a man walked to the mattress–a Gian, one of the few who got off work early and sometimes came in the afternoon. He took Zana's hand and led her off towards the back rooms; Arlinda and Kaltrina watched her go.

Clarissa moved over to them and exchanged a few words. Clarissa wasn't one of them, Majlinda knew: she might never understand why they told the stories they told. She would listen, though; and with luck, so would others. Majlinda had to leave now, but those she left behind would be more of a family–and so a little safer–for having known her. That truth was only a small jewel, only a little ray of light in a world of perpetual night; but it was hers, and she was glad of it.

She tried to keep her thoughts on it as Madame Vaccaro and the Madame's men climbed into the van. Majlinda tried to focus on what she'd accomplished, and to remember that Miriam and Lule were here with her.

But as the van drove out through the Factory's walls, all Majlinda could think of was Murat–Murat and his blue silk shirt–standing in the white room and forcing her down, and bringing her to the Factory, and selling her. She was leaving, but she couldn't escape his face or his clean smell, his pressed trousers or his sure smile, or the jaws that had forced hers open like a lever forces a hinge; and most of all, she could not escape the image of his blue silk shirt, billowing with a rhythm she could not stop.

Chapter 11

The Pretension of Indecency

"Prostitutes," "hookers," and "whores" are the women; "Johns," "Clients," and "Patrons" are the men. Hawaiian brothels prior to the second world war had different entrances for white and black patrons, so each would have the illusion the other race hadn't been with the girls they bought. [5] Image is everything.

"I HAVE BOUGHT YOUR BOND," said Madame Vaccaro. "That means your debt." She sat behind a small, old desk of white oak. A laptop on one corner almost made it seem she was a reputable businesswoman, and a series of ring-stains suggested she hadn't been raised around wood furniture. Amongst the ring stains sat a glass of ice water; slowly the tears of its condensation slipped down the outside of the glass to wear a new stain in the old, good wood.

Majlinda and the others sat in modestly comfortable chairs–the chairs didn't match, but each was wooden and held a padded cushion. It felt as if the mattresses of the Factory floor had been raised on four little legs, and the tight black shirts and skirts had been replaced by the falsely soft whiteness of their robes.

"And you owe me the value of that bond. Have you any idea what it costs to bring you in from out of the country? Or to buy from cruelty like Murat's? He'd rather keep you to himself and hurt you more." Madame Vaccaro cocked her head to one side with a frown.

"I don't enjoy hurting, but I also don't hate it. It is what it is and it makes me money, and I like money. You should like money too. If you earn enough of it to pay your bond, you'll be free to go.

"We collect the funds, of course–though sometimes a Gian will give you a tip, and those you get to keep until the end of the week, when we'll put it down against your debt."

Money. It seemed odd to Majlinda that such little pieces of paper should determine her fate, should be the reason so much had gone wrong. No, she thought–Murat was the reason. Murat and others like him. And the Gians, and Madame Vaccaro. Money could tempt and influence, but each man's sins were his alone.

"But you must work well," continued Madame Vaccaro. "You'll have almost anything you could want, if only you work well–good clothes and good food, comfort and rest. But cross me, and I'll whip you or send you back to Murat, or do something more creative. Don't fight–we prefer not to force you, but we have the means and the will to do so."

"This is Niut." Madame Vaccaro nodded to a tall girl who'd been standing in one corner. "She's been here for a long time, so listen to her. Go with her now. You'll begin working tomorrow night." She dropped her eyes to her laptop and began fiddling with the keyboard.

"Follow me, girls," said Niut. She wore a white silk shawl–smooth and almost transparent–over a loose grey blouse and a pair of black jeans. It was an odd assortment of clothes, and it made Majlinda wonder what she would wear here, if there would be more clothes than the white robe, and what they might be like.

Outside Madame Vaccaro's office, a small corridor reminded Majlinda of the corridors at the Factory; but a blue carpet covered the floor here, tickling her feet as she walked, and at the end of the hall was a sitting room with two couches and a window seat.

"Let's take a seat here," said Niut talkatively. "This shouldn't take long, but I'll tell you about everything." The words rolled off her tongue all bunched together in quick jumbles. "Or at least about most things–you'll figure it out fast enough, I'm sure. It's not hard." Niut sat on one of the couches. Miriam sat next to her, and Lule sat on the other couch, but Majlinda moved across the room and sat quietly on the cushion in the window seat, looking out into the street.

She had seen the street when they'd driven her here in the van, but it felt different to see the street from inside the world of the brothel and to realize that both worlds existed together. It was only a thin pane of glass that separated the two, and they were really one. It wasn't even tinted glass like the glass in the van.

For all that the worlds were separate in her mind, Majlinda realized, they were the same world: the world where she worked in this brothel was the same world where her father worked in his shop, was the same world of the universities and the towns and the mountains. Majlinda didn't know whether to despair or rejoice at that knowledge: for it meant that the hopeful world was real, but it also meant that that other world let this one exist, that the street and the city harbored knowingly the very worst depths of man's darkness, harbored the Gians who let their own veneer of civilization give way to their grunts and cries.

"A lot of the time here, you're on your own," Niut was explaining behind her. Majlinda's ears twitched, wondering what little freedoms might be found in 'on your own.'

"I mean, you can't leave the house," continued Niut. Majlinda glanced over her shoulder, studying the girl thoughtfully. "Not without one of the men, anyway." Niut was talking to them all, but she seemed mostly focused on Miriam–perhaps because Miriam was slightly taller than the others. "We're on our own each day, to clean and dress and eat and all that. There are eight of us here, by the way–sometimes one or two more, sometimes one or two less, but always about eight. About ten clients come per girl per night–more on weekends. This is a high class establishment, so dress well, and clean up as much as you can between clients." Niut smiled. "I'll show you the closet in a moment. It's a big walk-in closet at the end of the hall, and there are lots of great clothes there."

She was smiling about clothes, thought Majlinda: clothes to make them beautiful, so that men would take the clothes away. Ten Gians a night was a wonderfully low number, in its way. She was glad to be gone from the Factory, and for a moment she wondered if she'd begun to earn out the debt that Murat and Madame Vaccaro had spoken of–if it was not a lie at all, but if she might slowly earn her way to better and better conditions, to fewer Gians, and then to none, to go free. But what would she do if she were free?

"We clean the beds when they need it," added Niut. "After the clothes I'll show you your rooms, and the kitchen, and everything like that. Am I forgetting anything? Oh, silly me! What are your names?"

"Miriam," said Miriam. "This is Lule, and that's Majlinda."

"Well then, Mir," said Niut, "let's get going, shall we?" She stood and led them back down the hall. A print on one side and an oil painting on the other were both landscapes, ironic glimpses of freedom in a house of slaves. The vanishing points here came far before the canvas began: rather than being at the end of a river or a furrow, fading into the landscapes' horizons, here the vanishing points were outside this brothel, set all about its boundaries to keep it invisible to the world that did not wish to see it.

"Madame likes art," explained Niut, who'd seen Majlinda looking at one of the paintings. "She decorated the place herself, and once every few months she'll move things around or get a new painting. That particular painting was a gift from a client. Madame serviced him herself."

Majlinda blinked. Miriam and Lule had stopped to watch her, and Niut was still looking at the landscape. It was of mountains behind a plain, with a river flowing down on one side and a small town set on the other. Olive-skinned men drove carts and olive-skinned women drew water from a town well or carried children through the square. One of the few shops drawn well enough to be visible was a bookshop, and a shadow in its window that might have been a poor stroke of the paintbrush reminded Majlinda of her father.

"She services the Gians herself?" asked Majlinda, lightly touching the painting's frame, unwilling to touch the paint. It seemed her father was looking out at her, watching her as she was given a tour of the whorehouse which would be her home. "I thought she was a businesswoman."

"*Clients*," said Niut. "Always clients, never Gians. She is a businesswoman, and bodies are our business."

Our business, thought Majlinda. Niut had clung to Madame Vaccaro and had found some legitimacy in her. Perhaps that was why Niut had been here for three years. "Always clients," echoed Majlinda. "She is a businesswoman." She had grown used to saying what others wanted her to believe–it made life easier, and she wouldn't stop now. She didn't know if she'd be able to stop even if she were free.

"Down here," said Niut, leading the way to the end of the corridor, where she opened a closet and began pushing her way into a thin open space between hung garments. "There's lace and leather and cotton and silk, sorted in that order. Gowns, dresses, bodices, vests, pants, lingerie–some of this is quite tricky, but I can help you learn to manage it. Gerda loves these things–she's probably downstairs now. She's German, you know–Germans are more expensive, unless you're willing to take the drug-addicted ones, but there can be enough demand for them that occasionally it's worth it."

Majlinda shuddered at that casual announcement. She wondered if Niut had come from the Factory, or if somehow she'd chosen this life. It was hard to imagine someone choosing this life, but Majlinda knew there were those who had. Perhaps it did not matter–regardless of how she had come here, Niut was now Madame Vaccaro's creature. Majlinda should warn the others not to trust her, for she had become something worse than an unwilling whore.

The clothes did interest Majlinda slightly, she admitted. She was no longer confined to the color black, nor to the color white which she now wore. It felt good to be free of that shackle; but at the same time she frowned to think of it as a graduation, that she was somehow being promoted until one day they sought to make her like Niut.

Perhaps she was being too cruel to Niut; but she would warn the girls about her, all the same–it was far better safe than sorry, in this world where there was no forgiveness.

●　　　　　　●　　　　　　●

Rice was inexpensive, explained Niut. Pasta was inexpensive. Microwaving was easy. Set the washing machine to warm water for the bedsheets. Clothes were washed in different ways, and she'd explain how as they needed cleaning. At the end of the evening, if other girls were still working, you could join one; the client might give you both a bigger tip then, but he might also divvy up a tip he'd have otherwise given to one girl, or not give a tip at all. They should give a part of a tip gotten then to the first girl, and finishing early to go tip-fishing, if at the cost of a dissatisfied client, was not acceptable.

A single client could make them change clothes twice, but the third time cost extra, and most didn't want more than two, or even that many. A client could try on the clothes if he wanted, but that cost extra. Niut would teach the girls how to give light massages, and there was a Jacuzzi in a large, tiled room on the first floor. Clients could hit you or hold you tightly–but not so hard or so tightly as to leave a big mark. That cost extra too; this was a distinguished establishment.

The windows were nailed shut, Majlinda learned, and some of them had the curtains permanently closed–they were stapled to the walls.

Perhaps Madame Vaccaro feared someone would look in, see six couples on the beds in the upstairs rooms, and get suspicious. It seemed unlikely. Majlinda wondered what the Italian authorities would do if they found this brothel.

She thought of the Factory, of all the men who had travelled its halls and partaken of its product. Had none of them been lawmen, she wondered? Police, or sheriffs, or lawyers for the state? Doctors who were sworn to help, or at least not to harm? Wasn't it a harm to let something be, when that something hurt so many every day? When girls younger than Lule were coerced and forced? How could all these men hate Majlinda and her girls so much that they would leave the girls to this? And if the authorities caught her without her passport, what would they think of a whore?

How would they know? Majlinda blinked at the thought. How would they know she was a whore?

Murat would tell them.

A shiver ran through Majlinda's body.

No, she was past Murat. He was out of her life, now. He would tell police she was a whore if he learned they had her, perhaps; and he might send word of her life to her father and her village. But she was Madame Vaccaro's now; Murat was gone.

•   •   •

Some time after she had arrived at Madame Vaccaro's, Majlinda found herself sitting in the living room late one morning–the living room was really more of a waiting area, a reception room in the front of the house. A guard was always on duty here: Carmine, now, watching the television–a Saturday morning cartoon. Majlinda sat near him reading a finance magazine, something a client might read if all the girls were busy, or while he waited for a particular girl.

It had articles about what it called "The New Italian Economy," and it talked about skyrocketing property values in a few coastal towns, and about inflationary pressure. It was the first thing Majlinda had read in a long time, which was a large part of why she kept reading something so wholly irrelevant to her life.

When a commercial came on, Carmine got up and left the room. Startled, Majlinda stared down the hall after him. He disappeared into the bathroom, and the door closed behind him.

The other girls were upstairs, or in the kitchen in the back of the house, or doing laundry in the basement. She was alone in the front of the house. Nothing stood between her and freedom. Nothing except for her passport–what would they do to her without a passport? Where would she go? There was no place for her to go, and no home for her any longer.

But that didn't matter; it flashed through her mind in an instant, and she was at the door. Her hand closed around the handle, and it turned! It turned! It was all the way over, and she pulled–

The door didn't budge. Majlinda pushed and pulled quickly, and the time it took a man to use the toilet and wash his hands–no, it was Carmine, maybe he didn't wash his hands–suddenly tick-tocked in her mind. The door wiggled but didn't open. A bolt just over her head caught her eye–a keyed bolt-lock. She wouldn't be able to open it. A toilet flushed behind her. Frantically she moved across the room to the window, but blocks of wood screwed into the track kept the bottom from lifting high enough to squeeze through. Majlinda dove for her magazine, which lay splayed on the floor, and scrambled into the chair by the inner corridor. The bathroom door opened, and out came Carmine. His hands weren't wet, she noted; that could be important later.

Later? She tried to control her breathing, make it seem she'd only been reading. Carmine ignored her and sat back on the couch just in time for one last commercial–a Volkswagen commercial–to play.

Could the top of the window pull down, wondered Majlinda? They'd put wood blocks in the upper track to keep the window from opening upwards, but maybe they'd forgotten that it could open down. If not... She straightened her back, sucking in air resolutely, still pretending to read the magazine. The cartoon began again on the television, and Majlinda's eyes darted up to Carmine–his eyes were glued to the animated pictures. She looked over to the door swiftly, and then swiftly she looked down again. The hinges, she'd seen, were on the inside. If she couldn't get the window open, maybe she could get the hinges off the door. What if the deadbolt was too long? It might keep her from angling the door out of its frame.

It would have to be quick, she thought–the men might leave the room alone, but only rarely. Where would she go? Now that the opportunity was no longer so immediate, that question reared its head again: where could she go?

Maybe it didn't matter. So long as she was not back at the Factory or in the white room, she would rather be anywhere than here. She would do what she could to be ready, and when she could, she would go.

Swallowing, Majlinda stood and put down the magazine. She smiled at Carmine, and then she left to find her girls.

Chapter 12

The City of Virgil's Death

B RINDISI. Majlinda's father had never been here before, but he remembered another name, *Brundisium*, from when he was a boy. A schoolteacher had told him: according to Homer, Diomedes had founded the city after the Trojan war, after he'd been betrayed by his wife. Founding a city in a new land had been an attempt to put his past behind him and to live in peace. But for Diomedes' crimes in war–notably his theft of the Palladium from the Citadel of Troy– Dante had placed him in the eighth circle of hell. Myth and history were hard things, thought Majlinda's father.

Papola-Casale Airport was not a myth; it was only an airport. The bus to the city center was only a bus, yellow and square and with three sets of doors on the side. And First Star Employment did not exist.

Majlinda's father stood on the sidewalk, looking out from under the beautiful, green tree fronds and the tall, black streetlamps, at the spot where the agency should have been: at Via Persa 19A, 72100 Brindisi, Italia.

There was not so much as an alley between Via Persa 19 and 21.

Majlinda's father turned his head to look away from the spot, his fingers tightening on the handle of his ancient, battered suitcase. Apartment buildings a few stories in height decorated both sides of the street, their old masonry in a dozen different designs and light colors: slightly different shades of yellow and off-white and pale pink. The colors might have seemed normal in the midday sun, but in the moment's evening light they made this seem a sickly place.

Where was Majlinda?

Her father walked up the front step of Via Persa 19 and knocked on the grey door. A moment later, a little Italian woman opened it. Her mid-length hair was black, save for a small bit of silver growing in at the roots. The skin about her dark eyes was wrinkled, though Majlinda's father could not have said if the wrinkles were from age or worry.

"Yes?" asked the woman.

"I'm looking for First Star Employment," he explained, trying to smile. He did not wish to smile, but he was a salesman, and smiling was important in a first impression. "I was told they were near here."

The woman's lips pursed thoughtfully. "Nineteen A?"

A sudden stillness came to his breath. It had all been a misunderstanding, he thought: this woman would know all about it. "Yes," he said quietly. He was suddenly aware of a cold hand wrapped around his heart; it loosened now, for the first time in weeks. "Can you help me?"

"You're looking for your daughter," she said softly. The lines around her eyes sloped downward in sadness, now. "I'm sorry. There was another here like you, last week. For a week he stayed at a hotel near here. He wanted to stay longer, but he ran out of money. He didn't find his daughter."

The hand was back around his heart, wrapped as firmly as ever. He felt dizzy. He reached out an arm to lean against the door frame, and he closed his eyes.

"Would you like to sit down?"

Majlinda, he thought. "No. No, I can't. Did he talk to the police?"

The woman nodded. "They couldn't do anything. They said they'd call him if they found her, but that would probably only happen if she were involved in a crime."

Majlinda would never be. "Thank you."

The woman nodded gently. Majlinda's father echoed her motion once—it felt odd, nodding yes after all this time. Many of the younger generation in Albania—particularly the urban youth—were nodding like foreigners now, like Majlinda's father had nodded long ago. He had adapted to Albanian customs half a lifetime ago, but now he had left Albania. Would Majlinda be nodding when he saw her next? If he saw her again?

"I must," he said quietly. "I must."

The woman nodded gently one more time. She glanced to the right. "The hotel's a few blocks that way, on the right. You can't miss it. It's not the nicest, but it's cheap. If you need to stay for longer..." She tossed her head lightly to one side, as if thinking. "You could stay here for a day or two. On the couch."

He blinked. "I will find the hotel. You are generous. Thank you." He turned away and off the step.

"I have a daughter too," said the woman from behind him. "If I can do anything..."

"Thank you," he said, raising a hand in farewell as he walked away. Majlinda. What had happened to Majlinda?

Chapter 13

Freedom's Touch

"VIVIE: You were certainly quite justified–from the business point of view.

MRS WARREN: Yes; or any other point of view. What is any respectable girl brought up to do but to catch some rich man's fancy and get the benefit of his money by marrying him?–as if a marriage ceremony could make any difference in the right or wrong of the thing! Oh, the hypocrisy of the world makes me sick!

...

"It's far better than any other employment open to [a poor girl]. I always thought that oughtn't to be. It can't be right, Vivie, that there shouldn't be better opportunities for women. I stick to that: it's wrong. But it's so, right or wrong; and a girl must make the best of it."

–Act II, *Mrs. Warren's Profession*, 1894

"Play *Mrs. Warren's Profession* to an audience of clerical members of the Christian Social Union and of women well experienced in Rescue, Temperance, and Girls' Club work, and no moral panic will arise: every man and woman present will know that as long as poverty makes virtue hideous and the spare pocket-money of rich bachelordom makes vice dazzling, their daily hand-to-hand fight against prostitution with prayer and persuasion, shelters and scanty alms, will be a losing one. There was a time when they were able to urge that though 'the white lead factory where Anne Jane was poisoned' may be a far more terrible place than Mrs. Warren's house, yet hell is still more dreadful. Nowadays they no longer believe in hell; and the girls among whom they are working know that they do not believe in it, and would laugh at them if they did."

–*Author's Apology to Mrs. Warren's Profession*, 1902, George Bernard Shaw

"FREE?" asked Lule. "Where would we go?"

"Anywhere." Majlinda looked steadily at the younger girl. "Anywhere not here. It might be hard, but at least we'd be free."

"Free for them to find us," said Miriam. "Or free for the police to pick us up. I can't imagine we'd be treated well–how well would Italian whores be treated in Albania? Modestly well, if they were very lucky... but most police just wouldn't understand. Most *people* wouldn't."

"But we wouldn't be here," insisted Majlinda. "It's not right that we're here."

Miriam turned thoughtfully to look at the bed–they were closed in one of the bedrooms upstairs, where they'd come for privacy. Amazing to think that a bedroom could be used for privacy. "I'm not saying we shouldn't leave," Miriam said. "I'm saying that if we do, we should know where we're going."

"I don't know that we should leave," added Lule.

Majlinda frowned disbelievingly. "You want to stay?"

The younger girl turned away from her thoughtfully. She walked across the room slowly and stood over the bed; then she turned round and sat on the mattress, looking back at the other girls. "We have food and interesting clothing. We're well-treated. Here we have everything we need."

Miriam shook her head. "We're slaves, Lule."

"Slaves with means. Slaves who were wrapped in warm white robes and saved from the Factory. Slaves with jobs. Even if the bit about earning out our debt is a lie, we know that people can make a life here–look at Niut."

"Niut's been here for three years," said Miriam. "A lifetime is longer than three years, and a lifetime spent inside the same four walls isn't living. I'll never take the sun or the moon for granted again–they're a gift, every day, and they've been stolen from us."

"We can see them through the window," insisted Lule. "Did you know, Niut can go outside? Sometimes she goes to the supermarket or a clothing store, and she buys things for us. She *buys* things."

Majlinda felt an urge to argue, but instead she turned and looked out the window–they were in one of the rooms where the curtains opened. Miriam was already arguing Majlinda's position, and Majlinda didn't want Lule to feel the other two were ganging up on her.

Miriam shook her head. "Always with a guard. She's no more free than we are, Lule: she just thinks she is. That makes her more a slave than any of us." She frowned thoughtfully. "I grew up in Berat. We have a saying there: it is better to die standing than to live bending. Më mirë te vdesësh më këmbë, sesa të jetosh më gjunjë. Niut is bent so thoroughly that she could not find the sky with eagles to guide her, and I've bent too far already." Miriam's eyes burned with shame at that admission. "It's time to go. I don't want to bend anymore. I don't want to be Niut."

"She might be Madame one day," said Lule, looking away from Miriam, looking down at the bed and running a hand lightly over the sheets. "I heard her say it–she spoke of being Madame after Vaccaro retired, or of starting her own brothel one day. Can you imagine being your own Madame? You could give the girls everything, like we have everything."

Miriam frowned. "We don't have–"

"You like her," said Majlinda simply, glancing over to Lule. "You like them both, because they saved you from the Factory, they give you a soft robe, and they only make you sleep with about twelve different men every night." Lule frowned. "They brought you from a concrete-floored brothel to a brothel with floors of wood and carpet. They changed your uniform from stained shirts and skirts to laundered ones, from simple cotton to leather and silk and things with straps. Now you can walk from one room to another without being raped. Isn't it a wonderful thing she's given you?" The tone wasn't condemning–she could not condemn Lule. She could only hope that Lule would understand. "It's still a brothel, Lule. We are all still slaves, and whores. There's a better world past these windows, and we're not allowed out." Was it really better? It had to be. "There are better men than Gians–and they are Gians, even if you call them clients and pretend to be refined. Maybe it will be hard, and maybe people won't understand, and we can't go home, and in a way we'll be alone. Maybe

it will be hard to eat, or to work, or to live. But we won't be whores."
It was not shame she was feeling, Majlinda realized; it was anger.
Anger at Murat, anger at her father for letting her go and at herself
for wanting to believe the handsome stranger. Anger at Odeta for
telling her it was safe. Anger at Armand, and Peppino, and Carmine,
and Madame Vaccaro. At Niut who wanted to become like them; at
Anna who had said it wasn't so bad, really.

"Are there better men?" asked Miriam. "I mean, I agree we should
go–but do you really think there are better men? Even men who aren't
Gians let it happen."

"Somewhere," said Majlinda, turning from the girls to look out
the window again. She raised her eyes above the short apartments
on the other side of the road, raised them up to see the sky and the
shining white of the cumulus clouds that passed low and massive across
its wild blue drapery. "They want to come, but something prevents
them. Ignorance, or fear, or something else. Maybe even selfishness.
Even a good man is selfish, until he overcomes it." She reached out
one hand to touch the glass, to trace along the contours of a cloud
that touched the sky.

"You don't have to come, Lule," said Majlinda. "We could fail, or
we could get caught, or it could be hard, once we leave, to live. But
you don't have to come–it's up to you. It's your choice. It has to be
your choice, or we won't have learned a thing. You can stay, and we
can say goodbye; but I will try to leave. I will leave, eventually; or
they will kill me. But I will not die a whore. It doesn't matter if the
floor is cement or carpet, nor if the clothes are soft or taut: we never
left the Factory and we never left the white room before it. I intend
to leave."

A creak sounded behind her–the door to the room opening.

"There you are!" Niut's voice. How much had she heard?
"There's a leather theme this evening, you know. The first clients
should be getting here in a little while, so let's get moving! There's a
bodysuit that should fit you nicely, Miriam. Oh, and Lule–there's this
leather set with arm and leg cuffs that would look absolutely adorable
on you. It's too small for me. I'm so jealous! Come along, let's go."

Silence. "Why are you looking at Majlinda? I'm sure we'll find
something for her too. Come along, now." The cloud Majlinda had
traced had almost disappeared behind the building across the road,
but the bright blue of the sky was still beautiful to her. A single

hawk, flying high above the building and yet nearer than the cloud, seemed to cry out to her in its wildness and its freedom, though she could hear no cry.

"I'll be there in a moment," said Majlinda, lightly tapping the glass under the hawk.

•   •   •

The days passed quickly with the girls' anticipation of escape, and yet at times every moment seemed an hour: there was still rape. The girls had to endure it as if they accepted it, and as if they had no thought of escape.

When she was not being raped, Lule spent time in the closet up-stairs, learning more from Niut about how to care for the clothes: really she was picking clothes to leave in. Everything in the closet wasn't bodices and lace camisoles: there were cotton shirts, and jeans, and other simple clothes that would not make them seem the whores they were. Some clients liked to pretend the whores were ordinary girls, that they'd met them at the mall or at a club or a coffee shop. Other clients paid extra to hit them or tie them down. Some wanted you to resist, and others didn't. Some wanted you to dress like a schoolgirl and ask them to give better grades. The clients here were a cut above the Gians at the Factory, sometimes–but only a cut. It was all the same story.

One of the other girls–Althea, a Greek girl a little younger than Lule–refused to service a client, once. He was ugly, but clean. He'd brought a bottle of vodka, and he'd paid a bit extra to have a little leeway with Althea. He drank, and he made her drink too. She threw up eventually, but not before she called him names in Greek and bit him on the ear. It bled, and he stormed out, and Madame Vaccaro refunded his money and gave him a little extra. The Madame let Althea dry out and shower. The next morning, she took Althea down to the cage in the basement. It was a sturdy cage: a sort of mini-dungeon built to satisfy the fantasies of some of the more eccentric clients.

Madame Vaccaro took more than Althea to the basement: she took four pairs of handcuffs and a whip. And she took Carmine and Niut. The other girls huddled worriedly at the top of the stairs for a little while, listening to the screams that echoed up out of the brightly lit basement. Soon they wanted to leave, but Umberto stood over them and made them listen. He was one of the Madame's men, like Carmine, but not so nice.

The *crack* of the whip stopped after a while, and the screams faded, but then they were replaced by a near-rhythmic keening, laced with returning screams and thumps. *Carmine*, thought Majlinda. She knew the sounds too well to be terrified by them any longer, but she felt her lunch work its way upward in her stomach. She ran to the bathroom and leaned into the toilet, the rice from her lunch heaving sickly from her throat. The taste of it was unclean, though not more filthy than some tastes she knew. Still, in a brothel as clean as this one, it felt especially dirty.

She rinsed her throat at the sink, flushed the toilet, and sat on the floor. Umberto wouldn't make her listen if she was in here, though sooner or later he would remember she hadn't come back.

The door next to her opened suddenly, and in came Miriam. She, too, ran for the toilet, and lost her lunch, and rinsed out her throat. Weakly, she came over to the wall and sat next to Majlinda. There was little room next to them, now, for the door to open.

They were silent.

After a moment, Miriam said, "Umberto got bored. He went back to the front room. The others went upstairs. To get away from the screaming."

Majlinda nodded.

"I never told you," said Miriam.

Majlinda looked over to her curiously. Miriam had her hands drawn up around her knees, and her neck was stretched forward and a little low, as if to let it air out after the taste of her lunch had come up. Her eyes locked on some point on the floor, but Majlinda thought she was looking far beyond that.

"You saved me," explained Miriam. "When we were at the Factory. No, before that." She squinted. "It was in the van, wasn't it? They'd taken our lives away. I was just a girl, and then–then I was a whore. I was never a woman. I would have been like Anna, I think, or like Lule is in danger of becoming, if it hadn't been for you."

Miriam's eyes were still glued to the light cracks in the dark green tile floor: to the grout, between pieces of ceramic, that held it together. "Thank you, Majlinda."

"Kaltrina," whispered Majlinda. She didn't need to whisper, but whispering had been for so long a part of the ritual. "Kaltrina. Lule.

Arlinda. Zana."–Miriam's eyes came up from the floor to catch hers–
"Miriam. Majlinda." She smiled softly at Miriam, and it was the sort
of honest smile that was so precious in a house like this one. "Thank
you, Miriam."

Miriam smiled back, reflectively. "Will you pray with me?"

Majlinda's eyebrows shot up. "Pray?" How long had it been since
she'd seen someone pray? How long had it been since she had prayed
herself? "Do you pray often?"

"I haven't prayed, not since they began raping me," said Miriam.
"There wasn't time, or... No, that's not it."

Majlinda cocked her head sadly to one side. "Do you believe in
God anymore? I could understand where it would be hard."

"Of course I do." Miriam shook her head in a vigorous Albanian
yes. "It's me. You're supposed to be clean when you perform salat.
You're supposed to be pure, and I'll never be pure again. You helped,
Majlinda; I'm a little better because of you. I think... I think I
wouldn't even want to pray, if it hadn't been for you. You keep trying
to remind us who we are." Miriam squinted painfully. "As it is, I'm
worried: what would God think of me if he saw me now? What would
Allah think? I'm"–she winced–"I'm a whore. I want to pray, but I'm
afraid to."

Majlinda reached out and squeezed Miriam's hand. "Bismillah
ar-rahmaan ar-raheem: Al-hamdu lillahi rabb al-alameen," she began
softly.

There were small tears in Miriam's eyes, and slowly her lips began to echo Majlinda's. Together, they continued: "Ar-rahmaan ar-
raheem', Maliki yawm ad-deen, Iyyaaka naabudu wa iyyaaka nastaeen;
Ihdina s-siraata l-mustaqeem, Siraata l-latheena anamta alaihim ghair
al-mughdoobi alaihim wa la daaleen."

"You're not even Muslim," said Miriam.

Majlinda smiled slightly. "But I had friends who were, once."

"Thank you, Majlinda. Thank you more than..." A smile and a
frown seemed to be warring on Miriam's face. "Can we do it again,
properly? A little later? I'd like to wash, first. I'd like to be clean."

When we're free, Majlinda thought. *We'll be clean when we're free.*
But what she said was, "Yes, Miriam. We can."

● ● ●

It was Majlinda's job to scout the hall. Slowly, so as not to arouse suspicion, she began to spend more time there. She read the magazines or

watched the television with Carmine. Never with Umberto–Umberto was far less kind. They would escape when Carmine was on watch, she was sure, and she hated to abuse his kindness so; yet his kindness did not excuse his business.

The upper window was rigged so it wouldn't pull down, she discovered–that meant they'd need to pull the hinges from the door or get the key. Getting the key seemed problematic–they could probably do it: one or more of them could seduce Carmine and another could rifle through his things for the key. But if they did that, they'd risk being discovered, and then Madame Vaccaro would punish them and be sure they never had a chance to escape.

That left the hinges.

There were no tools in the house save a locked tool chest in the basement; it occurred to Majlinda to use a knife from the kitchen. They weren't sharp knives–the only sharp knives in the house were locked up and kept for the use of clients–but Majlinda managed to wedge one into the door's lower hinge. The spike slipped up an eighth of an inch. She pried it quickly a little further; it took effort, but it moved. She tapped it back into place with the butt of the knife and hurried back to her seat before Carmine returned.

The next day, she repeated the process with the upper hinge. She was satisfied she could dismantle them in very little time. The knife she buried in the upholstery of her favorite downstairs chair–how odd, she thought, that waiting Gians would sit on the instrument of her freedom.

The other girls would need to be downstairs, she knew, and it couldn't seem unusual that they were there. Niut couldn't be around, or she'd try to stop them. It could be in the late morning, thought Majlinda, when Carmine was on duty and before most of the girls were up.

So Majlinda and Miriam and Lule began to wake early each day, so it wouldn't seem strange for them to be up the day of their escape. Miriam and Lule made brunch in the kitchen while Majlinda sat, reading in the front hall, next to Carmine. It was tiring to cut into their sleep, but it let them get their chores done early and steal a little nap in the afternoons.

They didn't know the neighborhood well enough to know where to hide once they escaped. The apartments across the street seemed too near: the time lost finding a front door was locked would be time the girls were visible from Vaccaro's, and could get them caught again. They decided they'd be best to look for a church or a mosque, for they couldn't imagine Madame Vaccaro or her men in a church or a mosque; also, there were supposed to be lots of churches in Italy–more by far than there had been in Albania.

Majlinda almost wanted them to look for a bookstore; the bookstore in the painting upstairs had so reminded her of her father. But a bookstore was not so easy to spot as a church spire, and the men went into bookstores sometimes. Carmine did, at least. He read *1984*, and he gave it to Majlinda to read, afterwards. She read all the time, and he was considerate enough to think that maybe she was bored with the magazines. Maybe he thought she liked him, and that that was why she spent all the time in the hallway. If it hadn't been for Althea's keening, Majlinda might, almost, have liked him. He wasn't more cruel than he needed to be, and he was even generous at times when he didn't need to be.

He asked her about the book once. She closed it and looked down at the cover thoughtfully. It was the first book she'd read in a long time, and she wasn't used to thinking about books. It wasn't something she'd read before, and it wasn't like the romances she'd used to enjoy–this book was more serious, and, for all its fiction, was more real, if not so real as the men who came to her bed each night. "I think it's very sad," she said quietly. "It's sad that entire peoples should lie to themselves so well and so thoroughly. They believe the lie. It makes me wonder..." She frowned, wondering how much it was safe to explain. "What does it mean, 'a place where there is no darkness'? Do we live in a place like that? Darkness can be important sometimes, and this book seems..." She ran a finger lightly along the spine of the book. It was a new copy, no doubt bought and paid for by profits made from the sale of her body. "The whole book is a darkness, I think. A foreshadow. It's meant to be a warning, isn't it? A warning, and a preview of things to come?"

Carmine nodded. "I think so. You put it well." He raised his bushy eyebrows thoughtfully and ran his eyes over Majlinda. It was not the leering glance of a man who wished to sate himself, but the gaze of a man who wonders about the person under the skin. It was the first time Majlinda had felt that gaze in a long time, and it thrilled her slightly. "You sound like my daughter did when she read the book," he added.

"You have a daughter? I didn't know."

Carmine smiled softly. "At university. Gabriella–it means 'Devoted to God.' She speaks like you do, about sadness, and what things are trying to say. You would like her."

Majlinda smiled softly, thoughtfully in return, feeling the palpable words that lingered unspoken in the air: *Bring her one day. We'll talk about the book.* Bring his daughter here to see what he did every day, to talk over lunch with a whore. How could a man with a daughter do his job, knowing each girl here was the daughter of another man? She could not understand, even as she could not understand the Gians who came and abused her and felt no sorrow. She knew what they did, knew the sickening thrill in their eyes and the rush of power it seemed to give them; but she still could not understand why, and that lack of understanding troubled her.

Carmine stood, pulling his eyes away from hers, and walked past her chair. Majlinda blinked. She heard the bathroom door from the hallway behind her before she realized that this was her moment.

She plunged an arm down between her seat cushion and the chair's frame, grasping at the hidden knife-handle. The knife caught on something, but she forced it up through the fabric, stood, and ran to the door. A terrible *squeak* sounded as she pried the spike loose in the upper hinge. Her hands pushed against the flat of the blade as she used its back to *pop* the spike out.

Miriam and Lule came running quietly through the hall behind her, anxiously throwing glances towards the bathroom. Majlinda jammed the sharper edge of the kitchen knife into the lower hinge and pulled with all her might. It sprang up and she fell backwards; Miriam caught her and pushed her to her feet. The toilet flushed behind them.

They pulled at the door; it barely moved.

"Put the hinges back in!" said Lule. "Quickly!"

"No!" Majlinda jammed the knife in between pieces of the hinge, and tried to pivot it. Miriam's fingers caught at the hinge edge and pulled again. "Help, Lule!" urged Majlinda.

Lule joined Miriam, thrusting her fingers in under the hinge and pulling, and pulling. A rush of water behind them–He was washing his hands! He was finally washing his hands. He never washed his hands. Light came in through the edge of the cream-colored door, and they had it out at a little angle. "Sideways," said Majlinda. "There's a bolt! Pull sideways, towards the hinge!"

They dragged the door across the floor, and its corner dug into the blue carpet and tore a hole down to the cheap, white linoleum below. As soon as there was enough of an opening in the doorway, the girls dropped the door against its frame. Miriam pushed open the screen door outside–it wasn't locked, thank God–and squeezed out of the brothel. Lule was behind her.

The sound of running footsteps came from the hallway. "HELP!" shouted Carmine.

Chapter 14

Let Him Be a Hero

HIS FINGERS CAUGHT AT MAJLINDA'S SHOULDER, but she pulled away, darting to freedom out the narrow hole that was too small for a man.

She ran, and it felt like her footfalls echoed on the square cement slabs of the front walk, crying out "Here runs a whore!" Miriam broke left at the end of the walk; Majlinda and Lule broke right. That was part of the plan: they'd be followed quickly and would be harder to catch if they split up. Majlinda had been hesitant to split up, but she saw the wisdom in it and Miriam had been willing to take the risk of fleeing alone.

Every touch of her sandals on the sidewalk jarred at her. Clover-spotted grass on either side was green and vibrant and danced in the wind, and Majlinda wanted desperately to dive into it and roll in even the little patch of grass between the sidewalk and the road: it was the first green growing thing she'd been able to enjoy since before the white room.

She tugged at Lule's arm, and the two of them ran across the street. A car screeched to a stop mere inches from them–Majlinda's hand jarred on the hood, and she looked up at the driver. Madame Vaccaro! It was Madame Vaccaro, driving a Fiat. Madly, Majlinda stuck out her tongue. A shadow came over the Madame's eyes. Behind the car, Carmine was running towards them.

Majlinda and Lule darted off. A street led to the left; they followed it. A nice soft grass edging and a lovingly cared-for hedge beside it took the place of a sidewalk, but Majlinda ran in the street. She had to get someplace populated–someplace where they couldn't kidnap her. Carmine was a big man, but not out of shape–could she outrun him? Could Lule?

A car came down the road in front of her–a Volkswagen. Majlinda waved her arms and ran in front of it. "HELP!" The old lady inside looked at her as if she were crazy and drove around her quickly.

Majlinda looked back: Carmine just now turned the corner–the lady hadn't seen him chasing the girls.

How fast could she run? To the left a shadowed alleyway barely wider than Majlinda cut through the block. "Lule!" Majlinda ran that way, scraping elbows against the narrow walls, her sandals' muted *clap-clap* sounding on the old stone beneath her. She darted with Lule past tiny windows on both sides, over a storm drain and to the other side of the block. They turned away from Vaccaro's. Ahead of them, Miriam was running on the opposite side of the street: she turned a corner to the left, and was gone.

Majlinda bore right–she could not follow Miriam. This was a neighborhood, she thought–people *lived* here, and were letting a man chase her in the streets. "*HELP!*" she cried. It was hard to cry while she was running. "*RAPE! HELP!*" It wasn't right, she thought, her mind racing–Carmine had never raped her, and had never even slept with her. She swung right at the corner.

A car came into sight at the end of the block, driving casually towards her along this quiet residential street: a blue and white car, with lights on top. The large, blue letters of "POLIZIA" stretched across the driver-side door. How odd, Majlinda thought: a police car so close, only a block away, driving by when she escaped. It slowed now, and the officer inside looked out at her. He pulled to the side of the street in front of her, cutting off her run. She turned swiftly to look behind her. Carmine was nowhere to be seen–he hadn't turned the corner yet, or he'd seen the officer and turned away. Lule's arm still clasped hers, and the fifteen-year-old was shaking.

The officer's uniform reminded Majlinda of the sameness of the girls' clothing at the Factory. She stood before him, breathing heavily, panting next to Lule who was filled with terror. He was the first man she'd seen since before the white room who might be a good man, who didn't earn a living raping women or arranging for them to be raped, who might not pay to rape them. He was the first man she'd seen in ages who might not be worse than the whores that she and her girls had become, and she was filled with shame for what they were, even as she thought, *please, let him be a good man.*

"Help us," Majlinda said. "A man's chasing us. Help us." There were still good men in the world, she thought: she used to tell that to her girls in the stories, the stories out of Albania and out of her imagination. There had been fewer stories since the Factory, where it had seemed they'd been needed more and there'd been more girls to hear; but she still told stories sometimes, and she still believed that there were good men in the world. *Let this one be a hero.*

The officer raised his eyes to look over her shoulder, where no man appeared from around the corner to follow her. What had happened to Carmine? Could he have seen Miriam and run after her? Majlinda desperately hoped not–she hoped he'd been cowed by the officer, or that he'd tripped and twisted his ankle. Not worse than that–she promised herself suddenly, here while her future might still be in the balance, that she would never wish great pain on anyone. It was a free choice, and she loved that it was; she was free, here, in this moment– she might be free forever, or she might never be free again.

She knelt down at the side of the road and pushed her hand onto the earth, rubbed her palm into the naked green grass, into the free soil that basked under the sun and showered under the rain and knew not how to beat a girl or hurt a soul. "Help us," she said again. "It's been so long since I've touched the grass... they've held us prisoners." She lowered her nose to the ground, and smelled the green. The stalks there tickled her cheeks.

Let the officer think her crazy, she thought–if she was free, then she would feel the grass.

"There's a house on the Via Solare," said the officer. "We've been getting reports for a while, now. It's about a block from here. Are you from there?"

Shame wanted to burn in Majlinda's cheeks, but the freedom of the grass tickling them wiped the shame away. She rolled over, letting her dark hair splay open behind her, its fine, free strands intermingling with the free green stalks that now seemed its brethren. The sky was blue above her, and it was a blue she could have died in, for her joy at not being inside, at not being a prisoner. "We are from there," she admitted freely. "We are not there any longer."

"Someone's chasing you?"

"A man," she answered, though she watched only the sky, and not the face of the police officer who stood over her and looked down at her, and whose head blocked a cloud. "He works at the house, and we escaped, and he chased us. He's not a good man, but he's not particularly bad. He raped Althea, but he never raped me."

The officer blinked. He glanced towards Lule. "You're from there, too?"

Lule looked down at Majlinda. Majlinda nodded lightly. "She is."

"We can all go downtown," said the officer. "The three of us together. If you make a statement, we can close down the house with the statement as evidence. And we can protect you from the man who's following you."

All of the girls would be free, thought Majlinda. Niut wouldn't like it. Would the police treat them well?

The police officer was helping Lule into the back of his car. She went meekly, and she had not touched the grass. How could you be free and not touch the grass, not smell the green things that grow or look up at the sky and the clouds? Majlinda gingerly dug her finger into the soil beneath a small clump of grass, and pulled up the stalks lovingly. She slid them into her jeans pocket–she might get in a car now, and travel to a police station, and make a statement, and maybe eventually they'd try to send her back to Albania and to her father. She didn't know if she wanted them to, but they might try. She would know soon enough–but before she stepped into the car, she wanted the grass in her pocket as a reminder of her freedom. Carmine hadn't appeared, and she wondered if she would ever see him again. Had she endangered his job by running away? She would soon, she knew. If the police came, how would his daughter get through college? Who would pay for it?

Of course it mattered, Majlinda knew–it mattered that Carmine's daughter go to college. But against the cost, a college education wasn't worth it. Majlinda didn't need to have gone to college to know that; she had learned it in a brothel.

When the officer offered to help her up, she waved him off. She stood on her own. Lule was looking at her expectantly, tucked back against the opposite door inside the car, her young eyes uncertain. Majlinda wanted to run–wanted to run wild and free until she found a field filled with grass, or at least a park with trees under the sky–but when the officer left, Carmine might appear; and Lule still needed her, and so did Althea. Did Niut? She didn't know.

So Majlinda took a deep breath, felt the tender grass in her pocket, and stepped down into the back of the patrol car. The officer smiled at her and closed the door, and he slipped back into the driver seat. He hadn't stopped the engine, and he closed his door and put on his seat belt.

"We don't have any papers," Majlinda told him. "We're Albanian, but they smuggled us here. They still have our passports somewhere, but we don't have them, because they took them. I'm sorry we don't have them."

"It's all right, Majlinda," said the officer. "It will all be all right."

A tight ball of dread formed suddenly in her throat. The freedom of a moment ago turned to ash in her mouth, save for a small echo of it, save for the desperate clutch of the grass in her pocket. *She had never told him her name.* The car pulled away from the curb.

Quietly–quietly so he wouldn't know–she reached to her door and pulled at the handle, but the door wouldn't open. A metal grate– a screen to keep prisoners here–sat between her and the front seat. There was no control to lower the window.

On her right, Lule was oblivious. Her eyes were not innocent–they would never be innocent again–but they were almost hopeful now, and there was a spark in them Majlinda had never hoped to see. Lule was finally beginning to believe she'd escaped.

Majlinda slid over on the seat and held her gently, sliding an arm around Lule's waist and secretively using it to try the other door–but that door, too, failed to open.

"Whatever happens, Lule," whispered Majlinda, "whatever happens to any of us, remember it's right we tried. Remember what it is to be free, whether it's for a moment or a lifetime. There's a world beyond the walls of the brothel, and it's worth fighting for." She swallowed. "There are good men in the world, Lule. It's just that they don't know, or that they're kept away. They exist. Just like there are good women."

"Can you drive us around a little bit?" asked Majlinda of the officer in front. "We haven't been outside in months. Just... just around a few blocks, something new to see. Anything?" She tried to keep the desperation from her voice, and Lule did not seem to notice; but the officer looked in his rear-view mirror, and he met her eyes, and he knew: he knew that she knew.

"We've had no fresh air," she added. "You don't know what it's like. You can't know. They take you and they force you and they use you. What if it were your daughter? Your sister? Please, just drive us around a little. Take your time, before we go–" Her thoughts flitted back to Lule. Let Lule believe they were still free, for a while yet. "before we go where you take us."

There was a troubled look in the man's eyes. She remembered him now, she realized: he had been a Gian, though she couldn't remember when. She thought that he'd been violent, that he'd called her harsh names in Italian and bitten her legs and maybe done other things she had forgotten. She thought he'd done those things, though it was hard to know–there had been too many Gians, too many faces. She wished there had been fewer.

He turned right, rather than left–away from Madame Vaccaro's, not towards. They passed two blocks of houses, and then a little book store, and a coffee shop, and a little outdoor restaurant. She saw a church spire a few blocks away, and wondered if Miriam would seek it out, and if she would find help there.

The windows startled her when they came down–only an inch or two, not enough to slip through–but enough to smell the air. It was chill–colder than she'd realized running from Carmine. It must be tending towards winter, she thought. Had it been less than a year since she'd been kidnapped? Since Murat had come with his shirt and Odeta had come with her contracts? Or had a winter come and gone while Majlinda was in the white room, and this was a new year? How long had she been at the Factory, or even at the brothel? Surely it had not been a year, and yet it could have been. Was she eighteen, now? Nineteen? Was young Lule young?

Majlinda slipped her fingers into the space where the window was open, and she tried to pull. Nothing happened. She caught the officer's eyes in the mirror, and he shook his head. He would let them have air and a ride, to assuage his conscience; but he wouldn't let them go.

Majlinda pulled her knees up sideways onto the seat, and leaned her cheek over Lule's head. She reached one arm around the young girl and let the other run lightly over the grass in her pocket, remembering how she'd felt lying in the grass's greenness for the first time in months, even though it had been on the side of the road in a city. Her nose caught a whiff of the chill, and the scents of free air moving past the car. It was a thing one might not miss until one had not scented it in what seemed like a long age of the world. Her eyes darted lightly across everything she could see, across every shop and lamp-post, and the faces of those men and women whom she saw. There were not many—perhaps the chill kept them indoors, or perhaps the officer drove this way because there would be so few to see his crime—but there were some.

Did they know about the underworld which existed? How many of them had been Gians, like the officer who drove her? How many knew and did nothing, and walked about in their shoes, the shoes they took for granted that saved their feet from the hard cement beneath them? Majlinda hadn't owned shoes in months. She wore sandals, now—communal sandals, taken from the closet this morning.

"You could let us go," said Majlinda. "We'll disappear. We won't come in to the police, or tell anyone about you, or about the Factory." If he let them go, she wouldn't tell anyone about him. Her other words might be lies—she didn't know or care. She had grown used to lying, though the lies were most commonly to men who wanted to hear the lies. Even the most educated would believe that you liked him, or that a smile was genuine, or anything else you told him, if only he wanted to believe.

But the officer shook his head again. "I need to take you to the station," he lied, his eyes flickering over to Lule in the mirror, and then away from the mirror and back to the road. "You need to give a statement."

A lie for a lie, thought Majlinda, *like an eye for an eye—unjust.*

"It's all right, Majlinda," said Lule. "It will be all right. I can give a statement, like he says. It started with Odeta, didn't it? With Odeta and Murat? And then Armand, that first night." Lule shuddered. "I remember. I'll tell. It's all right."

So Armand was Lule's Murat, was the man who'd raped her first, on that afternoon so long ago. Majlinda had not known that. "No," she said. "It started with neither Armand, nor Murat, nor Odeta. It started with the Gians."

Lule frowned. "But they only came afterwards. We were already—" Her eyes glanced worriedly towards the police officer in the front seat. She lowered her voice. "We were already what we are, when they came."

Majlinda nodded. She turned to look out the window, trying to see every tree and every house, to steal every moment she could of a world that ought to have belonged to her. "Look out the window, Lule.

Armand and his kind could never alone despoil a world so beautiful. We are created for the Gians, and the Gians pay for us and for our breaking. Some think we're already what we are, and others don't care. Many don't want to think about how we became the whores they know, or they lie to themselves about it. They don't stop to think that every time they pay for us, they pay for the industry. They pay for the white room where they rape us and the ship that carries us across the sea. They pay for the time it takes to kidnap us and the readiness to kidnap a new girl when we're gone. It's a business, Lule. And none of this–none of it–would be possible without the Gians. The Gians buy, and it begins with them." She shook her head. Why think of this now, in their few moments of almost-freedom? "Look out the window, Lule."

They watched the walks, and the road, and the few people whom they saw; they saw beautiful stained-glass and old stonework on the side of a church, and Majlinda wondered if Miriam might be inside (though she did not speak of it–Majlinda didn't want the officer to hear); they saw nice little houses, and they saw apartment buildings that grew more and more familiar; and then Lule screamed, and the windows rolled up.

Lule pulled at the door-handles. The handles pulled towards her, but the doors would not open. To the right was the front walk to Madame Vaccaro's. The brothel's screen door was closed, and behind it Umberto held the inner door upright, and Carmine studied the hinges.

The officer in the front seat turned his head to look at the girls.

"You don't have to do this," said Majlinda firmly.

"You're a whore," he said accusingly. "Don't pretend you know what I have to do."

"I'm your mother," said Majlinda simply. "I'm your sister. I'm your neighbor. I'm the person you're sworn to protect, and you're sending me back into hell. I don't know you, officer; but I know you don't have to do that." There was no fear in her voice or in her breast: there was only a profound stillness. Was there any chance at all that he would help them? "You can save us. You can be a good man, and you can save us."

"I am a good man," he said angrily, "and you're not." He turned away and stepped from the car.

Lule had stopped screaming. Now she sobbed great, raspy cries that ought to have broken Majlinda's heart; but Majlinda had no time for tears. She pushed her shoulders back against the rear seat and kicked against the grate in front of her, the one that turned the back of the car into a cage like the cage in the grey van. The cage barely rattled under the desperate kick of her feet.

She sprang up and studied it–it was held in by bolts at the edges. She tried to grip one, but it was on too tightly, and her fingers couldn't twist it at all. Besides, it would have taken too long to take them all out. "Help me, Lule!" She spun sideways on the seat and leaned her back against Lule. "Hold steady!" Her sandals she kicked hard against the glass of the window, but like the cage, it barely moved. Something in her pocket jammed into her side.

It was the kitchen knife! She pulled it out quickly and swung the heavy end into the glass. It *thump*-ed, but didn't even leave a dent. This car was built to keep criminals apart from innocents by locking them away. Now it was working too well, in the wrong direction.

Carmine and Umberto were walking towards the car, following the officer. Desperately, Majlinda plunged her knife into the back of her seat. It plunged through the dark upholstery only to *clang* into a metal barrier. She tried driving it sideways, against the door–but it was only a kitchen knife.

Carmine opened Lule's door. He and Umberto had come, had come to take the whores back to their whorehouse.

EUROP Magazine reported police accompanying trafficking victims to a bus that would go to their home, but the driver wouldn't take them if they couldn't pay for the ticket. The men who'd abducted them arrived shortly thereafter and bribed the police, taking the women back into slavery. [7]

Victor Malarek reports police in Tel Aviv sometimes get discount rates because of their good relations with brothel-owners, and some–at the extremes–are even involved directly in the buying and selling of slaves, or the returning of escapees to their brothels. He also reports a pattern of the accepted and/or ignored use of trafficked women by peacekeepers, UN workers, international police, and US defense contractors. [14]

Peter Landesman in *The New York Times Magazine* reports a $200,000 weekly payoff shared among 10 senior officials in the state of Sonora, Mexico: their graft from the trafficking trade. [12]

"Several U.S. women reported that police officers or undercover cops had asked for sex in exchange for dropping charges against them.

'Police officers - they were abusive. The undercover cops asked me to have sex with them - straight and oral - in order to drop the charges.'

'Police are frequent customers, though, and they walk in like they own the place. In fact one of the cops ran his own house somewhere in Brooklyn and was always trying to get me to be part of his posse.'

"Another U.S. woman commented that her first 'trick' was a policeman. She was not arrested, because he let her off."

Sex Trafficking of Women in the United States
Raymond, Hughes, & Gomez, 2001 [19]

"Traffickers cannot create demand, and criminal businesses tend to be opportunistic rather than developmental. Poverty and corruption frequently go hand in hand; trafficking and modern-day slavery thrive in corrupt environments. Trafficking cannot exist without a degree of participation from the government, the police, and the judicial system. This is the ugly face, the dark side of globalization."

–Julia Ormond
UNODC Goodwill Ambassador [18]

Chapter 15

Helen's Call

A NEW BOY STOOD at the desk. His hair was neat, his clothes were plain, and his name tag said "Roberto."

Majlinda's father hesitated. He had been about to leave Brindisi, thinking he might go north along the coast and stop in another city. Here, no one on the streets had known Majlinda's name; no one had recognized her face. There were many more cities to search, and no guarantee Majlinda had even been in Italy. *The whole world to search,* thought her father, not for the first time. She hadn't called his phone yet, and the police had found nothing.

He approached the boy at the front desk. "I'm looking for a girl," he began. His voice was that of a salesman, though he was a worried father. This was a sales pitch, after all, for the boy's attention and for his memory. Majlinda's father's head nodded slightly up and down, even as in Albania it would have bobbed slightly from side to side.

"How old?" asked Roberto, smiling back. "You're in room three-oh-six?"

Majlinda's father nodded. "Seventeen years old. Her name is Majlinda."

"Majlinda?" Roberto mouthed the name silently, then jotted it down on a piece of paper. "All right. She'll be in your room in about half an hour."

Majlinda's father blinked. "What? How?"

"Half an hour, room three-oh-six. It's no problem. It's done. Unless... is half an hour too soon for you? Would you like to see Majlinda this evening, maybe?"

Majlinda's father squinted, not quite believing his ears. He should ask more, but he feared to break the fragile surreality of the moment. "No, half an hour is fine. My room, you say? She'll just knock on the door?"

"Leave it unlocked and she won't even knock." Roberto gave him a knowing smile. "But she'll lock it behind her when she goes in."

"I'll..." *Don't question the impossible.* "I'll go wait for her."

"Excellent!" Robert looked down at the notepad where he'd written Majlinda's name, and then he picked up a phone.

•   •   •

The door slipped shut behind her. She was a young German girl with golden hair, wearing a sheer blue dress that hugged her body in suggestive ways. If it had been a better dress, or if Majlinda's father had been less expectant, it might have been a display of beauty; but here, after daring to dream that he might see his daughter, he could see only a young girl in a too-cheap dress.

"I'm Majlinda," she said. "I'm seventeen years old."

For a moment the surreality of the conversation at the front desk held, and his mind refused to do more than halt, dumbfounded.

Then he lowered himself to sit on the edge of his bed, holding his head in one hand. "No, no. Majlinda is my daughter. I'm looking for her."

"You're a kinky one. Hello, Daddy."

Majlinda's father squinted painfully, his eyes closing for a moment. Where was his baby girl? "No. There's been a mistake. I'm not looking for a... a working girl. I'm looking for my daughter. My real daughter. I thought she might be here in Brindisi, and the desk clerk said he could find her. I didn't understand. I didn't believe him, but I didn't understand." He pulled his fingers away from his eyes–there were tears in them now: from strain, not from sobbing. "I still don't, it's just–" His shoulders hurt. Why did they hurt? He'd been filled with such tension waiting for her, and now it was only a working girl. "I'm sorry, Miss. It's really a mistake."

The girl frowned, and suddenly she seemed to him much smaller, and the makeup she wore seemed like paint spilled by a child. How old was she? "I have to go," she said. She turned to leave the room.

"Wait," he asked. "Have you seen her? I have a photo."

"I have to be making money," said the girl. "I have to go–"

"I'll pay for some time," said Majlinda's father. "Just a few minutes. Have you seen her?" He held out one of the photos he had of his daughter; it had been taken months ago, at her school graduation. At seventeen, she'd graduated a year early, and her father had been proud. The young working girl studied the image for a moment, seeming sad and somehow a little worried. Taking it from Majlinda's father, she walked across the room to a chair by the window, where she sat and considered the picture thoughtfully. She sighed.

"Please, do you know her?"

The girl shook her head. "No. I'm sorry." With her eyes still on the photograph, she added softly, "Her father came looking for her? Fathers don't come looking. I'm told mine never looked for me. He wouldn't like me now. Not with my job."

Because of her job? A working girl. A prostitute. Her father had never come looking for her. Majlinda's father let the thought wash through him, and he didn't know how to respond to it.

His daughter's disappearance still throbbed in his mind like an open wound, but now he worried too about the young girl who stood in front of him. Why was she here, and why had there been such fear in her eyes when she'd said she needed to make money? It had been surreal, but now it was real.

Majlinda, he thought. Majlinda wasn't like this girl. She would never have sold her body. He remembered how that stranger, Murat, had looked at her months ago in the store. She'd liked that, and she might have been tricked or seduced or even given herself too easily, but she would never have sold herself to someone like him. It was hard for a father to admit his daughter could be seduced, but he believed too strongly in Majlinda to think she could ever sell her own body. She could be raped, though.

He swallowed at the thought. She would be too smart. She wouldn't let herself be put in that position. She would ask too many questions–

Like I asked questions of Odeta? The thought stung. The money had made him blind. His drinking had made him blind. His daughter hadn't simply disappeared or made a wrong decision: she had been stolen.

His eyes caught on a print on the hotel wall: a hundred ships– triremes and war galleys–were being tossed by waves in a storm at sea. Some were crashing into each other, and men on all of them were running or carrying or crying, holding for their lives to rope or stay or oar. In the middle of it all, one woman seemed calm: she stood on the deck of a great ship and looked out of the painting, towards the viewer, as if to pretend that the waters of the storm posed no danger to her, and to warn the viewer not to save her. A hundred ships were stormed and sunk about her, and she did not wish to see more die. Was she Helen, wondered Majlinda's father? Or was she only another nameless girl, another nameless daughter? He found his fingers hovering just above the surface of the print. *I'm coming*, he thought.

Swallowing, he turned to face the girl in the corner. She was holding Majlinda's picture, sitting back as far and as deeply in the cushions of the chair as she could go, and looking out his window. Now that he looked more closely, he saw bags under her eyes, and it was exhaustion, not only sadness, which was hidden under her makeup. She had worn a guard when she'd walked into the room: a second skin of lies and smiles meant to entice a man and earn her money. Now she was herself, and it seemed to Majlinda's father that what was left of her was small and hard to see, was a nugget of what might have once been a beautiful daughter, but had been dried and used and fallen away. If that could happen to this girl, what could happen to Majlinda? Would Majlinda be the same when he found her?

He could not know unless he found her.

He let his eyes pass sadly over the young girl in the corner. Quietly and gently, afraid that the question might hurt, he asked her, "Who was your father?"

Chapter 16

Freedom's Cost

"The project interviewer observed that this U.S. woman had a particularly noticeable eye injury that she hadn't mentioned in her interview. It was only when the interviewer asked about the woman's eye, that she explained that 'she had completely forgotten about that.' This survivor of prostitution had been attacked by a buyer with a shard of broken glass that cut her eyeball in half. She now has only limited visibility and weak muscle control in her left eye. What the interviewer saw as noteworthy, the interviewee saw as one almost forgettable example of the many violent experiences she had suffered in her lifetime."

Sex Trafficking of Women in the United States [19]

IT WAS NOT SO BAD, really, as Majlinda had thought it might be: they put her in the cage in the basement, and they turned out the light. Niut brought her bread and water once in a long while. The bread was dry–Majlinda thought they microwaved it–and she was often hungry, but she did not starve. There were no windows down here–not even little ones near the ceiling–so she didn't know when the days passed, and the darkness about her was complete. Water would run in that darkness, when upstairs a toilet flushed or a shower ran. Sometimes she wished she could reach the running water in the invisible pipes, to drink, but she couldn't: her arms fit through the bars of the cage, and she could touch two pipes, but there were no faucets. One pipe was cold, and if she was very thirsty, she would wipe drops of condensation from its side and touch them to her lips.

The room smelled of dampness from the laundry or the pipes, and sometimes it smelled of the bedpan Niut brought her with her food.

She wondered what had happened to Lule. Girls came downstairs to do laundry, but they never spoke to her, and Lule never came down.

Umberto came down every now and then. He slapped her, and he left bruises on her chest and her legs and he raped her–but the bruises faded quickly, if in the little light she had she could see well enough to judge. He hit her, but he didn't hit her hard. He might have thought he was being cruel, and Majlinda let him believe; but he had never known Murat, and had never known the touch of Armand's cigarette.

She had light–dim light–only when others came to the basement. Madame Vaccaro didn't come, but Umberto sometimes brought down a Gian who wanted a girl in a cage, or who was rougher than normal. Sometimes she'd be given a wet sponge first, to clean herself. There were fewer Gians here than she would have had to service upstairs, even though they were rougher–so it was not such a terrible punishment.

Majlinda heard Anna's words echo in her thoughts sometimes: "It's not so bad, really." It was bad, she knew: it was simply not so bad as it could have been. She still couldn't close her mind to the sensations of a man who drove her legs apart or bit her or beat her, but she now knew that even such absolute wrongs were relative things: they could call her trash and leave her in the dark, but they could not, here, drive her from herself.

She told stories to herself. She did it quietly, because she had no water. She spoke again of Bukura e Dheut, and of Tomor, and of the tree over the river, and many more stories besides. She made new ones up–what else was she to do, in the dark? She whispered, as each story ended, "Kaltrina. Lule. Arlinda. Zana. Miriam. Majlinda." Sometimes she added Althea to the list, or Clarissa. Sometimes it would be Anna. She wondered if she was losing her mind.

In the darkness of the basement she found a refuge, for a little while. If she was insane, she thought, then all the world outside, all the world that purported to be good and true and to care about others and about hope and bright morning and sunshine, all the world that knew what it was to smell the grass and sit beside a river and laugh at its waters as they sang–if she was insane, then all that world was insane. Far better it was to be insane with that world than to be sane with the one she knew.

In the light of the rooms upstairs, there had been times when it had been easier to forget about the world outside–to pretend it had never existed. In the bright lights of hell it is hard to believe in a soothing heaven. Here in the dark, where she belonged to neither hell nor heaven, she could believe as she wished: she did not choose hell.

Once, the lights in the basement were all turned on. The cage was filthier than she remembered–it hadn't been cleaned in all the time she'd been here, and the light made that obvious. Dust matted over the bars where they met the floor, and she wished they'd given her something to clean it with.

Umberto lead a client down the stairs. The client examined her closely before he raped her: he made her strip down and turn around under his gaze. It reminded her of how Madame Vaccaro had studied her in the Factory: this was a buyer, she thought, not merely a Gian.

Some hours after he had gone and Majlinda had been left in the darkness again, the kitchen door at the top of the steps opened, and a few thin rays of light slid down the stairs. Footfalls echoed lightly from the wooden steps, and dimly Majlinda saw Madame Vaccaro come down to stand in front of the cage.

Both were silent for a moment.

"You have cost me a great deal of money," began the Madame.

Majlinda stood and walked forward until she touched the edge of the bars. "Lost profits," she said. "Lost profits from your whorehouse."

"I treated you well. Why did you run away?"

"You caged us," said Majlinda. It was the first time she had ever spoken so frankly to her captors, almost the way she would have spoken to her girls. It was different, she knew, than the way she had spoken long ago. Much had changed her. "You caged us. We are *Albanian*, Celia Vaccaro. Not by an accident does the eagle fly on our flag, and not by an accident is our land the land of the eagles. We were not meant to be caged."

"'Not meant to be caged' my foot! You're not meant to be caged? And Murat's innocent as a schoolboy. I've never kissed a man! The sun is cold as an icicle! You're *in a cage*."

"I am watching Shqipëtar hunt in the mountains under the sky," answered Majlinda. "I am sitting on the banks of the river Besim. I have known the touch of the grass. You can kill me, Celia Vaccaro; but you cannot cage me."

Madame Vaccaro stepped across the floor and pulled a chain that dangled from the ceiling, and a light bulb flooded a pale light across the near basement floor, leaving stripes of shadow across Majlinda from the bars of her cage. Majlinda squinted in the sudden light.

"Are you mad?" said the Madame. "Or blind? You're an unwashed teenager: caged, dirty, naked, and worse–unprofitable. All your being Albanian means is that you're a bit cheaper than a German or an American."

Majlinda stepped slightly back from the dark cage bars, her eyes still aching from the new light. Slowly she moved to the side, letting the cage's veil of light and shadow move across her face until its stripes shielded her pupils from the light. "Were I Egyptian like Niut," answered Majlinda, "I might speak of the mythical phoenix or of the eagle on Egypt's flag. It would only change the story a little, and you're right that it barely matters where I'm from. I would still know I'm not the one in the cage. You are. Can't you see the bars you build around yourself, the life you lock yourself away from? Do you know what it is to have a purpose that is more than making money?" Majlinda smiled sadly. "Some things are too precious to be bought and sold."

"This is madness," answered the Madame. "Madness and more. Did you learn nothing at the Factory?"

"Madness?" asked Majlinda. "It would be kind to call this" she gestured to the bars around her and the brothel above–"madness. But you can stop living in a mad world. Open the doors and let us go. There's more to life than this brothel of yours. This place is just a chain, for us and for you."

Madame Vaccaro shook her head. "You're mad as a virgin, girl. Remember yourself, or you'll die in a cage and no one will care. Lule might die in one, too–but she might make it. She might earn out her debt after all. She services a dozen Gians a night now, and she's sorry for running away and will never do it again. You could learn a lot from her. She could save you."

"The debt is a lie, and I thought you called them clients."

"*Enough!*" snapped the Madame. She frowned, the wrinkling of her brow casting shadows on her plump cheeks, and when she spoke again her voice was tightly controlled: "How did you convince Carmine to leave?"

Majlinda closed her eyes in the darkness. Carmine had left. She hadn't known that. "I reminded him of his daughter. Did you know he had a daughter?"

Only silence answered her.

"What of Miriam?" asked Majlinda after a moment. She opened her eyes again. Madame Vaccaro had turned half away from the cage, as if to leave and head up the stairs again.

"We caught her," answered the Madame. "She tried to steal food at a restaurant. We know the owner."

The corners of Majlinda's lips tugged upwards, and a little spring of joy came into her heart. "She would not steal. She escaped, and you have not found her."

After a moment, the Madame nodded. "You're a strange girl, Majlinda. There's no market for strange here, but the Germans aren't so particular. I'm selling you to them. You're to shower in the morning and leave in the afternoon." She pulled on the cord that dangled from the ceiling, and the light went out.

"Goodbye, Celia Vaccaro," said Majlinda. "I hope you are not caged forever."

Chapter 17

The Ceremony of Innocence

"Not one woman wanted to see her children, family, or friends end up in prostitution; and some spoke of society's need to de-glamorize the experience as it is portrayed in the media and see it bluntly for what it is. '*Prostitution stripped me of my life, my health, everything*,' said one. Despite the traumas, violence, and hardships these women had suffered, many expressed hope for their future to get on their feet financially, to help other women in the same situation, to stay 'Clean and Sober,' to get their children back and to be a better role model for them. The capacity for hope and the sense of still having a chance at life–something less evident in the Russian/NIS women's responses–is very likely due to the support and direct services offered by a survivors' support organization, Breaking Free, through whom they were contacted and interviewed."

A Comparative Study of Women Trafficked in the Migration Process [20]

ALESSA STOOD ON THE WALK before a window, and she looked at the hair of her reflection. It always managed to become dishevelled when she was talking with survivors. It did so because she grew distraught, though she worked hard not to show her discomfort; and she noticed it because she had a soft spot for her hair. When she had been a slave she hadn't been able to care for it properly; now that she was free, it was important to her that her hair be clean.

Opening a small leather purse at her side, she pulled out a brush she kept there for emergencies. A dozen strokes tucked her stray dark hairs back into place; then Alessa walked across the street to her office.

The little lobby that doubled as a reception area was unmanned now, though a bell on the counter could summon Marta from the back. Across from the counter were three dark wicker chairs, and in one of them sat the same man who'd been there when Alessa left this morning. He looked up as she walked in, and she smiled uncomfortably at him. "Hi," she said.

"Will she be all right?" he asked.

How in the world could she answer that question? "No. She has a chance, but she's not all right."

The man nodded slowly. Alessa slid around the small countertop and, seeing his filled out incident report sitting on it, began to read. His Italian wasn't perfect, but it was good for a foreigner.

"What..." His voice trailed off. Alessa raised her eyes to him without raising her head. She rarely felt comfortable with men, and his presence in the small lobby grated at her slightly, though she knew not to fear him. *Not to fear him,* she repeated in her mind.

"Yes?" she asked.

"What happens to her?" he asked hesitantly. He was concerned. It didn't seem voyeuristic or cruelly curious, but only worried and earnest. He'd said that he'd met her recently and that he'd never touched her, but Alessa wondered if he'd fallen in love with a woman he'd bought. It would not be the first time.

None of Alessa's Gians had fallen in love with her. She sighed and tilted her head to one side. "Withdrawal," Alessa said. "She goes through withdrawal, and that will be hard." She looked back down to the report beneath her fingers.

"Withdrawal from what?"

Alessa looked up again. He really wanted to know? She wondered which of the brochures would explain about drugs and pimps, but there were too many brochures and she couldn't always keep them straight.

"It'll take time to explain," she admitted. She could trust this man, she reminded herself. And she would feel better in a less confined space. "I'll explain over coffee, if you want to know. There's a café on the corner."

The man nodded.

Alessa picked up a phone from the counter and pressed a button. "Marta? Yes, I'm back, but I'm going out again. Coffee on the corner, with the man who brought Kristen in. We'll be fine. No, she's still at the hospital. Artemis will stay with her. Okay."

The man held the door for her when they left, and she wasn't sure how to feel about that. It felt good to be outside, even though the wind was a bit chilly. She should have brought a coat. She shivered, and the man offered her his; but she shook her head and nodded towards the café. She was glad all the indoor seating wasn't taken at this time in the afternoon.

She insisted on paying for the coffee–he had saved a girl, after all– and they sat down together at a little table next to a window. The café was warmer than the lobby of her office: customer's body heat all day long, perhaps, had made it so. Alessa picked at a speck of lint on one of the sleeves of her green turtle-neck. Then she took a sip of coffee.

"She is going through withdrawal?" asked the man.

Alessa nodded. "The needle-marks on her arm gave her away. They're doing blood work now, and she hasn't admitted it yet, but she was on drugs."

"She couldn't be diabetic, or on medication for..." His voice trailed off as Alessa shook her head.

"Pimps. Society makes pimps sound good–in slang, or at theme parties, or with songs and such. There's more of that in English and German than in Italian, but there's too much in every language, and there's getting to be more. Artemis says we're letting it legitimize pimps. You can get talking dolls that pretend to be pimps, did you know that? Real pimps are bad people. They control girls with drugs– girls like Kristen. And they control them with fear and beating, and with starvation." Alessa still remembered the first time she'd been locked in a closet for two days without food.

The man was looking down at his coffee, distraught. He said, "Kristen was free to come and go. She came with me to find you. Why would she go back to what you're describing?"

"Don't you get it yet?" Alessa asked. *Calm down,* she told herself. *This isn't his fault.*

"No."

She sighed. "When it's with drugs," she explained, "they need to return to the pimp for more. They need to make money to buy the drugs from him, and he charges them rates that keep them in debt. If they don't make enough money they're not given the drugs and maybe they're beaten. But the addiction's impossibly strong, like a habit your body craves no matter what your mind thinks, one that hurts you if you stop doing it, even though in the long run it destroys you if you keep doing it. So the girls go back to the pimp because they need more drugs, and because they don't know where else to go. When Kristen agreed to come with you to our offices, she did something most girls could never do. Probably she lied to herself about how hard it would be. Even so, you helped her. She needs a lot of help from a lot of people, but you were there first. Thank you."

He still had not looked up from his coffee. He was still troubled. It was hard for people to acknowledge this, Alessa remembered. It was hard for them to understand: they hadn't lived with it. They didn't even know what it was like to be raped.

"How common is it?" he asked. "Is it... is it rare? How can men do this? She's so young. She said she was kidnapped, two men just pulled her into a van, and..." His eyes flashed up to meet Alessa's briefly, but then he looked away again, this time out into the street. He took a sip of coffee.

Why hadn't she brought some brochures? They had numbers in them, at least. "No one really knows how common it is," she said. "It's a crime. It's not like there's a Gallup poll. 'Hi, do you have any sex slaves? No? Thank you and have a nice day.'"

He frowned.

She shook her head and added, "It's part of a larger problem: human trafficking. More slaves are bought for labor than for sexual slavery.[1] I only work with the sex slaves." She frowned. "Sometimes we can help the survivors, but their lives have been destroyed. Some can't go home because their parents would spit on them; others go home and are trafficked again. Some turn back to prostitution of their own accord, to support a child born from rape. Others do it because they have no vocational skills." She sighed. "There are programs to teach them some, but how do you tell a girl she makes as much in

---

[1]Statistics vary on this point. There is also a significant overlap between the two groups, as many slaves bought primarily for labor will be forced to engage in sexual acts from time to time, and vice versa.

a month as she used to make in a night? Even if her pimp took all the money, she saw it. And now she has a child to support, and her family's abandoned her." Reluctantly, she admitted, "With some of them, it's their family who sold them in the first place."

The man shuddered.

Alessa reached up and tugged slightly at the neck of her shirt, slipping her cooler fingers against her skin. "The government's better than it used to be–Rebuilding Our Lives is only one of the government-assisted NGOs that helps survivors. We teach language courses and coordinate residency permits and the like. Survivors need so much help–medical, psychological, social, food and shelter. Safety from traffickers. We do what we can, but it's hard, and we can't help them all. We don't even know where they are.

"Even when we can find them, sometimes we can't help–many trafficked girls are here illegally, and when the government finds them it may force them to go home without more than a token effort at providing treatment or protecting them from traffickers. That's been especially bad with some of the Nigerian girls of late. Again, Italy's not as bad as it was a few years ago, but there are still major problems. We should be charging traffickers with kidnapping, rape, and assault, for every girl they have, for every day they have her. And we should be doing more for the victims of labor trafficking–that's not my area, but we have a lot of it.

"There are the Roma children." Alessa grimaced. "The EU made Romania close its large orphanages, theoretically to move children to smaller homes, as a condition of Romania's bid for EU membership. Since then we've seen a lot of Roma children trafficked here for begging alongside the ones who were trafficked for sex. And there are other victims–men from Poland trafficked for farm work, for example."

The man was looking out the window. Was she rambling too much? "Are you listening?"

"Yes," he said. "How could I not be?" The skin around his eyes was bunched up in pain and thought, and his hands were both locked around his coffee cup. "This... trafficking. Is it new? How long has it been happening here?"

Alessa cocked her head. "Here? Since the Roman Empire, maybe? Probably longer. It's been around in one form or another for a very long time, so long as there have been poor people in one place and less poor people somewhere else. But slavery isn't just an Italian problem–

it's worldwide. The girls we see—when they trust you enough some of them begin to talk about where they've been and what they've seen, slave-brothels from Moscow to London and streetwalking in cities from Amsterdam to Dubai. Not that any girl I know has worked in all those cities, but when you put all their stories together..." She frowned. "It's really one story. It's an economic problem."

Alessa raised a hand and ran a finger through her hair. *An economic problem,* she thought. *Rape is an economic problem.* When her boyfriend had raped her and sold her the first time, that had been an economic problem. She swallowed. "Girls are taken from poor countries to rich ones, because the price of a week's cheap sex in a rich country is a lot more than the cost of a kidnapping in a poor country. So girls are stolen, or their families sell them, or their fiancés do. It's hard to catch traffickers because the girls rarely escape. The girls are far from their homes, and the only person they know is their pimp. They're told they owe money." *I bought you that lingerie,* Emilio had told her. *Do you know what it cost?* "Your world is not their world. You take your life for granted, but you can be made a slave in the blink of an eye. It's easier than you think. First you're a person with rights and hope and a beating heart, and then you're nothing." *What a dirty, worthless whore.* "And you're shamed, and you can't go home, and who would know you at home?" *Your parents would hate you, little girl.* "You're illegally in a foreign country, and you're taught to fear the police." *They'll throw you in prison, bitch.* "You don't know that NGOs exist to help you, or that your embassy might. You don't know where to go, and you can barely see past the next rape." *Turn over, slut.* Hot coffee spilled down over her hand, and she stared at it uncomprehendingly.

She had squeezed the cup. The man held a napkin out to her hand, but hesitated, looking at her to ask permission. *Breathe,* she thought. She let out a deep breath and let go of the coffee, then raised her hand to the napkin. Gently, the man wiped the coffee away. "It isn't always obvious when a girl is a slave," she said. Delicately, generously, he moved the napkin between her fingers and over her hand. "Men don't even want to admit a girl's orgasm is fake. Now tell him the girl under him is a slave. A real one—not a pretend one. That makes it rape. He won't admit that. He won't admit that the girl he bought, he slept with, or he saw on the computer screen might not be willing to do what she's doing. He certainly won't report it." Her hand was now clasped loosely around the man's, sitting on the table with his. His hand was the older, but it seemed strong to her. She thought it a forced steadiness: sexual slavery was a hard thing to hear of, she reminded herself. "Some men wouldn't care even if they knew. Some say the girls deserve it. If they were duped by their boyfriend, they deserve this, because they were stupid." She forced herself not to dig her fingernails into the man's flesh. "Others will buy girls who are twelve or thirteen years old. What excuse can there be for that? There's a premium on younger girls these days, because they're less likely to have HIV. And there are places where people believe sex with a virgin will cure AIDS." What else? "It's racism, too. Nobody likes to talk about that part: the girls are taken to foreign countries not only to keep them in line, but because governments and locals will care less about foreign girls than they would about their own daughters.

"Can you imagine the outcry if thousands of American girls were kidnapped for work in the U. S., and thousands of German girls for work in Germany, and thousands of Israeli girls for work in Israel? But when it's Koreans and Moldovans and Russians who are slaves in those places, suddenly it's a little less important. I don't mean Israel and Germany and America and the other destination countries don't care about this at all–they really do try sometimes. But can you imagine the outcry?"

Alessa had to struggle to keep her voice calm, but she felt her tension seep into it: "What should it matter where a slave comes from, if she is a slave today and she lives not an hour's drive from your home? But it *does* matter: think about that. *We* and our governments let slavery happen, because it matters that it's happening to someone else's daughters."

The man raised his eyebrows slightly. "You sound, and I feel, angry and sad."

Alessa blinked. "I am," she admitted firmly. "I am angry and sad. But you can't always let yourself feel that way–we have to be determined, too, and even brave. We need to fight it; we need to stop the trafficking. Because if there's a country without slavery today, I don't know where it is. Slavery is everywhere. We all pretend it's someone else's problem, and it's not. The daughters of the poor are sold to the sons of the rich, and everyone else watches in silent consent. People say they can't do anything about it, so they never even try. They forget that they can make a difference. So there are countless more rapes, and new victims every day. There are hundreds of thousands of us. Maybe millions. And everywhere people let it happen. Everywhere." She blinked. *Us.* She had told him she was a survivor. Should she have done that? His hand did not leave hers, but neither did it tighten in tension or in patronizing judgment.

His blue eyes were glazed in thought, and there was a tear in them. Quietly, in English and as if to himself, he said, "And everywhere the ceremony of innocence is drowned."

Alessa did not feel nervous with him any longer. "Thank you for helping Kristen."

He started to shake his head, but then he nodded slightly. "You're welcome."

She tilted her head to one side. "That was lucky. And all because of a mistaken desk clerk."

The man nodded. "I was looking for my daughter, Majlinda," he began. His hand, so gentle a moment ago, now tightened ever-so-slightly, seeking whatever reassurance she could give. Ice and sorrow mixing in her veins as she heard his story, Alessa suddenly feared she could give none at all.

GERMANY

Germany has legalized prostitution, thereby granting the government sizable taxes from a multibillion dollar industry and increasing sex tourism. As a rule, the legalization of prostitution causes a larger demand for prostitutes, which yields more illegal trafficking and more legal exploitation of poverty-stricken foreigners. With the Netherlands and a few other countries, Germany tries to decouple trafficking from prostitution in the popular mind. [14][13]

A particularly nasty chapter of the Hell's Angels moved into trafficking in Hamburg. In less than two years it ran twenty-six brothels and two strip-clubs named Pascha and Eros. When their crime ring was broken by police many thousands of rapes later, a plea bargain bought the traffickers sentences ranging from sixteen months to four years eight months in prison. The sixteen-month sentence was suspended. [14]

Chapter 18

Iskra's Choice

"Economic conditions in Russia, and the ways in which traffickers prey on poor women affected by the economic collapse in the country, form the background for the rise in Russian trafficking. One quarter of the Russian population now lives below poverty level, and it has been estimated that women account for two-thirds of those unemployed–among them many former doctors, professors, scientists, and engineers. In a country where 98 percent of the women are literate, many women are driven by the economy, the collapse of Russian social services, market-based sex discrimination, and sexual harassment on the job to leave their country to seek jobs abroad (Human Rights Watch, 1995: 307-29). Many of these women ultimately end up in the traffickers' networks."

Sex Trafficking of Women in the United States [19]

A HAND SHOOK HER SHOULDER, but Iskra ignored it. *Another minute,* she thought, though she didn't say anything. *Another minute of sleep.*

Cool metal pressed suddenly into her neck; her eyes shot open. Past the smooth silvery barrel of a handgun, Rudalf was looking down at her. "New girls," he said. "They start with your shift. Show them around."

Silently, trying not to scream, she nodded.

He turned and walked away, passing through a crowd of nine or ten girls and out into the hall.

Iskra closed her eyes, letting herself breathe. "English?" she asked quietly. "*Deutsch? Russkiy Yazyk?*"

"English is fine," said a girl's voice. "I'm Majlinda. This is Donna, and Pili, and Jendayi. This is Ramira, and Sofia, and–"

"I'm Iskra," said Iskra curtly. "And I just woke up. Follow me." Reluctantly, she opened her eyes. The adrenaline of a moment before hadn't quite worn off, or she would have fallen asleep again; instead she pushed herself up to sit on the side of her bed. *Get this over with,* she thought. She stood and led the others into the hallway.

Cheap fluorescent lights whined softly over the dark brown carpet. Iskra winced at their hum–another girl mightn't have noticed, but the hum always bothered her and made her headaches worse. "Shower's here on the right. Dirty clothes go in the bins there, and when we've washed we get clean clothes from the end of the hall."

A clanging began suddenly from a grey school bell on the wall; Iskra gritted her teeth, feeling the sound echo through her skull for the long moment before it ceased. "That's the shift bell," she explained. "Our shift starts twenty minutes from now. We've that long to shower and change."

"How long are the shifts?" asked Majlinda.

Iskra frowned. "Until they're over. Then you come back here to the fifth floor to sleep." She walked into the shower-room. "Towels on the wall are pretty ratty, but better than nothing. Clothes bins are beneath them. Make your shower quick–we'll be crowded in a moment. The bell wakes the whole shift, not just us."

After they showered swiftly and dressed, Iskra led them past a young, blond guard at the end of the hall and into the stairwell. "This is the whorewell," she explained as they started downstairs. "Johns can use the Johnwell or the elevators, but we can only use the whorewell. Don't forget." A scream lanced through the wall as they passed the fourth floor.

"What's that?" asked one of the girls.

Iskra frowned uncomfortably. She'd never been to the fourth floor, and she never wanted to go. "*That,*" she said, "is why you shouldn't ask 'What's that?'"

"What?"

Majlinda tapped the other girl on the shoulder. "She means you shouldn't ask questions," Majlinda explained. "Because they'll get you beaten."

"You shouldn't sound too smart, either," said Iskra pointedly. "Guards don't like it."

Hedeon was the guard waiting for them, holding open the door to the main corridor on the third floor. Iskra forced a sleepy, empty smile onto her face, and she nodded gently to him as she slipped past. A hint of grey was sneaking in at the roots to his well-kept brown beard, but she'd not have told him even if he hadn't worn a nightstick and a switch at his belt.

Iskra led the new girls down the hall, past the line of bruised, tired women whose shift had just ended, who were waiting to go upstairs. "One girl per room on this floor," she explained. "Some days they sort us–by race, height, breast size, the usual things–but for now we'll just fill in from the end of the hall." She nodded towards a room on the left, the last door in the hall, not counting the stairwell at the end. "This is my stop. If you don't do anything too stupid or smart, I'll see you later."

•   •   •

Majlinda blinked. The girls who stood with her began dispersing into their rooms. In the middle of the door in front of her was a small pane of glass; Majlinda stepped forward. Through the glass, on the landing of a blue-carpeted stairwell, she saw a guard in a cheap suit sitting at a desk, sharpening his knife. A bowl of condoms sat on the desk in front of him.

Majlinda turned away and walked down the hall and into the first available room. Her sandals she took off near the hall–better to leave them there: she'd be less likely to lose them or get them stained if they weren't near what she had to do, and she'd grown rather fond of wearing sandals. *Twenty minutes from the bell*, she thought. That wasn't much time. Majlinda might have five minutes to herself.

The brown carpet pushed softly at her toes, and she scrunched them into it, wishing it could have been green grass. A window on the other side of the bed had its curtains half-drawn, and she walked to it silently.

It had been nailed shut, she saw, though it had been designed to open. She wondered what this building had been intended for, long ago. Had it been a hotel that had gone out of business? Or an office building of some kind? Surely, the men who owned her now had customized it for their operation. What did they say to their carpenters, or to the plumbers they hired to build group showers? Did they simply pay them a little more not to ask questions, or were they, too, Gians?

She leaned her forehead against the window and looked down. The sheer edge of the building disappeared below her into the canal. In Albania, she knew, one had to be careful if one built too close to a river. She wondered how the Germans managed to build multistory buildings right over water like this. A two-lane bridge spanned the waterway, the same bridge the van had driven over on her way in. Three arches supporting it were large enough that small boats might pass beneath. Opposite her, the roadway disappeared into a tunnel under a faded brick building.

What might that building be? It, too, was built right up against the waterway. Support pillars at the bottom shadowed a walkway along the canal, a thing where people could, perhaps, enjoy the sight of the water. A woman ran innocently along it now, amongst the shadows, wearing a purple tank top and shorts. Majlinda could barely tell–barely because of the shadows–that the top of the tank-top was sweat-soaked a darker shade of purple than the rest.

What does she have to sweat about? wondered Majlinda. She sighed. Maybe it was good that the woman could sweat without fear, and run peacefully next to a whorehouse. Maybe it was good she didn't know what happened across the waterway.

Majlinda cocked her head sadly. There should be some people who didn't know about whorehouses, who thought the world prettier than it was; but only some such people, and as Majlinda waited for another man who she did not know–or want–to come and take her body, she wished that more might know about this whorehouse, about this whorehotel, and that they might come to save her. She wished the woman could always run innocently, and that the sweat of such exercise was the only sweat any woman need know; but selfishly, she also wanted to be saved.

Her eyes flitted upwards to the windows of the facing building, across the canal, and were drawn to the first on a height with her floor. A man and woman moved together against the window there: naked, and were they lovers? A motion on the floor below pulled at her eyes: through the window she saw a clothed man on a bed with a naked girl. Majlinda winced when the man struck the girl's shoulder, and she felt anger and sadness war with resignation in her heart. She glanced to the next window, and the next. Six windows on the floor, and behind five–far enough behind them that Majlinda needed her greater height to see–were men in their throes of lust, and women under them or over them. It was another whorehotel. She'd seen the acts before and had taken part in them; but it was different, here. Here she could see a grid of slaves and those who raped them. The sixth room was like the others, only the rapist was a woman; it took Majlinda a moment to realize that, for she hadn't seen the same in Italy. Gians here could be men or women. *Whoever paid*, Majlinda thought. They would service whoever paid.

How many more rooms might there be? Between these two buildings, and perhaps more, this was a larger operation than those she'd seen in Italy–larger than Vaccaro's brothel and larger even than the Factory. Even Murat's operation, with his raids across the Mediterranean Sea to Albania, and Egypt, and Greece, and more, barely compared to this. This was a machine.

A chill went down Majlinda's back.

For the first time, Majlinda truly considered that she might die here. The only future for her was here, and her life would end in one of these cells, inside this grid of slaves. Even if she held on to the part of her that told stories and remembered Albania, to the part that loved the sky–the sky that even now she could see from the window of her cell–what would it matter, here? She would only die a slave, one part of a vast machine of slaves. Madame Vaccaro had been right.

"*Warum sind die geöffneten Vorhänge? Ich mag die Vorhänge geschlossen, Dirne.*"

Majlinda sighed and closed her eyes, shutting out the light. "I don't speak German," she said in English.

"Stupid whore. Close the curtains."

•   •   •

Majlinda didn't try to keep track of how many men she serviced that day. She hid within herself, and she pretended her body wasn't hers. Like an ungenerous lover, it betrayed her to keep her alive: she felt that familiar betrayal each time it kissed a Gian or falsely moaned, and each time her legs were parted. By the time her shift was done, the afternoon sun had long since fallen across the sky, passed into night, and tripped up towards morning. Majlinda was sore and bruised in a way she wouldn't have been in a month at Madame Vaccaro's.

A woman came once, and that was strange to Majlinda; while the motions were not the same, nor so familiar, the light of power in the woman's eyes was no less terrible than that which came to the men, and her cruelty was no less. If anything, she was more cruel. *Only another Gian,* thought Majlinda.

That night, exhausted, Majlinda crept into bed alongside a girl she didn't know–there weren't enough beds on the fifth floor for her to have her own. She tossed and turned that night, and so did her bedmate. Each toss or turn caught at a different bruise or soreness, and it was hard to sleep.

The next day, Majlinda moved quickly at the sound of the bell–it wouldn't do to draw attention and be slow. She showered quickly and went downstairs, third or fourth in the line to do so, and began another day. She was fast enough that she had a few minutes to herself before the first Gians came, and she almost fell asleep on her feet, staring out the window.

Days and weeks passed in similar routine: Gian after Gian after Gian, exhaustion and abuse and exhaustion and abuse.

Few things tempered the monotony of Majlinda's rape. When she had her period, Majlinda would join other menstruating girls to do laundry and change beds and clean rooms, and to do whatever else needed doing. It was a miserable experience. Majlinda's own cramps and mood swings were manageable–she would gladly have borne much worse, since few Gians wanted a bleeding woman and she was raped only a few times a day–but the constant complaints of headaches and pain and misery from the girls she worked with made Majlinda feel ill.

And then the bleeding would stop, and the rapes would begin again.

Hedeon–the man with the well-kept beard–picked some girls each day to go down to the first floor. There were better rooms there, and a closet like the closet at Madame Vaccaro's, but bigger. The Gians on this floor were wealthier men, and they came in suits more often than in plainclothes. They spoke of arriving from Madrid, Moscow, or Paris. They had to be quick so they could catch a plane, or they were in town on a business trip they spoke of–though only in general terms, and never naming their names, nor the names of those they worked for or those they came to meet.

Most first-floor rooms had cameras, and Gians could buy a recording if they wanted. Cables led away from the cameras, and devices on the other end made copies of the movie. Majlinda overheard Hedeon explaining it to one of the girls, once, to make the girl feel shamed: the whorehotel kept the copies. Some they sold on the Internet, and others they kept to use as blackmail.

Other rooms seemed camera-less, but usually that meant the cameras were hidden behind mirrors, behind the one-way glass that hid an observation room from which those who ran the whorehotel could record and watch that which they sold.

Majlinda did not know what each whore cost—how much they cost on the first floor, the second, or across the canal. She didn't know what was charged for the condoms that most Gians bought, or what the taxes and maintenance costs might be on buildings like these. Even so, she knew what fortune her owners must make on the sale of her body and the bodies of so many others.

She imagined some part of that fortune would go to the men who watched, to Hedeon and Heinrich and Egor. But she had overheard enough talk to guess the truth. This wasn't like Madame Vaccaro's brothel or Murat's Factory: here, most of the profits would go far away, to some crime lord in a great mansion, sitting behind bought officials and corrupt governments, hidden in plain sight with countless millions or billions of euros in his bank. This place would be another investment, and each girl he owned would not even make it into his ledgers. They would be less than names to him.

The economy of it all filled her with a sickness worse than when Gians left hand-shaped, blue bruises on her breasts. She had often heard how large the black market was in her home country, but she could never in her darkest dreams have imagined this whorehotel.

•   •   •

Rape. Rape. Rape. Rape. Rape. Rape. Rape. Bathroom. Rinse mouth. Rape. Rape. Rape. Rape. Rape. Re-make bed. Rape. Rape. Rape. Rape. Rape. Rape. Rape. Rape. Rape. Rape. Rape. Rape: pretend to be a schoolteacher. Rape. Rape. Rape. Rape. Bathroom. Stick arms in shower. Rape. Rape: his beard scratches. Rape. Rape. Rape. A half moment alone; sore. Rape. Rape. Rape. Rape: he brought handcuffs. Rape. Rape. Rape. Rape. Rape. Rape. Rape. Rape. Rape. Sandwich. Rape...

•   •   •

Some days, she could slip from one shift of girls into the next—a few girls did it each shift, and Iskra taught Majlinda the rules: you had to ask the guard, first, and he'd say yes or no. Sometimes he'd want something from you—some part of your stock-in-trade. The guard most frequently on duty liked to wedge his rifle into your body, and it was always loaded; but enduring his twisted play meant one Gian instead of a shift of Gians, and it gave you sixteen hours of rest with only the one Gian in the middle—it was the only sort of real rest you could get, and the only time when you weren't truly dead on your feet.

It was in one of these rare double-rests that Majlinda told her story to Iskra. Surprisingly, and perhaps because she did not know Iskra well, the story came easily to her lips.

She told first of her parents, of how her father had visited Albania long ago and fallen in love with a local woman, a girl in a small mountain town he had visited. "He spent time in Tirana and Vlorë first, and in the farm country on the plains. But he found himself travelling more and more into the mountains," said Majlinda. She hadn't heard the story since her mother died. "The roads were bad, but the people impressed him, and he liked the mountains. They were beautiful, and he almost fell in love with them, but a girl stole his heart first." Why did it have to be 'stole'? "I mean, he fell in love with her. He'd been in the country for a week when he saw her near the Besim—a small mountain river.

"He was captivated by her beauty—" Majlinda's words caught, and she thought how odd it was to speak of being 'captivated by beauty,' here where beauty truly did enslave.

"He courted her, and he stayed longer than he'd been planning to. Her father was suspicious of him at first. But my father promised to return, and he did, faithfully for each of the next three years. Father didn't have much money—" Some things didn't change. He'd probably never seen a lek from Majlinda's 'work.' Maybe it was better that way, but she wished he'd had more money. She wished her mother hadn't died, too. "He didn't have much money, but the strength of his dedication impressed my grandfather.

"The fourth year after they met, my parents married—"

"Were they the same religion?" interrupted Iskra.

Majlinda shook her head. "Father was Christian, and Mother was confused. They loved each other, and interfaith marriages are common at home." She frowned thoughtfully. "He lost much of his faith, I think, when she died."

"What idiots," said Iskra.

Majlinda blinked. She and Iskra were whispering, lying next to each other in the dark in one of the bedrooms. "Idiots? Why?"

"He didn't have money," explained Iskra. "He kept making these trips to Albania for no good reason at all. He didn't have power. He wasn't from her culture. What advantage was there to her in marrying him? He was stupid not to find a girl at home, and she was stupid not to find a boy from Albania."

Majlinda frowned in the dark. "It was love, Murat." Why had she called Iskra Murat? "I mean Iskra. It was love–they married for love. He was dedicated to my mother, and she loved him."

Iskra barked a quiet laugh–one of only a few laughs not from a man Majlinda had heard in this place, but no less cruel than those– and shook her head. "I love twenty times a day. When they love that much, they can talk about love."

She doesn't understand, thought Majlinda. More quietly, though– more timidly–a small part of her wondered if Iskra might be right. Was love only an illusion, only a thing spoken of by those who had known less than she, who had never seen the inside of a brothel, and into whose wildest nightmares the simplest day of the whorehotel had never barged?

Majlinda shuddered, suddenly feeling very lonely. She hadn't any friends here. She knew names of girls, but not the girls themselves. There was no time for talk, no time to know them: she was always too tired. Even now, with her fifteen hours of sleep divided only by one Gian–the guard at the end of the hall–her muscles ached the ache of one who sleeps for so long after utter exhaustion that their muscles feel they will never move again.

"There are no jobs in Russia," said Iskra.

Majlinda's eyes flitted over to the dark shape of the girl she shared the mattress with.

"There are some for men," said Iskra, "and there are parts of Russia where it's not so bad–although it's not *good* anywhere that I know of. It's hard for girls to find jobs, even if they're educated. I have a bachelor's degree in Russian Literature, but it didn't matter. I lived with my parents, but they couldn't support me and I couldn't find a job."

Iskra grew silent for a moment. Majlinda wasn't sure if she was supposed to say anything, so she only lay in silence. She would speak if it went on for too long, she decided.

After a minute, Iskra explained, "There were ads in the newspaper for work. Foreign employment agencies where they'd find you employment 'waiting tables' or 'as a hotel clerk,' or any of a dozen other jobs. They were looking for women, and everyone knew what they meant."

She had chosen this life.

"It's harder work than I thought," admitted Iskra. "I thought we'd be able to pick our clients. I thought we'd be whores, but we're more than that, aren't we? We're whores and slaves, and that's worse." Iskra shook her head slightly. "I don't know about tomorrow–you know, the future, what happens. But I know about today–I know I get three meals. They're plain meals, but we get three meals. Do you know what it is to be hungry, Majlinda? To be so hungry your parents almost lost their ratty apartment trying to feed you, and they hated you for it?" Iskra shook her head, and the bed shook a tiny amount in the dark. "I did everything right, and it wasn't enough. So I came here. Now I have headaches and I feel sick half the time, but I get three meals a day. Maybe I don't know about tomorrow, here–but there I didn't know about today."

●   ●   ●

Majlinda had no sense of time. Ten days or a hundred days later, it was not one bell which woke them, but two. The girls who'd been here longer than she walked into the hallway, stripped their clothes from their bodies, and stood in a line along the walls. Majlinda followed and echoed them silently, for they all were silent.

Heinrich–the blond man on duty at the end of the hall–stood watching them, holding his gun and running his eyes unashamedly over their naked bodies. Another man–a shorter man with cropped, dark hair and polished glasses–walked down the hallway, stopping in front of each girl and examining her closely. He carried a flashlight that he shined over her lips, and he looked into her throat. He then looked thoughtfully at her naked abdomen, and might press at it once or twice with his hands, which were covered in clean, white, latex gloves.

With either of two markers–black or blue–he left a line on the shoulder of some of the girls. Most had no line, but some he marked once and some he marked twice. Majlinda didn't know what the colors meant, but she was glad when the man's fingers left her stomach and he moved on without drawing on her skin.

He came back along the line more slowly, this time examining the girls' pelvic area and their buttocks, using his flashlight and sometimes prodding methodically. Once in a while he reached back with his glove to push his glasses a little higher on his face, and Majlinda noted that he used the back of the glove–not the underside he used when he touched the girls. Again, he left ink marks on the girls' shoulders. This time the marks were purple or brown. Majlinda's was purple.

She swallowed when he marked her, and she wondered what it meant.

Heinrich came down the corridor after him, and sent girls to different rooms according to the colors on their body. The ones naked of color or clothing he sent to shower and dress and go to work.

Majlinda waited fearfully in one of the rooms with other girls of purple. One of the girls, she knew. "Margaret? What's happening?" Margaret had been at the whorehotel longer than she. "Why are we here?"

"To get shots or pills," Margaret told her. "Or to get a blood sample for an HIV test, or maybe to be taken to the fourth floor. Usually it's pills." She reached down suspiciously to poke at her stomach. "I hope it's pills." Quietly, with an eye to the door, Margaret added, "Don't swallow it. If it's a pill, hide it in your cheek. Watch what happens to the others. If they're all right in a few minutes, swallow it then."

Majlinda frowned, but there was no time for questions: the little examining man came into the room. He lowered a black bag to the floor, stripped off his gloves, and put on new ones. Then he pulled a glass jar out of his bag. "This is penicillin," he explained, unscrewing the lid. "Lean against the wall, butt to me. When I get to you, keep your weight on your left leg; you'll be getting an injection on the other side." He pulled a syringe out of the bag and stuck its needle into the top of the jar, sucked up a quantity of penicillin, and walked over to the first girl. "It won't hurt much, and it's better than leaving the disease untreated."

Some of the girls looked at one another worriedly, but all moved to lean against the walls. The examiner tapped the needle once, then stuck it into the first girl's rear.

"What disease?" asked Majlinda. The girls around her stilled suddenly: even their breathing had stopped, as if they'd never before heard a voice that questioned their captors in even the slightest detail.

"Syphilis," answered the man, injecting the next girl. "Called *the great pox,* by some. We should do labs to be sure, but that would take longer and cost more. It looks like syphilis, so we're treating you for syphilis. It's no shame in your line of work, and easily cured."

"I was not shamed."

The man frowned at Majlinda, and then shook his head and turned to the next rump.

"You might be sick for a day or two," he added. When he'd finished injecting the girls–about fifteen in all–he put his things back in his bag and left the room.

Majlinda wondered why Margaret had warned her about the pills. She started to turn towards the other girl, but Heinrich appeared and told them all to shower and get moving.

In the hall Majlinda passed Egor, who was just opening the door to the next room and going in, his light machine gun hooked over his shoulder and a large plastic sheet in his hands. Beyond him and the door he opened only for a second, Majlinda saw a head on the floor–Iskra's head, unmoving.

The door swept gently closed across the carpet, sweeping away the sight of the gentle curls that flowed in Iskra's hair. What had they done to her? What had happened to the girl who had chosen this life because it would be better? Majlinda hoped she only slept; but in her heart, she knew that Iskra was gone, that this girl with her degree in literature and her learning had died alone and friendless half a world from home.

Majlinda wondered how sick the injection she'd had would make her. Syphilis was a strange idea to her, a word she'd rarely heard. Diovanni's voice echoed in her mind: "You do not want to get diseases," he had told her, and "You do not wish to know the fate of a pregnant whore." Had one of the marker colors been for pregnancy?

A shudder racked her frame as Majlinda remembered there were chemicals that could end pregnancy, that could kill a fetus growing in her womb. Had the injection she'd received truly been penicillin, and would the sickness she'd been told to expect come from that, or would it be the fluid corpse of a baby unborn?

The idea made her ill; when she reached the floor she'd work today, she paused in the bathroom. Each floor had several bathrooms–you couldn't hide in them for long, but perhaps once every five Gians, you could get away for a moment. A few glassed-in showers were occupied now by girls who waited for Gians to come to them in the spray.

Majlinda wet her face at the sink and swallowed, and looked into the mirror.

She didn't know the girl who looked back at her. How long had it been since she was home? How long had it been since she was free?

"The grass," she whispered. "I was free in the grass."

One of her hands she reached up to touch the mirror, to touch towards the cheek of the woman on the other side. She was older now than she had been. When she pulled in her cheeks, the dimples that once had been a trademark of hers seemed shallower and more angular: much of her baby fat was gone, much of the newness that is so precious in a teen had faded, to be replaced with a different character and a new face. It was the same as it had been, yet different, aged by fate and time and rape beyond what she would have imagined, and yet was not so old as it ought to have been–she ought to have been an old woman with white hair and brittle bones, who knew not how to fight or laugh or read, but could only be bitter and old. If age and God and life had truly granted her the years that her experience had earned, she would long since have failed and turned to dust; but she was Majlinda.

Her shoulders rose, seemingly of their own accord, and her breath came full and deep and filled her chest. She was aged, and was not the girl she'd known: she was a woman, but she was still young. She was still free, and they could not cage her, not even in a hotel made for whores. Not even a thousand miles from her home.

She could not escape, now. There were men at every exit, and a routine that would defy exceptions. There was no simple Madame Vaccaro whom Majlinda could escape with the truth of her existence, but only the hard, uncaring walls around her in a hard, uncaring world.

Was Iskra dead? Majlinda hoped not. Iskra had not, perhaps, been honorable, but even a willing whore who could not understand Majlinda's parents' love did not deserve a whore's death, an unremarkable and unknowable death at the edge of the world. Majlinda, at least, would be careful of all pills, and should they come to kill her, she would die; but she would not die dishonorably. She would stand, and speak her piece, and die as who she was–not as who they sought to make her. *They can make me a whore,* she thought, *but they cannot make me any less Majlinda.*

Chapter 19

The Church of Saint Lucy

There are thousands who are in opinion opposed to slavery
and to the war, who yet in effect do nothing to put an end
to them... They hesitate, and they regret, and sometimes
they petition; but they do nothing in earnest and with
effect. They will wait, well disposed, for other to remedy
the evil, that they may no longer have it to regret.

–Henry David Thoreau, *Civil Disobedience*

MAJLINDA'S FATHER PUSHED OPEN the pair of arched double-
doors and stepped inside.

It was very small for a city church: only a few dozen pews, all
empty. Two candles burned in a recess to his left, under the gravely
troubled statuette of a young woman.

He had not been to a church since his wife's funeral. It had not
seemed right to him to return. While he hadn't blamed God for her
death, he also hadn't absolved God of blame for letting her die. God,
he thought, had not been watching the front of the store that day. It
had been a hard lesson. Was it happening again?

Majlinda's father walked slowly to the statuette. The two lighted
candles stood among dozens of dark, cold ones; he took one flame and
spread it to a new candle. *Majlinda.* He moved the flame slightly to
the right, and a second new candle caught fire. *Kristen.* Again to the
right, and a cold wick turned hot. *Alessa.* There was one more unlit
candle in the row. He lit it last. *Miriam.*

He'd found Miriam some time ago. Alessa had helped him make
inquiries about Majlinda, and Miriam had heard. Miriam was living

at *Regina Pacis*, a fortress-like compound run by a Roman Catholic priest, Don Cesare Lo Deserto. The site had been a children's summer camp; in 1995, Don Cesare had turned it into a refuge for the poor and the destitute fleeing Yugoslavia; in 1997 the collapse of the Albanian economy and rule of law led many to flee, and thousands of them had passed through Regina Pacis; and in late 1998 and the beginning of 1999, it began to help the increasing number of recovering girls who had been trafficked through or into Italy from Moldova, Romania, Russia, Ukraine, and dozens of other nations.

In the years since, Regina Pacis and the Diocese of Lecce had helped thousands of such girls. *Only a fraction of the total,* thought Majlinda's father. *Only the ones who are free.* Majlinda was not free. His hands tensed in worry.

Before the statuette was a kneeler; he knelt and made the sign of the cross. Minutes passed in silence. Above him, stained glass–mostly green–let a few rays of sun into the dark room.

Footsteps *clack*-ed on the stone floor behind him, and he looked over his shoulder. A short, fat priest walked slowly down the aisle in the middle of the church, looking from pew to pew. Every once in a while the priest stopped to put a missal or a book of hymns back in place.

"Father–"

The priest looked over to him.

"Are you Father Williams?"

"Monsignor Williams," corrected Monsignor Williams. "Yes."

This was the man who had referred Miriam to Regina Pacis. That meant Majlinda's brothel was near.

Majlinda's brothel. As he knelt here and wasted time on candles, Majlinda was in a brothel. He crossed himself hurriedly and stood. "I'm looking for a girl: my daughter Majlinda." He pulled her picture from his coat pocket and walked nearer to the priest. "Miriam knew her–you remember Miriam? Their brothel must be near here. Can you help me find it?"

For a moment, the monsignor stood perfectly still in the aisle of his church, eyes glued to the image of Majlinda. There was sadness on his face, and perhaps fear. Hesitantly he looked towards the confessional at the side of the church; then, slowly, he turned towards the cross at the head of the church. "Forgive me, Father," he said. "I can."

●   ●   ●

Monsignor Williams knocked again.

The door, a newly-painted blue-green, opened while his hand was still up, and he smiled politely at the middle-aged Italian woman who greeted him. "Pia, it's good to see you. Is Carmine home?"

She nodded. "Come in, Monsignor." She nodded towards Majlinda's father, who stood next to Monsignor Williams in the hall. "And..."

"A friend," said Williams. "He's helping me with something for the diocese." He stepped past Pia and smiled when she gestured to a cushioned seat. Majlinda's father sat down on a sofa nearby, and Pia disappeared into another part of the apartment.

A moment later, she reappeared with Carmine at her side. He smiled and nodded at Williams. "Monsignor! Welcome, welcome! Can we get you anything? What brings you here?"

"It's a matter of some discretion," said Williams, raising his eyebrows meaningfully and shaking Carmine's hand.

Carmine frowned. "Pia, would you get our guests some drinks?"

The middle-aged woman frowned momentarily before smoothing her lips into a smile and looking at the two visitors. "What would you like?"

"Water," answered Majlinda's father quickly. "Thank you, water."

"Whisky, straight," said Williams.

Pia shook her head. "I can do wine, but we're out of whisky."

Carmine reached into his back pocket and passed his wallet to Pia. "Can you make a run down to the liquor store, dear?"

Pia looked suspiciously from Monsignor Williams to Carmine and back. "Try to stay out of trouble. You reek of trouble." Her eyes tripped over to Majlinda's father. "Maybe not you so much, but the other two." She sighed, put on a coat from a wooden coat tree in the corner, and departed resignedly through the front door.

Williams turned to Carmine. "This man is looking for his daughter. Her name is Majlinda."

Carmine tensed visibly; his muscles flared and he seemed to grow larger, and Monsignor Williams was afraid.

"Of course you don't know anything about it," added Williams quickly. "I know that, and he knows that. You are a good man, Carmine, and I am glad to see you at church so often." Carmine was now coming three times a week. The first week Father Williams had not thought to ask why; but the weeks had passed, and finally

Carmine had confessed. "Majlinda's father is also a good man. He was praying for his daughter when I met him." Majlinda's father shifted uncomfortably in his seat.

Carmine's tension seemed to bleed away–perhaps it was the easy sound of the Monsignor's voice, or perhaps it was relief that he would not be accused for his crimes.

"But you are an imaginative man, Carmine. And so I ask you to imagine: if you had known where Majlinda was, and if this man's daughter had failed to escape from a place where she was held, would she still be in the same place? Can you imagine where she would be?"

Carmine swallowed. Hesitantly he raised his eyes to look at Majlinda's father. "You are her father?"

Majlinda's father nodded.

"She was a good girl," said Carmine. Now it was Majlinda's father's turn to tense; his hand closed tightly on the arm of the sofa, and anger and desperation warred in his eyes. "I mean, I imagine she was. But the trouble she caused, with that she would not be kept." He frowned. "She would be sold to someplace new."

"Could you find out where?" asked Williams. "They'd never tell me or her father, but they might tell you."

Carmine had not looked away from Majlinda's father. "You will tell no one I helped you?" he asked. "I have a daughter: Gabriella. You do not know what they would do to daughters." Shame burned in his eyes and in his heart.

"I won't tell anyone," said Majlinda's father. His hands were balled in fists and a mighty anger was written on his brow, though he was not a violent man. "And I have already been told what they would do to daughters."

Chapter 20

Salt Again

O N THE TENTH DAY after Majlinda received the injection, two bells rang in the morning.

She knew it was the tenth day because she'd started to count them, because it seemed a small gesture of defiance to bring time into this timeless place.

When the two bells sounded, the girls rose from their beds and went to the hallway, and sleepily disrobed and stood in lines. This time it was not the medical man who came and looked them over, but Ivan.

Majlinda had rarely seen Ivan, and she didn't think she was supposed to know his name; but she'd been on the first floor once when Ivan had come to inspect the whorehotel, and she'd overheard one of his bodyguards talking to Heinrich. The bodyguard's name had been Hortensio, and Majlinda still wondered if Ivan realized that whore was a part of that name.

She studied Ivan from under drooping eyelids, trying to force her mind to wakefulness despite her sore and exhausted body. Ivan's broad face was clean-shaven, and it lived under a neatly-trimmed, full head of hair. His shirt was a smooth silk like Murat's. Majlinda wouldn't call him a large man, but he seemed strong, like some middle-aged Olympian who had been cast down by Zeus to the underworld, and then had returned bearing some part of its darker terrors to the surface of the earth. "Turks," he said, and his voice was like a rock that would brook no resistance and expected none. "Turks, step forward."

Immediately a small handful of girls and women stepped forward.

137

Those in line nearest the handful grew especially still, either out of fear or out of a wish to avoid notice.

Ivan nodded to Hortensio, who walked to the nearest Turk and slapped her hard across the face; she cried out fearfully and fell back against the wall.

Hortensio moved to the next Turk and slapped her as hard; she fell back against the wall but didn't cry out. When she turned her face back to Hortensio, Majlinda saw blood bubbling at the corner of her lip and a hatred in her eyes. Hortensio stepped forward, raising the back of his hand, and she dropped her eyes and cowered against the wall.

"Enough," said Ivan coldly. "She'll do. Stand at the end of the hall, girl." He nodded towards the whorewell. The Turkish girl stood, still eyeing Hortensio angrily, and walked down the hall.

"Step back, Turks. Italians, step forward."

Hortensio repeated the procedure, knocking down five girls until he found two whom Ivan chose–they were the ones whose eyes raised in anger when Hortensio hit them, the ones who showed spirit. Whatever Ivan was doing, he wanted people who showed spirit. The sight of morning brutality had awakened Majlinda fully: the sight of blood on girls woke her in a way that even the barrel of a gun couldn't have. She could suddenly, eerily, see every hair in the hallway–every bead of sweat or quiver of a girl's fearful hand. When blood and life and death were in the hall, Majlinda's eyes could see better than a hawk's.

"Albanians," commanded Ivan. Majlinda swallowed, and every little detail of the hall was vivid to her: the soft, dark brown carpet, brown to hide the stain of blood? The yellow walls and dimly humming bright lights, and the school bells on the wall below the lights. Ivan watching the rows of girls, from which no one had stood forward. He frowned thoughtfully, no doubt thinking there were no Albanians here.

Majlinda stepped forward, and she met his dark brown eyes. *The same color as the carpet,* she thought, *to hide the blood he's seen.* In her peripheral vision, Majlinda saw Hortensio moving towards her. They wanted girls with spirit, did they? Majlinda remembered how she'd said no once, in the Factory, and how she'd brought the one man to his knees. Her eyes flashed fire, and she turned towards Hortensio, breathing deeply and feeling a sudden wakefulness in her muscles and her frame. Hortensio approached her clumsily, thinking her just another girl to push aside. He would think differently, before–

"Stop, Hortensio," said Ivan.

Hortensio turned to look at his boss.

"She'll do. Go to the stairs, girl."

Like a cat bitten by a bee in mid-pounce, Majlinda's gaze snapped suddenly, uncertainly over to Ivan. "Ukrainian girls," he said, his eyes trailing over the line of women; he had already forgotten her.

A few minutes later, Heinrich led Majlinda and the others who'd been chosen down the whorewell. She let out a little sigh of relief when they passed the fourth floor, and a mite of hope dared to fill her heart when they reached the garage: they were leaving, and she didn't know where they'd go, but mightn't it be someplace better than here?

•   •   •

In the back of a cream-colored van, inside a cage like the one Murat had used to take them from the white room, nine girls were taken through and from the streets of Hamburg. A panel kept them from seeing to the front of the van, where the windows would have shown them motion and given them light; so there was only the cage in the darkness, and each other.

There was silence in the dark. But then one of the girls cursed at her captors in anger, and another cursed them more; whores learned well how to curse, for they heard others curse them every day. Men paid for their bodies yet tore down their souls: it was hard to hear every day from so many lips how worthless you were, and to have to kiss those lips. Different girls responded in different ways, though all were terribly changed by their abuse. These particular girls–excepting Majlinda–had survived by their anger.

She alone now found herself filled not with anger at her captors, but with sadness for those around her: Niut and Anna had shown her how a girl could risk accepting this world, but these girls here embraced it by rejecting it, and became in their anger misshapen impressions of the very despots whom they would destroy.

To become like them, Majlinda thought. *To hate, or not to care.* Years ago, when she'd been a child, she had caught a young boy shoplifting. The Albanian boy had said he could steal because Majlinda's father was a dirty foreigner worth less than spit. Majlinda had hit him, and the two children were scuffling about on the floor when her mother walked in.

Afterwards, her mother had knelt beside her and said, "If the boy hates your father, and you hate the boy, and because you hate the boy his father hates you, and because his father hates you I hate the father, then there's no end to hatred. Hatred can't be stopped except by little girls." Majlinda's mother had smiled. "I would have you defend your father, but he can't be defended with hatred. If you want to defend him, to defend yourself, and me, and the whole wide world, then remember, Majlinda: only you can decide not to hate."

Majlinda remembered how, when she'd escaped from Vaccaro's, she had decided she would never wish great harm on anyone. For a moment, here in the dark, she felt a tiny thrill of pride at that memory; but then the pride faded: Majlinda knew well enough that such memory had no place here. Pride belonged to a moment, and in the choosing of a valiant heart–but it did not lie in remembering the choosing, for remembrance of pride is only vain, and today and tomorrow matter more than yesterday.

Where were they going, Majlinda wondered? Where would the van stop and what would she find there? These were not her girls around her, and she felt very lonely. These girls were so angry. *The moment,* thought Majlinda again, *and the choosing of a valiant heart.*

"We don't need to hate them," she said in her storytelling voice– soft and strong and smooth, it cut through the rage of voices in the van, through the curses of girls who knew only anger. "They are fools in want of money, and they don't understand what they're doing. They know the fact of it–the brutality, the moment, the power and the lust that they feel–but they don't really understand what they do, no more than they understand how beautiful the world can be." She was in the dark in a cage in a van full of whores. "They might know they are evil, or they might tell themselves they're not, but what they've done doesn't really matter to them–it can't, because they don't understand it and they rationalize it away. It is normal for them, and they no longer see it as a crime–if they ever did." The other girls were silent, now: listening. Were they uncertain? Angry at her for saying so? She could not see their faces, and she did not know them in the dark. "I do not say forgive them, but we need not hate them. They might yet learn to be better than they are. And even if they can never learn, if they live and die as beasts, we need not become like them."

"We're not like them," said a voice in the dark. "They're bastards."

"Egor held a gun to my head while four men raped me," spat

another. "They did it from behind. You want to *redeem* him? Damn you, girl. Get a clue."

"We need not become like them," said Majlinda again.

"Shut up," said a new voice. "You must be new. Try talking like that when you've been there a week. They deserve to die. That Hortensio–I'd have hit him, if I weren't so afraid."

Only silence came out of the darkness now, as the last voice's admission lingered in the air. It was what they all felt, Majlinda knew–they were all afraid, and all turned to their anger out of fear.

She shook her head determinedly. "There are good men in the world, still; and–"

A hand *thwack*-ed across the back of her head. "*Ouch!*"

"Shut up, I said."

Majlinda frowned sadly. She could tell her stories, but they would not hear her. All they cared about was their anger, their shame, and their fear. *Power,* thought Majlinda. *They are powerless. That is why they fear, and what they fear.* "When you hate them"–she ducked low in the seat, and a hand passed through the space where her head had been–"you give them power over you. We need not become like them." The hand landed hard against the side of her face, knocking her cheek against her teeth and her head to the side.

She was silent, then–she had said what she'd needed to say, even if she had not told a story. They wouldn't have understood a story. They'd think they had, but even if they took the time to try, they wouldn't know how to listen.

Majlinda reached one of her fingers into her mouth, to trace along the cheek where it had been smashed into her teeth. There might have been drops of blood, but her mouth was too moist for her to be sure, and in the dark she couldn't see the color of her finger when she held it before her eyes. *The taste,* she thought. She ought to be able to taste blood's salt.

Hesitantly, she brought the finger back towards her lips.

There was salt, she thought–she smelled it. She could taste it now, and her tongue had not yet touched the finger. How could she taste it? She inhaled deeply.

It was not the warm salt of blood that she scented, but rather it was the cool salt of the sea. In her mind she remembered crossing the Adriatic, and how Murat had told her not to fear the sea, and that Albania would be waiting for her when she returned.

She had no home to go back to, but the scent of the sea was still strangely reassuring. It was an illusion that seemed like home to her. It was a wild thing, a free thing that could never be tamed, and that knowledge filled Majlinda with hope and great joy, that she was like the sea.

They had broken her body. They had raped her and made her learn to accept the rape, dozens of times a day: to be numb to the false and lustful attentions she had, terribly, grown used to. She knew how to please a man, and she knew better how to sate his crude desires. She knew where to stroke and where to lick, and what stains washed out and how to wash them. They had made her a thing that once, she would have viscerally despised, a thing she would have run from and refused to see. She would have clung to her romance novel or hidden behind her father, and would have closed her eyes against the whore she would become.

In a way, they had destroyed her.

But what would she have become without this life? How many girls had she saved, if only for a little while? Miriam would still be a slave, but for her. Desperately she hoped Miriam had not been recaptured; yet as the sea salt played under her nose and called to her of what could not be tamed, she believed in her heart that, somewhere, Miriam was free.

There had been nothing wrong with being a girl in her father's shop, or reading romance novels on the shores of the river Besim—although there would have been something wrong about closing one's eyes to the whore Majlinda had become, merely because it was uncomfortable to open them. Living a life where the grass was beneath her feet, and her eyes were open, and her heart was full, would indeed have been a beautiful thing; and yet Majlinda was glad that in this life she had been able to help her girls.

No, she thought. She would not glorify this life. Even now, she was sore in a way that would have terrified her once, and there were bruises on her thighs from last night and the night before. She was glad she'd been able to help her girls and glad she'd been able to free Miriam; but this was a terrible life. She thought of Iskra, whom she'd last seen in that unblinking state upon the floor. She thought of Armand and his cigarette burns, and how he had first taken Lule in the white rooms. She thought of Murat and his smooth blue shirt, and how first he had pierced her. Had the shirt been blue? Almost, she could not remember. She wondered if it mattered any longer. There was no glory, here: only terror. Only pain. Only animal death.

It was true that Miriam had escaped, and that no man like Murat could ever truly capture Majlinda, despite all that such had done to her; but Miriam and Majlinda were not the norm. How many girls had disappeared from the Factory while she had been there, or from the whorehotel? How many girls became like Niut, and how many were whipped like Althea? What if Majlinda had had a disease worse than syphilis, and it hadn't been cost-effective to treat her? Even if a girl escaped, where could that girl go? Where could any of them go?

There was a tear on Majlinda's cheek. She felt it, and wondered how it had gotten there–she was not crying, she thought. She caught it and brought it to her lips. It tasted of salt.

ENGLAND

Anna was 12 when she made friends with a man and ran away from her home in Albania. He bought forged papers and took her to Hamburg, where he forced her to work in prostitution. Four years later, she was hidden in a lorry and trafficked again, this time to the UK. Here she'd face 15 or 20 customers a day, and nearer to 30 come Christmastime.

I Was Sold for 2,000 Euros, BBC [2]

Chapter 21

The Hand of LeGree

"The reality is that not everyone survives this ordeal. These people are often functionally invisible. They lack either birth records through lack of birth registration, or citizenship, or they lack legal status in a country. Not surprisingly, invisible people are incredibly disposable. Victims and survivors and NGOs ask that I carry their message to others that may be in a position to effect change.

"I have met with many girls and women from many shelters, some girls so young it was just hard to comprehend their fate. Girls as young as 5, 7, and 12 who had been victims of rape, then sold into prostitution.

"There is a specific phenomena in this era of the HIV/AIDS pandemic. Clients seeking HIV-negative assurances will pay large sums to buy very young girls, who are promised to be virginal. Over the period of the week, these girls are raped repeatedly by their client. The girls then are returned to the brothel, only to be taken to clinics where they are sewn up and sold again. This cycle can be repeated as many as eight or nine times before the girl enters a life of forced prostitution."

–Julia Ormond
UNODC Goodwill Ambassador [18]

THERE WAS A REASON Majlinda had smelled the sea: she was to make an ocean journey.

On a great barge whose name she never learned, she was taken with the girls around her to sit in a dark compartment: a single dim room with a smaller bathroom to the side. The only light was in the bathroom. Its dim rays reached uncertainly out the door to watch peeling grey paint crawl along the floor and sneak up the walls. The girls picked at the paint–there wasn't much else to do. And then some of them fought with each other–over a poorly chosen word, or a question of race or thought or pride, or over anything at all that they could find to be angry about. Sometimes they only argued or cursed, and sometimes it came to blows. Majlinda tried to stay out of it.

While the girls argued, the barge steamed up the cool waters of the Elbe and into the colder, deeper waters of the North Sea. Its brown hull sliced silently through the dark waves, and there was nothing sinister in its steaming to suggest that its cargo was larger than its manifest, and that it carried lives away.

To the south and west it steamed, down, down to the Straits of Dover, between the white cliffs and Calais, where the English Channel met the North Sea; and when they turned and hove to at Dover, no one would notice a few invisible girls slipped past what might have been a vigilant constabulary at one of the busiest ports in the world.

Another van awaited them: it was not cream colored like the one that had taken the girls from the whorehotel, but was pure white, white as driven snow, white as Murat's first van, long ago, had been. Like that van, rust grew around the handles, grew around the tail-lights and ate away with its little filings at all the whiteness–whiteness that ought to have lasted better than it did. Even white paint could not wash away what this van carried, could not wash away its uses: the veneer was too thin to hide it from the sea.

And so Majlinda was carried among whores who hated and feared and so became the men who had made them; she was carried by sea and by van, by road and by bridge, by the Gians of the world; she was carried into England, over the mighty Thames where Conrad's Marlow had spun his yarn, and into the city where the true Marlowe's Tamburlaine had been spun centuries before, and where the Lord Chamberlain's Men had first played the plays of Shakespeare. For better than a thousand years, London had seen and moved the world; now, in a want wholly, sickeningly, insultingly irrelevant to all the best parts of this grand old Lady's honor, the Gians of London wanted whores.

Spirited whores.

Somewhere more to the east than not, buried between the whims of urban and suburban life and crammed into the larger ambiguity of urban sprawl, their van entered a two-car, brick garage. When the van doors were opened, Majlinda let the others crowd out first–she didn't hold back out of fear, but rather because, for some reason she didn't fully understand, she wished to differentiate herself from them in her mind.

There was a rusted-out hole near the wheel-well, and Majlinda had been able to see the sun shining on pavement as they drove. Now that the door was open, she saw only the panels of a closed garage door, lowered and locked and with no windows, pale under the sickly cast of cheap fluorescence. She stood, stooping slightly so as not to bump her head on the van's ceiling, and stepped out onto the rough cement of the garage floor.

"This way, cherries," cracked a voice, splitting the air like a whip of tough leather. "This way pomegranates. Into the house–no waiting. Need to stretch like that, eh? I didn't pay for a need to stretch–get your hide moving, or I'll move it for you. Apples need eating, and I'll find a tiger to eat you if you don't hustle."

Majlinda passed the edge of the van door to see a golden-haired little man watching the girls pile through a doorway in the wall. On his face grew a beard as light as dawn, and yet it seemed scraggly and unkempt, and new. He was shorter even than the shortest of these girls, and yet whatever height he lacked in fact he more than made up for in quivering: it seemed in him a great torrent had been stored, and in his light face and pale pink eyes that torrent was ready to drain forever, to rain down destruction on whatever opposed it. Against his skin the yellow of his blond-dyed hair seemed a dark, dark thing; for his skin was pale as if he had never seen the sun.

"Inside!" he said, and his voice gnashed at her more strongly now that she saw the little man from which it came. "Or you'll see the inside of a box soon, and I don't mean a lorry. Box! You'd be lucky to get a box, you would–you'll get a ditch. Not worth a ditch."

Majlinda slipped through the door, past walls of brick a sanguinary red, into the main part of the building. The ceilings were high here– perhaps eight meters–and the walls were made of foam or something else light. They'd been added to an older building, and stretched less than half the distance between the mosaic tile floor and the arched roof.

"Forward, there, and left! Hurry, now–men here in a little while, need to have you ship-shape." They passed down the narrow corridor of white walls, under the tall ceiling, and turned left where the corridor met a longer one near the long one's end: looking swiftly around, Majlinda saw that it perfectly bisected the short hall; the corridors were t-shaped. Behind her, doors dotted the makeshift walls all the length of the long corridor, and Majlinda knew well what sort of rooms they would contain.

"Go hurrying, do–the others are waiting. Front door, there!" A slap on her thigh made Majlinda hurry–she half-tripped onto the tile floor as she climbed the two stairs in the middle of the hallway, and then she scrambled forward, towards the door and behind the other girls. This door was in a wall as insubstantial as all the others, but the wall here stretched to the ceiling.

Majlinda stopped dead as she reached the threshold of the door. Inside, the girls she'd travelled with stood near the front of a crowd of other girls–perhaps twenty others, all naked–and in the air above them, between two great wooden beams that vaulted up past the brick wall of the building and supported the massive roof, was splayed a young girl.

Her hair was red, and long, and beautiful. It trailed down over her shoulders and past her outstretched arms. By rope around her wrists– thin, harsh, brittle rope that dug far into her skin and bit at the blood of her body–she was suspended Y-like in the air. Her feet dangled straight and helpless above a clear, green stone in the otherwise tiled floor. As her near lifeless eyes passed over the door where Majlinda entered, a shudder wracked her naked body; her legs convulsed, and her arms thrashed as they could, though they could thrash but little, tied as they were; and then the convulsion stopped, but still she weakly breathed.

The *slam* of the albino's fist into Majlinda's back sent her over the threshold, to the floor of the room. White and grey and blue tile looked up at her; she pushed herself half-up from the floor and looked upward, looked upward from the eye of the great Madonna mosaiced in the tile. Her eyes followed the ropes, darting through the pulleys and back to cleats screwed into great beams on either side of the building. She scrambled to her feet and was halfway across the room when a tall, thin man seemed to appear out of nowhere. He slipped a loop from the cleat and let the rope go.

Majlinda dove for it as it ran upwards under the weight of the red-headed girl. All she caught were the tiles of the floor, coming up to *crack* at her elbows. Her eyes twitched to the right before she could stop them, and the naked girl–the naked pregnant girl, she realized with a sickened horror–slammed into the cold brick of the outside wall with a *CRACK*.

The contents of Majlinda's stomach–meager though they were–came suddenly up through her throat and mouth and nose, down over her forearms and her scraped elbows and the ends of her coal-black hair, down over the tile of the floor. Desperately she wanted to turn away, but all she could see was the girl dangling by a wrist.

The albino was at the other cleat now. Majlinda wanted to close her eyes against what she knew was coming, but she pushed off the wet and sickly tile beneath her and–

Crash went the redheaded girl, plummeting down next to where the albino stood. He pulled a gun from his belt and aimed it at her belly.

"Here's one earned a lot of money. Men like the redheaded girls, and she'd a fine figure. She got with child, and she was worth more. But one day she said no. She said no to a client, and she said no to Gerald." The albino nodded towards the tall man who had slipped the rope so easily from the first cleat. "It's mean to say no to Gerald. He's a nice mute, and he's no way to talk back. So she says no." The albino turned his eyes to look over the new girls–the strong, spirited new girls that had been brought to him. "We want you to fight, sometimes. You fight when we want you to. But she says no. That's fine, everyone can say no. But saying no costs. Saying no makes you useless to me. It makes you just another mouth to feed."

Just another mouth to feed, thought Majlinda. She knew what was coming. She tried to dash across the floor, but the tall mute–Gerald–grabbed her from behind and forced her back down to the tiles. He held her down with one knee, and held her head up by grabbing her hair–he thought she would look away, she realized. She would never have looked away. Not from this.

"A baby," added the albino, "is just another mouth to feed." The silenced barrel of his handgun jammed into the side of the redhead's belly. A little *pop* came from the gun.

"NO!" cried Majlinda–it was drowned out in a chorus of shouts from the new girls, a chorus too late, a chorus broken into silence when the gun turned towards them.

The silence too was broken–broken by the weak sobbing of the shot and broken girl upon the floor. Majlinda twisted under Gerald's grasp and scratched at his arm, and tried to scramble free. His knee was still on her back. Gerald lowered both hands onto her head and pushed it down against the tiny tiles. She felt the grooves between them impress her nose and jaw.

The Albino's voice sounded chill in her unseeing ears: "Another mouth to feed. This is what happens, when that's all you are." Another quiet *pop* cut through the sound of nothing, and the little sobbing stopped.

"Every door is locked, and there's a guard on each. Do what you're told and you'll live. Fail, and you're another mouth to feed. New girls, put all your clothes in the garbage in the corner. Then follow Gerald."

There was a brief sound of shoes on tile. When Gerald let Majlinda up, the Albino was gone. The twenty-some whores who hadn't come with Majlinda talked quietly to one another. The new girls hurried to strip and throw out their clothes. Majlinda–feeling as wretched as she smelled–walked across the room and went down on one knee before the redhead, whose body still sat broken and mangled on the floor. "I'm sorry," whispered Majlinda. The words seemed terribly inadequate, and almost she wished she could have called them back. "I'm sorry," she whispered again, more firmly. The girl's eyes, open, stared up at her from beneath a bullet hole. Majlinda reached down and closed the eyes.

A hand grabbed at her torso and tossed her the way a child tosses a rag doll. Disoriented for a moment and with a slight pain in her shoulder, she realized Gerald had thrown her against the garbage can. She picked herself up and quickly dumped her clothes, even the sandals she'd worn from Madame Vaccaro's, the ones she'd managed to keep all her time at the whorehotel.

Gerald led them back into the garage, to the empty half of it beside the van. He turned a hose on them–Majlinda wasn't the only one who'd vomited to see the redheaded girl fall. The cold pressure pushed and tickled. The water and the dirt of travel flowed down from their bodies almost as if they could truly be cleaned, but it could not clean their eyes: all Majlinda could see was the redheaded girl falling into the wall again, and all she could hear was the *CRACK* of that fall.

Water dripped slowly off the girls as Gerald herded them back into the main part of the house, and one by one let them into rooms along the makeshift corridors, until Majlinda was alone in a room with only a futon.

Out of habit from the Factory, Majlinda shied away from the futon now that she was wet, and sat on the cold tile floor to cool. *Better for mildew,* thought some mechanized part of her mind.

She inhaled deeply, bringing her head up to look around. A girl was dead. One of her girls, even if Majlinda didn't know her name and had never spoken to her. There was nothing Majlinda could do for her now, but Majlinda herself still had to live. Where was she?

England, she thought. She was in England–she'd heard them speaking when they'd taken her off the ship, and that had been in Dover. Dover was in England, if she remembered correctly. And if she didn't, well, one country was much like another. She had to get out of this building before it would matter what country she was in.

The floor below her was made of the same tiny tiles that had been on the raised platform under the dead redhead. They were in the corridors, too–she hadn't had time to look closely, there. Here, the mosaic was of an angel with wings spread wide, hovering in a cloud and holding up a baby; but the artificial walls that divided this one great room into the rooms of a brothel sliced clumsily over the tile of the baby's neck, and his head would be sitting at the base of the next room. It was better, perhaps, that he would not see what would happen in this room; but Majlinda almost wept, that his eyes might see the next. She hoped they were hidden by a futon.

Her hand she pushed lightly into the foam of the walls–like cork or particle-board, there was little substance to them. She could break them if she needed to, but it would do her no good: she'd seen the outer walls of the building, and they were made of brick. She'd need to leave by an exit. And if the Albino spoke true, the exits were guarded.

The room's door opened abruptly. In stepped the Albino. Majlinda's eyes narrowed to see the pale face of her captor. He was so short and so alien that it was almost easy, in her heart, to keep from feeling hate–revulsion, yes, and maybe even a little pity, but not hate. Her thoughts tripped back to the redhead, and her pity disappeared. Who was this beast who stood before her, this white thing shaped almost like a man?

"Your name is Susan."

Majlinda blinked. "What?"

The Albino stepped forward and raised his gun–the same gun that had killed the redhead–to press against her breast. "Your name is Susan. Say it."

They wanted to take away her name. The barrel of the gun ground cold into her skin. Hate flowed into her from its mouth, hate she could no longer hold back: this man sought to strip her of her name, of the very last thing she had that was hers.

Let this be her moment, then. Let her die, here, but still keep her name. Let him shoot her, if he would–but he would shoot *her*, and not this Susan whom he tried to make her. "My name," she said firmly- "My name is M–" *Lule,* she thought. Miriam had escaped, but Lule had not. The redhead had not. Majlinda could do nothing for any of them if she were dead. Living, could she do anything at all? Might there be some last act that could help save the girls around her from the terror they knew?

Her face had frozen in the saying of her name, and the Albino's eyes fastened expectantly on her lips. The slightest of motions played in his hand: his finger, rubbing gently over the trigger of his gun.

The air and height and pride that had remained to her ballooned down out of Majlinda's shoulders, out of her breast with the gun upon it and the heart that beat within. "My name is Susan."

Chapter 22

On Angel's Wings

SHE FELT MORE ALONE every day, and every day her urge to do something stupid–something that would get her killed–grew stronger. The first time she thought of herself with the name Susan, she felt a powerful urge to find the Albino and shout her real name to him. The second time, she only wept. She forced herself to repeat *Majlinda* in her mind every time she heard the name Susan, until it seemed to her that her name was Susan Majlinda; but at least a part of that name was hers.

To her fake room, the clients came. Most were Englishmen, though England had grown into such a hub of commerce, and England's capital city into such a hub of tourism, that men of every nation and complexion came to buy Majlinda in the day.

There was no window in her room, so she didn't know when it was day and when it was night; but because there were no windows, she could choose which it was. When clients came, she chose the day.

When she could sleep, she slept, in a futile attempt to chase away familiar soreness. Once in a long while Gerald would come and take her with some of the other girls to hose her down and bring her back here again to dry. There was no shampoo, and rarely soap, and she felt that slowly the grime of every Gian deposited upon her, and she would never be clean again. Her hair–though still beautiful in a way– grew more and more brittle. They gave her a comb so she could keep the hair straight, but that was all she could do for it.

A small plastic chest next to the door held food and water for her: a water bottle, and some bread or granola, and sometimes some honey.

The chest itself had almost certainly been made for a child, for it was so short she had to bend over or kneel to open the lid, and in its bright red-on-red plastic was embossed the image of a little boy building a sandcastle on the beach.

The Gians here rarely brought condoms. Majlinda had felt no sicker in the mornings than she had on any morning of the past year, yet still she worried, sometimes, that she might get pregnant.

The routine here never changed, save occasionally when the Albino would take girls up the stairs to the room at the back where the redhead had died, and there he'd punish one of them for something she'd done and make the other girls watch. He whipped one girl, and he stuck another with a cigarette lighter fresh from the van. The burn it left was far larger than were the little scars Majlinda still had from her burning by Armand.

But then they'd be sent back to their rooms.

The Gians had little new to tell her. Their teeth bit at her neck–not nipped, but bit–and the sweat of their beards rubbed into her nose. It felt to her as if, little by little, the very last parts of Majlinda's soul were being swept away by the churning arrhythmia of carnal use.

She learned to slip carefully from her room. Down one corridor or the other she would step lightly, barefoot and unclothed, and seek a way out of her prison; but there was none to be found. The door into the garage was locked. Opposite the garage, the corridor led to another door, but that was barricaded, nailed shut with great wooden boards, and locked to boot. Sometimes Gerald would sit before the garage door, or the barricaded door, but he never saw her. She was always careful of him, because when Gerald wasn't torturing someone it seemed all the life drained out of him, and he was lazy and slothful. Fortunately for Majlinda, there was no joy for him in guarding, and no reason for him to lift his eyes or survey the corridor well.

The raised chamber–where the redhead had died–was sometimes deserted, but more often a girl or two would sit there looking down at the tiles, or would lie dazed against the wall and stare up at the only natural light that shone into this world: the little stained-glass blood-red cross that sat high in the wall at the back of the building. Majlinda had not seen it the first time she'd entered the room, because the redhead's body had blocked it; and now that Majlinda could see it, almost she wished that she could not. While its luminance waxed and waned with the hours of the outside world, its panes blocked every color but red from coming through to this dark place, and it seemed there was little or nothing of nature in the rays that made it through.

The girls told Majlinda why the corridors were not forbidden to them: where could they go? There was no exit, they said. There was no way out. These few girls spoke in tones so despondent that Majlinda felt herself breaking to hear them, felt her own walls and determination crumbling with each new word they shared. As she'd tried in the van, she tried here to speak her storytelling voice and return some hope to these girls. But they only listened to her tale–to the first tale, of the land of the Eagles–and their eyes were glazed, and their hearts were empty, and they did not care.

A set of great wooden doors led out of the building's main chamber and into a large anteroom. The anteroom was always guarded: there, sometimes another guard and sometimes the Albino stood or sat or raped a girl. Majlinda thought the doors on either side of the anteroom led out of the building.

It was when a guard raped her there–a particularly unpleasant rape, on the cold tile floor–that Majlinda learned of a smaller set of doors to one side of the anteroom, facing towards the great chamber that had been divided up into the rooms of this brothel, but distinct from the doors that led into the hall. Majlinda was just beginning to wonder more about it when the guard, Oscar, pistol-whipped her shoulder again, and she cried out in pain.

She started to turn over–to turn right-side-up–but the barrel of the gun jammed into the side of her cheek. "Down, pretty Susan. Wouldn't want to hurt your mouth. Such a pretty mouth. We'll find a use for it." She growled deep in her throat and pressed her cheek against the gun, felt the cool black metal and the hole in the middle of it press her cheek into her upper jaw. *No.* She could do nothing if she were dead. She turned her head away from him, down to face the cream-colored tile of the anteroom floor.

Chapter 23

To Buy the Beast

"Legalized prostitution brings sex tourists and heightens the demand among local men. Local women constitute an inadequate supply so foreign girls and women are trafficked in to meet the demand. The trafficked women are cheaper, younger, more exciting to customers, and easier to control. More trafficked women means more local demand and more sex tourism. The end result looks a lot like Amsterdam."

–Dorchen Leidholdt, Prostitution and Trafficking in Women: An Intimate Relationship, *Prostitution, Trafficking, and Traumatic Stress*, 2003 [13]

ALESSA SHIVERED in the evening wind.

For the third time today she asked herself why she had come. The man had somehow traced his daughter to Germany, even to Hamburg, but he'd had little more information at first. His daughter had been bought by a big organization, he'd said, so perhaps they should start with the bigger brothels.

The Albanian embassy had talked to the German Police, but the man would not say how he'd traced his daughter here. The police thought he must be grasping at straws, or that perhaps he'd sold his daughter himself. They'd promised to do what they could, but it did not seem like much.

Alessa paused for a moment and stood in the lee of one of the brick columns between her and the canal. A man watched her from across the waterway, and she worked hard to ignore him, though she was nervous. She hadn't been this close to traffickers in a long time. She turned her head towards Majlinda's father, who had paused next to her.

He, too, avoided looking at the man across the canal. He passed Alessa his mobile phone. "If I'm not back in forty-five minutes–"

"Call the news station, the NGO, and the police. I know." She ducked back into the column's shadow, so the guard across the way would not see her waiting. He'd have to walk into her line-of-sight to reach the bridge between them, though; she could run if she had to.

This was the fourth brothel they would investigate. The first three had been legal–prostitution was legal in Germany. A local NGO had heard a rumor of trafficking at one of the brothels on the Reeperbahn, and it had seemed a good place to start. A hundred euros had told them Majlinda had never been there. The next two brothels had yielded similar results, and the scope of the problem had begun to dawn on Majlinda's father. Next he had gone–without Alessa–into the Herberstraße, the street where countless window-prostitutes stood on display behind their glass, smiling alluringly at men who came from all over the world to buy them: the street which banned any woman who would not sell herself.[1] A beautiful blond woman, trying to be helpful when she learned of his daughter, had told him softly that there were well over a thousand pimps in the Saint Pauli district alone. "There are too many," she had said sadly. "Perhaps you should go home."

The next day he'd gone into a large strip club, where a day of spending money, artificing conversation, and playing the jovial foreign salesman had loosened lips that told him where he might find an Italian girl, or maybe even an Albanian, whose owners would let him rough her up for a small fee. He'd had the basic idea, and Alessa had added the need to rough the girl up. And now they stood across the canal from the fourth brothel.

It was a huge thing, Alessa thought: more like a hotel than like the brothels she'd seen. "Brothels this big don't exist in Italy."

"Miriam spoke of a Factory near as large."

That was true. Alessa had seen those reports; she nodded. "I've heard of things like that: Calle Santo Tomas in Mexico City, or the Breaking Grounds in Serbia. I've never heard of it in Italy before–

---

[1] While not technically legally prohibited, signs at the end of the street warn women (and children) not to enter, and the police strongly discourage entry.

Italy has more streetwalkers, and little brothels with only two or three slaves. Places like this, or the Factory... They're the exception rather than the rule. The exception is a little more dramatic, but the norm is as bad or worse." She shook her head, frowning at the five story building across the canal. "This is dangerous."

Majlinda's father smiled. "I know." He raised a hand to scratch thoughtfully at his chin, but she caught it and squeezed it in worry. Why did he make her worry so? She pursed her lips to ask him, but he released her hand and moved purposefully down the walkway, turned at the bridge, crossed it, and disappeared into the drab grey building on the other side. The guard watched him enter, then lit a cigarette. Alessa backed again into the shadow of the column. She opened the phone and checked the speed-dial, but it was set. There was nothing to do but wait.

•   •   •

Thirty-eight minutes later. Twice she'd pretended to be on the phone when men or women had passed her. Always her finger was hovering over the speed-dial button, and she felt ready to run or to dial or to dive down into the canal or to cry for help; whatever she must do, she would do. She was calm in her mind, but her body felt coiled like a spring. She rubbed a shoulder through her sweater while watching the bridge and clutching the phone.

Majlinda's father emerged from the building. A well of Alessa's tension flared out of her, and she fell into step next to him when he passed her hiding place.

"Where to now?" she asked.

"She was there recently."

Alessa winced. "Was?"

The man nodded. "I payed for a girl, and she told me Majlinda had been there. For months, she thinks, but she has no sense of time." He swallowed.

Alessa nodded sadly. "It's like that. There's one moment, and then there's the next. That's how you stay alive."

"Her name was–"

"Stop!" Alessa shook her head. "Don't tell me her name. Don't repeat her name. Not if you want to save your daughter." She shuddered. Names. Names were important. "We'll tell an NGO anonymously. They'll tell the police, or a point person in the government. We're not involved anymore–we can't be, or they'd kill your daughter."

The man began turning his head–

"Don't look back," she said plaintively. "If you slept with her you slept with her, but don't look back. They're slaves. We'll report it to an NGO, but we have to focus on Majlinda. Remember? *Majlinda*." Why was she like this? Why was she saying his daughter's name like a prayer? And was she starting to cry? "Just–" Why was she crying? Too many slaves in a building like that. Alessa thought of the guard with his cigarette, and she remembered the burns on her thigh. Her eyes were buried in someone's shoulder; why was she crying?

Gently, Majlinda's father held her. "I didn't sleep with her," he whispered. "She's a daughter too."

• • •

They sat awkwardly on the bench waiting for the bus. Alessa had pulled away slightly, into herself. She'd apologized for suddenly acting distant, but old memories were surfacing. She swallowed.

"How much did the girl cost?" she asked. It was an economic problem, she reminded herself, and she should know how much it cost.

"Seventy euros. The expensive part was the guard."

She frowned, reaching up with one hand to wipe away the remnant of her tears–they were chilly on such a cold evening. "What guard?"

"Heinrich. I will give him one thousand euros this weekend, in a public place, and another twelve hundred when he finds out where they've taken her. He thinks she's somewhere in France or England, but he must ask–discreetly. It will take time, but I believe he is greedy enough to find out."

"Plus whatever you gave him today?"

He nodded.

"If you have that kind of money, why'd she take the job?"

Majlinda's father looked away guiltily. "Because we thought we were losing what we had, Alessa. Not enough money from the store means not enough money for the mortgage, and we would have had to sell. I would have sold, but this woman came into the store and answered our prayers: a safe and well-paying job for Majlinda, a life for her that would help us both. Why did I listen?" He shook his head angrily. "And I–" He looked ready to throw up. "I drank. Because of her mother's death, at first."

What had changed, that he had money now? "You sold your house," she said quietly.

He nodded. "I went back to Albania while someone was tracing Majlinda to Hamburg for me. He wasn't greedy like Heinrich; he had been an evil man, but he helped me willingly. My bank gave me a large loan against my house until they are able to sell it, which they will do soon, if it has not yet been done."

When would the bus arrive? It was getting cold. Without conscious thought, Alessa slid over on the bench and leaned gently against the side of the homeless man who spoke to her. Why had she come with him, she asked herself again. He'd visited Kristen in Brindisi, and then he'd come to her. He'd asked for a list of German NGOs he should talk to, and had said he was coming for his daughter. Why had she insisted on coming with him? It had been a foolish, impulsive thing to do. "You're a very stubborn man. Will you take your daughter back to Albania?"

He shook his head lightly, and when he spoke his breath was warm on her hair: it would snow soon, she thought. With a sad voice he told her: "I will never return to Albania."

Softly she asked, "What will you do?"

"I will save my daughter. And..." his voice trailed off. He lowered his head so that his cheek lay against the hair of the young woman who sought his warmth against the cold. "She's going to be mad at me. She hates it when I try to protect her."

Alessa smiled quietly, as a mother at a precious child.

"I've always been a shopkeeper, Alessa. I've never been anything more than that. But..." Again his voice trailed off.

Alessa wrinkled her nose. The night still smelled of snow. Would snow come tonight, and cover the dark streets in a cold curtain of brightness? If it snowed, it would feel so cold. Alessa didn't know if she wanted it to be cold. He had always been a shopkeeper, she thought. "But what?"

"But I need to be something else now."

Alessa felt a drop of water land on her cheek, but it was not from snow or sky; it was the single tear of Majlinda's father.

"It's the girls, Alessa. Not just Majlinda. Each of them is some-one's daughter."

Chapter 24

Saviour

"ARE YOU ALBANIAN?"

Why would Murat ask her that? He knew the answer; he was the one who'd stolen her. She shook her head *yes*, and she was in her father's shop, seeing him walking across the floor towards her. "*Stop*," she wanted to shout. "*I know what you are.*"

"Answer me. Are you Albanian? I ordered an Albanian." Majlinda's eyes blinked open. She was naked in the darkness, and the soft foamy mattress of her futon was beneath her. It was not Murat's voice that spoke to her from the darkness: this was another client, another Gian.

Majlinda sighed. In her mind, for a moment, she remembered sitting on the shores of the Besim, and how the water felt when it tickled your fingertips. If she'd been there, she would have jumped in and bathed all over, to wash away what her life had become.

The *clack* of metal-on-tile: the man had dropped his pants. A little rustling in the dark, and Majlinda knew his shirt was on the ground. Perhaps he didn't care whether or not she was Albanian. Maybe he thought it didn't matter in the dark.

A depression on the mattress beside her tilted her slightly to one side, and she felt the man's hip against her outer thigh as he sat. She started when a hand landed gently on her stomach. The hand tickled its way upwards over her skin; it was softer than most hands, and more gentle than any she'd felt in a while. Perhaps the darkness helped. Had he turned on the lights, perhaps he was ugly and fat, and leering at her. Maybe the darkness hid a nose the size of a mountain, even as it hid this man from himself.

Susan Majlinda was tired, but she caught the back of his hand with her palm and closed her fingers into the cracks between his. Both hands rested lightly over her heart, now. She wished she did not feel so unclean, she wished she were still on the shores of the river Besim, and she wished she knew how to escape this place. She wondered if she could make herself kill a guard. She didn't want to, but she wondered if she could. She wished she were still on the shores of the river. The tickle of memory reached around the edges of her mind and soul. She stroked the hand gently, wishing it could have been the hand of a good man.

But he was only a Gian. Still sitting next to her, he leaned his torso down over her top and pressed his lips to hers, giving gently, at first, to her lower lip, and then pulling softly on the top one, and pecking a light peck, and pulling away. It was a far softer kiss than many–than most–though not, perhaps, so experienced.

She would have thought it wonderful once, she thought.

The hand that wasn't in hers teased gently down her side, and again she thought of the shores of the river Besim. She thought of the summer when she was fifteen, so young, and Valdrin and she had teased and been so new–they hadn't really done anything, but it had felt like–

Her breath caught in her throat. That hand, still tickling down her side. The lower lip and the upper lip and the gentle pull away. She became so still she thought that she would die. "Valdrin?"

The tickling hand at her side stopped. Her client was still, here in the darkness. "Do I know you?" he asked. His voice was strained.

Majlinda moaned, a terrible deep moan that was half a sob as wide as the ocean. All her shame, all her life, all her pain came back to her like the roaring of a great sea, and he was holding her and she was talking and she was talking and she was talking.

"It's been so long. They took me, Valdrin. It's me, Majlinda. They stole me forever ago. It was Murat, Murat and his men and the Factory. And the brothel, and the... you don't know, Valdrin. Help, Help me." She was choking on her own tears. "There were my girls, and I helped Miriam escape. The others aren't free, and they're so far away from me. How can I help them? The redhead died. I couldn't save her–they held a gun to her head and they shot her. The Albino shot her. He shot her belly first, because she was pregnant. All they know is rape and pain. What's wrong with them? Help me."

His arms stroked hers gently, and he held her. She babbled on about the Factory, about the whorehotel, about what she'd seen and what she'd had to do, about the cage under Madame Vaccaro's. About the escape. About the van and the sickening crack of the redhead's bones. She didn't tell him about the syphilis, but she told him about Althea, and about Iskra, and about Arlinda and Zana and Anna and Lule.

It seemed an age he stroked her arms lightly, and he held her. She looked up at the face she could not see, in the dark, and he kissed her. She pulled away. "Not that, not now, Valdrin. Anything but that. You don't know what they've done to me. Help me. You can't stop them–they have guns. But bring someone here. Police, or the army, or someone who can stop them, someone who won't be corrupt and won't be afraid and can get us out of here. Just tell them we're here."

"Majlinda," said Valdrin, and his voice was strong, but a little afraid. "I knew a girl once, named Majlinda. I liked her, even. She's still at home, though. She probably hasn't left her father's shop."

Majlinda frowned. "It's *me*, Valdrin. It's me. How do I know your name? How do I know that you like to tickle a girl on her left side, or that your father's mobile phone never worked on the west end of town? How do I know that it hurt when you left for Durrës? I don't love you–God, I don't know what love is, anymore–but I know you. It's me. *Help me.* I'm Majlinda. Majlinda."

"The Albino said your name was Susan."

Hope died in her when he said those words. "He lied, Valdrin. He gave me that name with a gun to my chest. I can still feel where the barrel was. It wounds me every day. My name is Majlinda. You can save me. You can be a hero. Please." He was a Gian, even if he knew who she'd once been: he would never help her. "Please," she said again. "You know me."

"Oh, yes," he said chidingly. "Help the whore. I went to a whorehouse. I bought a girl, and I know her from home. Please officer, won't you help her?"

"They might. Let them help me."

"I'd have to make a statement. They'd ask me to testify, and they'd arrest me for buying love."

"For buying sex. And maybe they wouldn't–please, Valdrin, look at what they've done to me." She tried to stand, to go turn on the light, but he held her tightly in his arms. "Let me go!" She pulled against him, but he wouldn't loosen his arms. He was too strong. After a moment, she stopped struggling: she knew when a man held her too tightly for her to escape. She knew it well. Tears came into her eyes. "An anonymous tip," she whispered through the tears. "You could make an anonymous tip."

"And even if they saved you, you'd tell them who you told. You'd tell them I was here. They might kick me out of the country. I'd lose my scholarship."

"Valdrin," she growled angrily, "you should have thought of that before you bought a whore! Is your scholarship more important than my life?"

He pushed her away, back onto the bed, and stood. "I've bought a whore once a week since I've gotten here."

A black pit lived in Majlinda's stomach, under her tears. "Your money paid to bring me here," she said. "You did this to me."

"I asked for an Albanian," his voice answered out of the darkness. "I never knew it would be you."

"DOES IT MATTER?" Majlinda shouted. She jumped up from the bed and beat her fists against his bare chest. "You PAID for it! You stupid, stupid Gian!" His hands found her invisible wrists and closed around them tightly. "Every time you buy a whore," she said slowly, trying to check her rage, "you pay for it. You pay to make a girl a slave. Is that what you really want? I've been a slave, Valdrin. I am a slave. There's nothing beautiful about it. It's just about power and lust, and these stupid little boys who want to imagine they're in control."

"But we are in control." Valdrin's hands loosened slightly on her wrists. "We are in control, Majlinda." His was an academic tone, a debating tone, a mindless objection to the words of a thing without an appreciation for their meaning.

"You control nothing," she said, though the hands encircling her wrists would proclaim otherwise. "You do not control your urges, you do not control your fear, and you do not control me. You are a small, selfish child." A portion of her anger turned to sadness. "You could never be a hero."

"I'm not trying to be a hero," he said. "I'm trying to be an engineer."

Majlinda closed her eyes and pulled her wrists away; he let them fall. "Then that," said she, "is all you'll ever be."

• • •

"Are you Albanian?"

A chill ran down Majlinda's back–she was in the dark again, and had been about to sleep; but it was the Albino's voice that asked, and what could he want? "I am," she said.

The light winked on over her. She swivelled on the futon and sat up, her eyes–half-blinded by the sudden light–almost even with those of the small man who turned back towards the hall. "Come with me," he said, disappearing through the doorway.

Majlinda stood and followed. He led her down the hall and stopped at the door to the anteroom. "An Albanian's come to deal," he explained. "If he talks in Albanian you'll know what he says, and you'll tell me." The Albino tilted his head to one side, letting his eyes flit over to hers. He pursed his pale pink lips and stuck his tongue out to wet them. "You'll tell me, pomegranate. Or you'll be another mouth to feed."

Majlinda nodded. "I'll tell you." Her voice was surprisingly smooth and calm–death held little fear for her, even if she did not wish it. Valdrin had left, and no police had come. She'd dared to dream they would, for a little while; but now it was up to her again. She was alone.

Pushing open the large wooden doors into the anteroom, the Albino stepped forward. There, waiting inside the large chamber with a dozen girls beside him, stood Murat.

Arlinda and Kaltrina were among the girls. They seemed older, now, than Majlinda remembered. Majlinda was naked and they were clothed, but she stood tall and unashamed before them and felt a pride that they were still alive. She wished they weren't here now, and that they'd somehow escaped; but at least they were alive. Did they remember the stories she'd told? Did they remember Bukura e Dheut? Or why the stories mattered?

Armand and Peppino stood in the background behind the group of girls, their familiar, terrible shapes like bright shadows in the room. Armand's cigarette burned red in his mouth. His eyes met Majlinda's, and hers were fierce and full of memory, and yet also, somehow, almost forgiving: they were more noble than he knew how to face. He dropped his cigarette to the tile floor and looked down, and he stepped on it and turned to the side, pretending to study the walls or the sides of the room. Visibly he tried to shake off his discontent, and visibly he failed.

But Murat did not see, for he was facing the Albino.

Murat disliked the Albino. The Albino was too short, too strange, and too unprofessional for his tastes. A professional, Murat thought, would not carry a gun, and one sat at the Albino's hip. A professional would use rape and words and beating, sometimes starvation or confinement or a girl's bodily functions; but he never used a gun. He hired other people to use guns for him.

Still, the Albino's cash was good, and so Murat smiled, saying, "You ordered five girls, friend. Which do you want? They're all pretty enough to lie for." Wordplay to set the fellow at ease. The Albino didn't seem to relax, though. Fine. Business-only, then. "We'll need the rest of the money."

Gerald, tall and silent, stepped forward out of the shadows in the corner of the room with the sudden clack of hard heel on tile. Murat felt the tension in the room grow thick, and he heard Peppino and Armand shuffle uncertainly behind him. One of Gerald's hands rested on the holster of a gun on his hip, and the other carried a briefcase.

"Easy," said Murat to his men, in Albanian. "Easy, now. He's only carrying the money. A lot of money here." He brought his eyes back towards the Albino, but something familiar about the girl from the back rooms stole his attention: he knew this one. He hadn't thought to see her again. She was still pretty–prettier than he remembered, maybe–but you could tell she'd started to age. "Majlinda? I heard you made trouble at Vaccaro's."

She nodded. "I did what I could, Murat. That was a long time ago."

Murat furrowed his brow.

"What's that?" asked the Albino. "What do you say? Susan?" His hand closed tightly around her lower arm.

"Only that it's been a long time since I've seen this man," answered Majlinda in English. "I knew him once."

"Remember who owns you." The Albino released her. He walked up to the other girls, and he was shorter than they. "You," he said, tapping a Nigerian girl. "And you," tapping Arlinda. "You, and you," tapping two Murat had bought from Moldova. "And you." Kaltrina.

Five, thought Murat. If any had been especially beautiful, or if they'd been younger, he would have insisted on more money. He still had a few young Armenians to sell, and he knew a pimp who would buy them. But first, he'd prepare the five. "They'll be ready in the morning." Peppino's eyes trimmed sideways to run over Kaltrina's rump.

"No," said Majlinda.

All eyes turned to her. Naked and off to one side, she'd been forgotten. "You can hand them over today, Murat. Why wait until tomorrow?"

Because he wanted to say goodbye, of course. Because they still had to thank him for what he'd done. He'd brought them from poverty to a life where they had food and water, from lives of uncertainty to lives where they always knew where they stood, and they should thank him for that. But what he said was, "They'll cost less tomorrow. It's a markup if you buy them on the same day."

"So you can rape them?" asked Majlinda. "Haven't you done that enough already? You are cruel to them."

Murat stared at her in incredulity, then looked to the Albino.

The Albino's gun was clear of its holster, and its barrel pressed deeply into the side of Majlinda's belly. "Susan–" he began.

"Take me instead," she said.

Murat turned his eyes back to her. Why had she said that? Her nakedness and her earnest eyes seemed suddenly more appealing to him, though he did not know why.

"I'm jealous," she said, and her voice held the tinge of angry, lustful emotion. "I remember you, Murat. I..." She turned her eyes down–in shame, he thought. "I want those nights again. You can always have a girl you own. But I don't belong to you now. Can't I... can't I belong to you, for one more night? Give him the girls tonight, don't take them, and he'll let you... I mean, if it's all right–" she turned hesitantly to the Albino. "Can he... can we? It works better for you: it'll damage them less, and damage to one costs less than damage to five. It helps you. Please?"

The Albino, frowning uncertainly, pulled the barrel of his gun away from Majlinda's belly and sheathed it at his hip. He turned to regard Murat, but Murat's eyes were on Majlinda.

Her words had tugged at something within him, and it was not only lust. She was not his, and she could be his, and... she wanted him. He found the thought–and her volunteering of it–strange and bewitching.

"Yes," said Murat. "You get five girls, tonight. I get one night with Majlinda. And the money."

The Albino frowned, as if puzzled. "Susan," he mumbled under his breath. He nodded. "Very good. Very good. Gerald, sweet, pay the man. Pay the man. He gets Susan, tonight."

Majlinda, thought Majlinda.

•   •   •

He was only a man. For all her memory, for all his clean shirt and his silver tongue and his cruelty, Murat was only a man. He had broken her once, a long time ago. He had broken her in the white room, had kissed her and she had thought she was so lucky that he had, but then the kiss had died.

He kissed her now, here in another room of white, standing upon a floor of tiled angel, and her kiss was far more schooled than it had been: she knew how to kiss now, far better than she'd known then. She no longer knew how to take joy in kissing, but she knew the mechanics.

He kissed her again as he had then—first slowly, and then forcing himself into her mouth. She yielded her lips slowly to excite him, issuing the token struggle he would expect that would seem part of a larger acceptance; that acceptance in turn masked a still larger struggle and her true defiance.

Murat pulled away and kicked off his shoes and pulled off his socks so he was barefoot on the tile. Majlinda smiled softly—not for him, but for Arlinda and Kaltrina, and for the three whose names she didn't know. She'd saved them this, and from Armand and Peppino.

Murat's trousers fell to the floor, and the engorged thing that had so frightened her long ago stood naked beneath Murat's shirt and reminded her again that he was just a man. The shirt was still a blue shirt—Murat had not changed since the white room. He had always been like this.

"I remember you," said Murat thoughtfully. "You came from a tiny village. There wasn't anything there but you. Nothing worth keeping, at least. I threw out the towels I bought from your father."

How odd, Majlinda thought, that he remembered the towels. "They were good towels."

"You wanted to see the cities," added Murat. He reached out and squeezed harshly against the bare skin at the side of her neck. "You're not wearing any clothes. There's nothing to tear away." The fingers dug in tightly. His nails hurt no more than the nails of any other man, and Majlinda's smile did not waver.

"You offered me something more than a store in a mountain town," she said. "Italian cities, and work, and hope from hopelessness."

A frown came over Murat's face in a quick wave; but then his confident grin–the very same grin he'd given her long ago, that had made him seem so worldly–came over it. Looking down at her body, he reached out and cupped one of her hands in his, and brought both down together to run up his inner thigh. The hairs Majlinda's hand touched were trim and soft: he conditioned them carefully, she realized. Even here, he was so concerned about cleanliness, about appearances.

He was just an animal, bare before her. He wore the blue silk shirt, but that couldn't hide him any longer.

Majlinda's hand squeezed untenderly against his thigh, and he laughed cruelly.

"I promised you work!" Murat grinned. "You like your work, don't you, Majlinda?"

Her smile slipped. "I thanked you for it once."

Murat grabbed her wrist away from his thigh, pulled it up to his mouth, and tore against it with his teeth. She knew the strength of the bite–enough to leave a mark, but not enough to break skin or to hurt greatly. He had not planned it so, she knew: he merely wanted to bite her. Behind his confident grin and well-conditioned hair, beyond his pressed shirt and his scented skin, he knew less than she and less than her. She'd learned since the white room, and he had stayed the same. He would never learn. He was just another Gian, tonight. And by him, she would save her girls.

Majlinda smiled again. "It's only an illusion," she said softly. "You told me not to fear the sea. You told me it would see me home again."

Murat pushed her down to lie on the futon, and lowered himself over her, his clean shirttails tickling across her unwashed, naked stomach. He pushed his knees inside hers, but he paused and turned his head slightly. She could see his face too clearly, and it seemed a brittle thing.

Murat was frowning slightly, now. "Home?"

Majlinda shook her head. "Home, Murat."

"I lied, Majlinda. You will never be home." He pierced her.

She grunted.

•   •   •

It was good to speak with Kaltrina and Arlinda.

Zana had been sold a month ago or more, but Arlinda and Kaltrina had been at the Factory all this time. Arlinda still told the stories on the mattress, and the little family Majlinda had created for them had grown. Anna listened, and Clarissa listened, and Irene, and Mariah, and girls whom Majlinda did not know. Now that Arlinda and Kaltrina and Zana were gone, Clarissa would tell the stories. She wasn't Albanian, but that didn't matter–what mattered was that the family still existed, that those stories could bring a little hope and meaning to lives utterly devoid of both.

Majlinda told them of her time at Madame Vaccaro's, and of the whorehotel in Hamburg. She didn't leave out the syphilis as she'd done for Valdrin–but she did leave out Valdrin; she didn't tell them she'd seen him, for she didn't wish these girls to think of boys from their own villages, or that they might be Gians.

And it was with these girls, finally, that she was able to plan her escape. They had been walked in through the front doors, which had not been locked–merely closed. The front doors led in through the sides of the anteroom as Majlinda had thought, so only one guard–albeit an armed guard–stood between the girls and freedom.

They had to overcome the guard, somehow, or distract him. Sometimes whoever was on duty would take a girl to the anteroom to rape her, and that could be their distraction–they could sneak up behind him and beat him over the head with a piece of wood from their futons.

"It's too light," said Majlinda. "We need something else."

But they had nothing heavier.

They could tie him up with the rope from the main room, the rope that dangled from the pulleys in the walls.

Majlinda shook her head *no*. "Could we hold him down to do it? Could we sneak up on him and together hold him down, or would he reach for his gun just in time?"

They could draw him into the hallway with a distraction.

"A distraction would draw all the guards," said Majlinda. "Suddenly we'd need to deal with all of them. And how would we slip past him to the anteroom and make our escape?" Something tickled at the corner of her mind: a vague memory or a half-formed idea.

"What would you do?" asked Kaltrina. "You shoot down every idea we have. How would you leave? If anyone can think of something, you can. You're the one who told us: 'Never trust them, never believe them, and remember we have a choice to defy them. There's a price for that defiance–in pain, blood, sweat, or screams–but there are times when it's worth the price. It would be worth it for any of you.'" Kaltrina shook her head defiantly, looking down at the tile floor of the raised room in the back of the building, where most frequently they talked about their plans. A Madonna stared back up at her, and almost she thought there were tears in its eyes. "We say the words every night," said Kaltrina. "We say what you taught us, and we teach it, and then we say, 'tonight I will tell you the story of such-and-such a legend,' or, 'tonight I will tell you the story of Majlinda, who saved Lule from burning, and who taught us that a whore can be a hero.' I wish we'd known you'd helped Miriam escape–it would have made the story better."

Majlinda's jaw dropped. She hardly believed anyone remembered what she'd said that day. She'd almost forgotten it herself. The girls recited it every night. They'd be risking their lives to do so; for a moment, Majlinda wished she could have warned them they were... but then she realized they already knew. They risked their lives every day, and only to remember her. *It's not worth it*, she thought. In her heart, she wondered what it could mean if a whore could be a hero. It wouldn't be her–but was there someone, somewhere, who could start in a place as terrible as the whorehotel and still make any difference at all in the world, push even so much as a grain of sand towards hope? There was so much darkness, she felt; and it hurt her more than just by scale, because she knew that such darkness did not have to be, that men and women chose to live in this world and to let the darkness be.

"There are doors," she said quietly, realizing what had tickled at her mind. "There are doors in the antechamber, beside the main ones to the corridor. The walls inside this main chamber are all simple, artificial things that could be cast down in a moment, if only you were not afraid to see what was behind them. We go to the room to the left of the big doors, the room that's even with the smaller set of doors into the anteroom. Quietly, we break through the wall and test the lock of the door. One of us seduces the guard, draws him somewhat into the hallway–but not too far into the hallway, lest he feel the need to turn back to his post. The other two slip through the hidden door into the antechamber, where they leave by the side door.

"Whoever escapes can't go to the police," added Majlinda. "The police here may be good men or they may be corrupt. And if you find one officer, maybe he's the wrong one. We found the wrong one in Italy, I think. When Lule and I escaped, we trusted an officer, and he took us back to the brothel. He betrayed us, and it was the last time I saw Lule. She was terrified when they dragged me away."

For a moment, the girls sat silently. The half-muted sound of a loud fake orgasm reached them through the door.

"Where do we go?" asked Kaltrina. "Where, if not to the police?"

"What happens to the girl who's left behind?" asked Arlinda.

"We go to the newspapers," said Majlinda. "We're naked, so we can't get far–people outside wear clothes. Those of us who escape find a house–a house that's empty, or one with a woman, with no men about–and get clothes. I hope there's a woman there, so you won't have to steal." *Stealing.* It was odd to think about stealing, after so long: about rules that society placed on you, expectations that were not backed up so thoroughly by the force of a gun or the closing of a fist. "Use the phone to call a newspaper or a newsroom. Get two newsmen.

"Tell them the story quickly. Get them to record it if you can. Send one back to his paper with the recording while the other goes with you both to the police. Ask the police to raid this place. Remember where it is, when you leave, so you can tell them where to come." Would that work? "If you can't find a house quickly at the beginning, find a woman with a cell phone." She thought it might work, if only they could escape. If the hidden doors were unlocked. If a Gian didn't come in while the girls were trying to go out. If the Albino didn't happen to walk in on them. If the guard was willing to be seduced. Too many *if*s for her liking, but better than not trying at all.

"What happens to the girl who's left behind?" asked Arlinda again.

Majlinda glanced up from the floor to meet the worried eyes of the other girl. "There is a price to that defiance," she said softly, sweetly. "In pain, or blood, or sweat, or screams–but there are times when it is worth the price." She smiled lightly and shook her head. "They cannot touch me, Arlinda. And they doubly cannot touch me if you are free. What can they do to me that has not already been done?" Her smile spread determinedly. "I have been raped, and broken, and groped, and prodded, and bitten, and burned. Every part of my body has been taken from me, all at once and a piece at a time. I could never close my eyes to that–you can't close your eyes against sensation, against the feel of a terrible man as he rides inside you and all your fight does nothing to him. Closing your eyes doesn't hide the soreness of your skin, or the feel of his teeth that you cannot chase away. But for everything they've done, they've never touched me. They don't know how." Majlinda's smile turned away to look upwards, up to the great wooden beams that licked up through the brick walls of the building and supported the ceiling, the great beams from which the redheaded girl had hung and beneath which she had died. "They are children, Arlinda. Terrible, cruel children, but children all the same. I wish..."

She shook her head lightly. "I wish the world were different. I wish that Murat had never learned to rape, and that the Albino knew what it was to feel the touch of the sun. I wish he knew why it mattered. But he doesn't–he's just a small man who never learned what beauty could mean or why the sunlight mattered. He's a murderer. He knows how to kill bodies, but he will never in his life touch a single living soul. Almost I pity him." The image of the redhead girl, *CRACK*-ing into the pillar, replayed itself in Majlinda's mind. "Almost."

"I'll stay," said Arlinda. "You go. I'll stay."

Majlinda shook her head. "I couldn't leave you here. I'd turn back for you, and be caught, and then Kaltrina would be alone. You two should go together, so you won't be alone. Get help and come back." Majlinda feared, shamefully, that she lied–that she could leave Kaltrina and Arlinda, and could run and run and run and never stop running, just to feel the grass again. "If you succeed, and escape, and bring help, I'll be fine. And if you don't, we'll find another way." She knew they wouldn't have another chance, but these girls would perform better if they didn't face how much rode on this escape. How much did they believe in her? Could she convince them?

"Kaltrina," Majlinda said softly, almost lyrically. "Lule. Arlinda. Zana. Miriam. Clarissa. Althea. Iskra. Margaret. Donna. Jendayi. Rose. Pili. Sofia. Leigh. Anna. Irene. Mariah. Niut. Celia Vaccaro. Murat. Armand. Peppino. Carmine. Rudalf. Heinrich. Egor. Hedeon. Oscar. Gerald. The Albino. The Factory. Madame Vaccaro's. The whorehotel. Here." Had she forgotten anyone?

"Majlinda," added Arlinda softly.

"Majlinda," agreed Majlinda. She was silent for a moment. "We need to escape. This is what I need you to do–will you help me?"

Chapter 25

Of Endings

"I know how lucky I am to have been born into a different generation. To have been born when and where I was–in a country where no one is shooting at me, I face no unnecessary risk of dying of HIV/AIDS, nor do I lack access to clean water. But merely through a twist do I hear about rather than experience the horrors of trafficking and slavery, because I know in my heart that 'there but for the grace of God go I.' I know that the victims are victims of circumstance. All of us must change that circumstance, and change it we can."

–Julia Ormond
UNODC Goodwill Ambassador on the Abolition of Slavery and Human Trafficking [18]

MAJLINDA KISSED Gerald when she passed him in the hall. It wasn't a hard thing to do, save that he was a little tall. He looked at her in puzzlement, and she smiled a small, secret, teasing smile at him and went on.

It would be best if the guard she seduced was Gerald, she knew–he was large and strong, but he was also mute–he could not cry as quickly for help when he realized the girls were gone. Would he even realize it?

She kissed him again the next time she saw him. He reached out to hold her this time, but she danced backwards out of his grasp, smiled softly, and winked. He did not grab her–but he seemed puzzled by her, by a girl who would give herself willingly.

When she kissed him the third time, he held her to him when she tried to pull away, and after a moment she turned her struggle into a mock-struggle, and she let out a little-girl-sigh when he released her. She was lucky he'd let go. She couldn't do this again until the girls were ready to leave.

On each of the next four days Majlinda forced herself awake at midmorning, while those around her slept. She walked down the hall towards the anteroom to see who guarded it, wearing a practiced look of exhausted distraction. If the guard noticed her, she yawned and then scratched her head as if she'd forgotten something, and she loitered for a moment before retreating. And on the fourth day, finally, the guard was Gerald.

Majlinda smiled a sleepy smile at him, and yawned her tired yawn. And then she went to find her girls.

"It's time," she told them quietly. "Wait two minutes, and follow me one at a time. The last door on the left, remember." Kaltrina swallowed, and Arlinda nodded; Majlinda smiled to reassure them before stepping back into the hall. She walked towards the anteroom, but slipped through the last door on the left before she reached it. This room ought to be in line with the hidden set of doors which, she hoped, would be found behind the artificial walls of this place.

Turning on the light revealed a girl–a German girl, she thought, with long blond hair–lying on her side on the futon here, too exhausted to wake with the light. Majlinda turned quietly away from her and counted off paces from the hallway, along the wall, until she thought she'd reached the edge of the hidden door's frame. She drove a pen swiftly into the thin wall–she'd slipped the pen from a Gian's pocket two days ago, when she'd noticed it and realized it might help her escape.

The pen didn't penetrate the wall, but did leave a dent in it. The wall reverberated under the strike, and Majlinda reached out to touch it and stifle its noise. She struck at it again.

By the time Arlinda entered the room, Majlinda had a hole as wide as a hand. She jabbed and prodded and hooked until there was room for two hands, and the two girls reached into the hole and held onto the weak material, and pulled and pushed until the wall cracked: a streak lanced left through the board.

Majlinda and Arlinda slid their fingers along the crack and pulled again, and pushed and pulled, and jammed with the pen, and jammed with their fingers. It hurt their hands but they kept working. The air around Majlinda seemed oddly still, and she felt each slow beat of her heart. *thump. thump. thump.* Minutes seemed hours.

When they had a hole almost large enough for a girl and they could see the handle to the hidden door, the blond behind them woke.

"What?" she asked, in a voice too loud by half. "What are you doing?" Majlinda winced. "Why are you–" Kaltrina slipped in through the doorway from the hall, and the blond's eyes swivelled to her. "Who–"

"Sssssssshhhh," said Majlinda. Kaltrina closed the door. "Ssssh. Kaltrina, help, here." Kaltrina slipped across the floor and helped Arlinda with the wall. Majlinda came over to kneel on the floor next to the blond's futon. "There's a way out," explained Majlinda. "No more clients. No more Gians. No more teeth under the light bulb. The grass at your feet, and the wind at your back, and the outside world at last. You were in Hamburg, weren't you?" Majlinda couldn't remember the girl's name. "This is another bad place. But everyplace isn't bad like this is, like that was."

The girl stared at her for a moment in disbelief. "They'll find us."

Majlinda didn't have time for this–there was no way of telling when guards might check the halls or check the rooms. "Then stay," she said simply. "Choose this life and stay, if you'd rather. Or go with these girls and be free. But remain silent–we don't have time for more. All I can do for you is give you a choice."

The girl's brows furrowed down. "Go with them? Where are you–"

"Someone has to distract Gerald," explained Majlinda. "That's me." She looked across the room to her girls, who had enough of the door exposed to step through. They tried the lock. Gently, gently, ever-so-gently they turned its handle, and Majlinda felt her stomach winding with it. With each passing moment, she half-expected Gerald to burst into the room, grunting his tongueless cries and beating them all–but there was only silence, only grating silence under the harshly loud near-silent sounds of the door.

Slowly, slowly, slowly they turned the handle back, and then they released it. Arlinda turned and nodded to Majlinda. Majlinda stood and walked to the hallway door–a touch on her shoulder stopped her. It was Kaltrina, and she was crying silently. Majlinda hugged her.

Kaltrina's dark eyes could barely look at her. Gently Kaltrina kissed her cheek and stepped back, to let Arlinda step forward and do the same. "Because we don't have to," said Arlinda quietly. "I'm sorry, Majlinda."

Why do you love her? Clarissa had asked, a lifetime ago. Majlinda remembered.

Because we have a choice, thought Majlinda. "They cannot touch me," she said quietly. "It's all right, Arlinda. It's all right." She smiled then, and she turned, and she went out into the hall.

The hallway that surrounded her was as empty and artificial as was this world from which she sought escape: only the floor was real, the floor and the large, open wooden door at the end of the hall, beyond which Gerald would sit, guarding the doorway between the two worlds like a great mute demon guarding the gates of hell.

Walking forth from the entiled gauntlets of Saint George upon the floor, Majlinda was full of fear and purpose. At the threshold of the great door, where the mosaic ended and blank tile began, she stood and watched Gerald, and let a smile that was not false wash across her face. It would work, she knew as she looked at him. She walked to one side of the door's threshold and bent down to touch the woodwork lightly, pretending to examine it; but truly she meant only to show off her body. And she looked over her shoulder at Gerald to see him watching her. He licked his great, mute lips and stood.

Majlinda laughed, and it was a joyful laugh whose kin had never been heard before in the artificial walls of this building.

Gerald was a man as cold and terrible as any. He had let the rope go. He had made the redhead fall. But he was filled with lust as easily as a greater man might have been, and his inhibitions were far fewer: he came across the room to her.

She jumped lightly away, twirling on her soft feet against the hard tile, laughing lightly across the hallway, a little further from the door. She took the back of her hand and ran it quickly through her hair—men liked that—and took a big step along the wall, as if to run from him, but all the while looking him in the eye and laughing and smiling. Let him think she laughed and smiled for him.

The mute reached suddenly for her, and again she flitted across the hall, though not too far back from where she stood—she didn't want him to realize what she was doing. She ducked and rolled, more lithely than she would have imagined she could have rolled even on the shores of the river Besim, even in the wildest grasses of the world. And she smiled at Gerald and she laughed gaily and she kissed the air invitingly.

Again he reached out to catch her, and again she ducked and rolled across the hall. Past Gerald, a ray of sunlight–the first naked sunlight she had seen in ages–beamed against the cream-colored tiles of the anteroom floor. It blinked wide and faded again! The girls had escaped!

Her laughter was free now, and she turned, laughing, to face the mute who eyed her so eagerly. "You cannot have me," she said, and there were bright tears on her face. "You could never have me. You could never have anyone–not if you spoke with the poetry of the wind. Not if you moved with the grace of a courtier. I am not for you."

Gerald's great hand struck at her, but she dashed backwards. She still faced him, though, and she would not run. "I'm sorry she never loved you," said Majlinda, still laughing in her joy and with her tears. "I'm sorry your father beat you or your mother hated you, or the bigger boys taught you poorly when you were young, or they stole from you or they laughed at you."

Again he struck at her, and again she darted back. This time his hand caught at her wet cheek, but he could not hold her. "I'm sorry about whatever is so terrible that it should make you like this. But it's not all right, Gerald–not to murder, not to rape, and you should never have let go of the redheaded girl."

He lunged at her, and she pulled a door to one of the side rooms open and he smashed his head on it and fell backwards. Inside, a Gian looked up from the girl he was beating. Outside, stumbling back from the impact of Gerald against the door, Majlinda felt her back unexpectedly hit something almost solid. She looked down and took a better footing, and her eyes traced across the partial banner she saw in tile beneath her feet. *In Pulverem Reverteris*, it read. What could it mean? She laughed again, and turned to find the Albino staring up at her hatefully, the grip of his gun held in one hand; his other hand was the solid bit that had held her up.

"You cannot touch me."

"Whatever you say, sweetling." A quiet *pop* cut through the air, and her shoulder jerked backwards. She looked down in surprise at the red blood that began pooling on her skin, and how she laughed!

"I'm Majlinda," she said, her wide smile sure and not desperate, and perhaps a little insane. Her eyebrows rose, and the dimples of her cheeks were full and beautiful. "What can you do?" she asked, swaying on her feet. Gerald caught her from behind, and the Albino raised his gun to point at her arm. She reached up–laughing through the pain of her shoulder–and pressed her hand against its barrel. "What can you do, poor man? I'm Majlinda. I'm a whore, and I'm more than you will ever be." A small explosion knocked her hand backwards from the gun, and as she looked down at it she thought she could see the floor through the palm. Sticky, warm blood ran quickly down her fingers and drained onto the floor. She wanted to cry out that her girls were free–but she would not, she would not cry out and tell these fools the truth. "*I* am free!" she said. "You couldn't take that away. You could make me a whore, but you could never make me any less Majlinda." She squinted in pain and sudden dark thought, the full pain of her body reaching through her shock, and all her memory of slavery suddenly warring with the new hope in her mind. And then she fell to the ground.

•   •   •

When she awoke, her body was racked with great pain; but her heart was buffered by that indomitable spirit which, in the rarest of people, may rise from the ashes of sorrow and pain to become as brilliant as the sun after darkest night. Her girls were free; and so would she always be.

Her head dangled limply down on her neck, and her arms were held above her head and to either side. She opened her eyes to see a Madonna before her: the Madonna on the floor of the raised room. Majlinda's legs dangled freely in the air below her, and matting blood ran down them from her shoulder, even as she felt the sticky grit of it in her hand. She raised her head and smiled.

"*Liria i ka rrënjët në gjak,*" she quoted softly. "Liberty has its roots in blood."

"About time, sugar-lips," said the Albino, his little body sitting on the floor beneath her, his eyes looking upwards to her from under his light eyebrows. "Bollocks but I thought you'd die. Wouldn't want you to die yet–we always need examples, here. Some girls are gone, cherry, but I've still got most of 'em, and we'll find the others." He turned his head. "GERALD! OSCAR!" he shouted. "Bring the poppies in!"

Majlinda waited silently as the girls were roused from their rooms and brought to stand before her. Arlinda was gone, and Kaltrina was gone, and the girl with the blond hair was gone. As the room filled, Majlinda knew what was coming. She was the redhead, now–and red indeed did mat her hair, where it had touched her bleeding shoulder while she slept. She tossed her head, but couldn't unmat the hair. It didn't matter. "I helped three girls escape today," she said in her storytelling voice, only more weakly–for she had little strength in her body, even as she had a heart that was full of joy. A *clunk* cut through the air as Gerald closed the chamber's insubstantial door behind the last girl. The girls were listening. "I've helped others escape before. There's another world out there, and it's worth fighting for."

A bullet drove upward into her leg, and she cried out. Her joy was pierced, but like a gel it closed about the piercing, and as blood drained from her and pain remained, she spoke again: "They can't destroy you unless you let them. They are small men, and they have no power over you."

Another bullet, grazing her other leg. She cried out again, less deeply, and through her pain she heard a crash. Beneath her, the door to the chamber was broken!

Black-clad men poured into the raised room, shouting and with weapons drawn, darting around the naked girls and towards the three who guarded them. Gerald dropped his gun and raised his hands. Oscar shot at one of the men, but the men wore armor and Oscar didn't, and three of them shot him at once. But the Albino's eyes were only for Majlinda. He shot her again in the shoulder which he'd shot before, and she swung on the ropes; the Albino fell. Had he been hit by the bullets of men? Majlinda hadn't seen. Or had he somehow been felled by his own vehemence, by his own torrent of terror that did not understand the sun? The sun?

Majlinda thought she saw the sun, almost, but that would have been impossible. There was no sunlight here: only a brightness, dancing behind her eyelids, trying to entice her there to sleep. She felt a jostling of her broken bones and a motion of her body, but it wasn't worth her time to cry again: she had so little time, she knew. Hands–men's hands, gentle hands after all this time–were under her, and they lowered her gently to the floor, to the one green rectangle of stone in all the mosaiced floor of this building. Something pressed firmly against her skin: against her shoulder, her legs, and her palm.

"Majlinda?" It was a voice she knew. Her father's voice, she thought. No, that was impossible. Her eyes opened, and the face looking down at her was strange to her. He was one of the men, she thought, one of the men in their armored padding, and he was not her father. "I'm William Loch. You're safe, Majlinda."

"Majlinda?" asked another voice–a more familiar voice, a voice that moved Majlinda's heart to hear, yet a voice that nearly broke her heart by the woe with which it spoke: Arlinda's face appeared next to William's. Kaltrina was only a second behind.

"They insisted on being here," explained William. "They had the press with them, and well–" he shook his head, as if this was oddly difficult for him. Why would it be difficult for him? "We need to get you to the hospital."

"Do you have a recorder?" asked Majlinda weakly. "A movie camera? Something?"

William shook his head. "The hospital–"

"*No*," said Majlinda, as forcefully as she could. "I might die on the way. A camera, first."

"I can get one–"

"I have one." A new voice–also a man's voice. "Sam Hullworthy. Your friends called me." He sounded oddly hesitant. "Are you sure you want us to film this, Majlinda?" It felt so good to hear her name from the lips of an honest man. "It won't be pretty. We can record just the sound, if you want."

"No," said Majlinda weakly. "Record it all." Light danced behind her eyes again, and they closed.

"Majlinda?" Kaltrina's voice. "MAJLINDA!"

Someone was shaking her–it hurt.

"Are you recording?" she softly asked.

"Yes," said the second man–Sam Hullworthy, she remembered. "Because you asked us to."

"Thank you, Sam," she breathed. "We were taken from Albania by Odeta, by Murat. Murat took us by boat from Vlorë to get jobs in Italia. They raped us again and again in the white room, and then in the Factory. Arlinda can tell you." Why were there stars behind her eyes? Once, when she was a girl, she had always been able to see stars if she closed her eyes, but as she'd grown older they'd seemed to fade, until they were only a memory. Now she could see them once again.

"I will tell, Majlinda," said Arlinda. "You saved us."

Majlinda coughed, and blood danced up into her throat. It tasted of salt, salt such as she had not tasted since the sea.

"Celia Vaccaro bought us," she said weakly. "She had a brothel in the same city. Via Solare–we escaped, and a police officer told us the brothel was on the Via Solare, and he forced us to go back. Miriam escaped, but Lule was caught with me.

"Vaccaro locked me in a cage in the basement, but she couldn't catch me. I was flying over the mountains, and she couldn't cage me. So she sold my body again. To Hamburg."

There was perfect silence around her. Were they even listening? She knew that they must be, and she forced all her strength into her voice, into the truth of her words and the depth of her storytelling voice: now it told stories that were true. Would they listen, if the stories were true? "There was an apartment building, on a canal. It had five stories. A bridge nearby. Across from it was a brick building with a walk on the first story, under pillars. Iskra died in Hamburg. There are hundreds of girls there... Maybe more–there might–" she coughed again. A rag came to her mouth, darted in and tried to catch some of the pooling blood that slipped warmly against her tongue, and darted away.

"There might be more buildings than the two I saw. A man called Ivan was in charge. He sold us here, and a van brought many of us. The Albino and Gerald–Gerald is the tall mute–killed a redheaded, pregnant girl the way they would have killed me. And then Murat came and sold Arlinda and Kaltrina, and I remembered them. I love them like sisters. I helped them escape." What more could she say? What mattered? How could she help them to save the other girls?

Desperately, with the last of her strength and all of her joy, Majlinda forced her star-covered eyelids open, and looked into the camera that looked at her, and she smiled. "There are good men in the world, still. It's just that they don't know, or they're prevented. Maybe they're afraid to see the truth. It's easier to close your eyes. But you are a good man, William Loch. You are a good man, Sam Hullworthy. Save them. Save my girls. And show the other men"–she tried to shake her head, but it would not move; her voice itself was terribly, terribly weak, and yet was far stronger than she felt–"Don't hide or turn away. Show the other men why they cannot close their eyes."

Life fled from her body with her storytelling voice; dead and lifeless, all that was left upon the floor was the lump of still-warm flesh, broken and battered and destroyed, that had been sold across half of Europe. But the blue eyes of her corpse lay open, and no man would close them.

THE END

Author's Note

EVERY DAY, THOUSANDS BECOME SLAVES FOR THE FIRST TIME. A century and a half after the American Civil War, young women are bought and sold in Times Square as in Tirana, in San Francisco as in Thailand. They are bought and sold in Japan, Australia, Italy, Cambodia, Israel, India, South Korea, the United States, Canada, Mexico, Saudi Arabia, England, Belgium, Germany, the Netherlands, and many more countries beside. It happens within the United Nations and in the source countries[1] of Moldova, Ukraine, Bulgaria, Romania, Nigeria, Serbia, Albania, and more.[2]

From Vlorë in Albania, it is only 44 nautical miles across the Strait of Otranto to Italy: a night's travel in a rubber raft with an engine on the back, and a relatively easy–if unsafe–journey for slaves and slave traders. If the weather is particularly bad, their bodies may soon wash up on shore next to the craft that was too small or too badly piloted to handle the sea in a storm. And if authorities chase them, the slave traders sometimes throw women overboard to delay their pursuers.

This sea crossing is one of many routes used around the world by the modern-day slave trade [14]. For land crossings in Europe, Asia, the Americas, and Africa, traffickers are known to sneak across borders where there is no legal crossing. They also bribe border guards, find legal pretexts for travel, or use forged identification or papers drawn up by bribed embassy personnel to cross border checkpoints [7, 15] or board international flights. The girls being trafficked can be kept silent

---

[1] "Source countries" refers to countries which are primarily a source of trafficked women, as opposed to destination countries. There is some overlap. Women are occasionally trafficked, for example, out of the United States, which is considered a destination country. That being said, the vast majority of slaves flow from poverty-ridden countries to countries with larger amounts of disposable income.

[2] Modern-day slavery in every country listed here, and many not listed, is documented in one or more of the following works from the bibliography: [14, 15, 25, 26, 13, 19, 9, 21, 5, 12, 8, 18, 24, 22].

by threats against themselves or their families. They may not realize they're headed for sex work, or, like Iskra, they might not know they will be slaves. Sometimes they are coached to fear the border guards more than they do their own pimps.

Majlinda's story–the fact that she wanted to escape, and that she never surrendered completely to the world of slavery and forced prostitution–made it necessary to show her only in brothels where physical confinement was the rule. Often it is the rule: girls may be forced to live and eat where they work, and may be locked behind heavy security doors under the eyes of surveillance cameras and guards [16]. Often, though, girls are coerced and confined by debt or perceived debt [10, 19], by fraud, by threats of violence to themselves or their families [14, 19], or by drug dependencies [4]. They may be confined almost as thoroughly by an inability to communicate with anyone–being strangers surrounded by foreign tongues and culture–as they would be by cold iron bars. Fictional debt structures ensure that a woman who earns her pimp a small fortune every week will never pay her way to freedom [11, 19, 10]. Are these fictions, threats, and isolation, used to force a woman to accept perpetual rape, any less terrible than mere physical confinement?

Women are killed in this industry. If they contract disease, grow too old or too worn, or become pregnant or for any reason unprofitable, they may be discarded to fend for themselves in a foreign city. They are commonly resold to new brothels, and they are sometimes killed–as an example to other girls, or if they somehow become so uncooperative that beating and starvation and gang-rape fail to make them useful. Health problems and emotional scars that last a lifetime may encourage suicide even years down the line, and sexually transmitted diseases may kill quickly or may haunt an ex-slave's long life, only to be passed on to her children. Majlinda's death, though atypically symbolic, is not without common precedent [14, 18, 26].

Scholars point to many causes of trafficking: lust and greed; the existence of poverty; globalization; or the divides between the rich and poor, the "Global North" and "Global South," the First and Third World, or men and women. All of these pictures are both incomplete and overcomplicated. It *is* important to ask why, and to understand what makes trafficking possible and profitable. But at the end of the day, scholarship isn't enough: these women are being stolen, confined, coerced, beaten, bought, sold, injected with drugs, starved, broken, raped, gang-raped, and murdered. Are we to spend our time only in wondering why?

> "There are thousands who are in opinion opposed to slavery and to the war, who yet in effect do nothing to put an end to them; who, esteeming themselves children of Washington and Franklin, sit down with their hands in their pockets, and say that they know not what to do, and do nothing; who even postpone the question of freedom to the question of free trade, and quietly read the prices-current along with the latest advices from Mexico, after dinner, and, it may be, fall asleep over them both. What is the price-current of an honest man and patriot today? They hesitate, and they regret, and sometimes they petition; but they do nothing in earnest and with effect. They will wait, well disposed, for others to remedy the evil, that they may no longer have it to regret."
>
> –Henry David Thoreau, 1849 [27]

Majlinda is already dead, and in a way I mourn her; but she was an honest fiction created to die, to remind us of all the slaves who still live and die today, of the millions who know what it is to be a slave. They live in cages built of our ignorance, maintained by our inaction, and paid for by our fellow human beings.

The US Trafficking In Persons Report for 2007 acknowledges approximately 800,000 trafficking victims each year, worldwide [26]. For reasons of nomenclature and politics, this figure only includes slaves who are sold *across international borders*. For a more comprehensive picture of slavery, in a field where it is notoriously difficult to get reliable data, the report cites a range of estimates from 4 million slaves worldwide at any time on the low end to 27 million on the high end. To give a sense of the scope of the problem, the UN's Pino Arlacchi pointed out at the close of the 1990s that the decade had seen perhaps as many as 30 million women and children sold in Southeast Asia alone, or nearly three times as many slaves as were sold *in the entire 400-year-history of the African slave trade* [1].

These numbers refer to slaves of all kinds. Of the 800,000 internationally trafficked slaves referred to in the TIP report, about 80% are women and up to 50% are underage. Whether the majority of slaves worldwide are primarily sex slaves or forced-labor slaves is an open question, and many slaves of both kinds are children.

When we turn our eyes from this slavery because it is hard to watch, when we fail to speak of it because it does not feel comfortable to speak of, when we fail to act on what we know or have learned, we allow slavery to exist unabated.

The countless slaves and soon-to-be slaves alive today are human men, women, and children, just like you and I are and have been. In a different life, it might have been me. It might have been you. It might have been—it might still be—our children, our cousin, our friend.

Majlinda came to remind us that this crime is real. A moment's online search can tell us that and point to some of the places where it's happened, and a quick look at a satellite map can show us those places are real, and nearer than we think. They may be just across the river, or near where we work every day, or even in the home a few doors down from ours. The crimes are real. The beatings, the buying and selling, the murders and the rapes. The women locked in closets, and the seven-year-olds outside San Diego.

This is why it matters that we overcome discomfort, and speak. Today you are the hope of humankind; you are the hope that we can end slavery.

You will more than likely never know what a slave endures. You will never endure that death and irrelevance of hope, the split personality brought on by the need to distance yourself from constant rape, the health problems brought on by unending abuse, the utter disdain of society, or the beating and trauma and damage and death experienced by a completely disposable woman at the very edge of our world.

And you probably can't stop slavery. But ask yourself this: Are you willing to try to stop it? You—you who are a free woman or free man, you who know what it is to touch the grass and swim in the ocean and be the property of no one—Will you do your part?

The rules of polite society make sex slavery a difficult thing to speak of; we have an inner voice, an almost in-born hesitation, that tells us not to speak of it. It doesn't fit in our polite conversations, it rarely finds a segue from our How-are-you's, and we would rather speak to our friends of something joyful than of something sad.

But sometimes speaking of a thing, admitting we have a problem, is the first step to finding a solution. If we let the world remain largely ignorant of slavery, if we don't overcome our hesitation and speak of it with our friends and our co-workers, our families and our church groups, at our PTA meetings and even at our schools–if we don't make sure we all know about slavery, and we don't try to stop it, then it will continue as before in the recesses and shadows of the world, forever. It will lie forgotten on the shelf of your mind, with only you remembering, sometimes, what a terrible problem it is and how you read a book about it once, and shouldn't somebody do something?

Will you do your part? Spread the word, at the least? And maybe even do more? (See http://www.riverofinnocents.com/act/ for a few ideas.) Because *the crimes are real.* The beatings, the buying and selling, the murders and the rapes. The women locked in closets, and the seven-year-olds outside San Diego.

And if we do not even talk about it, how will we ever stop it?

Pass this book to a friend, or tell them of it: tell Majlinda's story. Read elsewhere about these crimes and what they mean, and how real they are. *Learn.* And then *act.* Do not close your eyes; that would be Majlinda's wish.

Her storytelling voice was written for her girls–to bring a shred of hope into a world devoid of meaning, devoid of sunshine and freedom, devoid of all the things we take for granted every day. Words alone don't save people–but they can be a start. Tell Majlinda's story.

Would they listen, if the stories were true?

Tonight, I will tell you the story of Majlinda, who saved Lule from burning, and who taught us that a whore can be a hero.

Trafficking Emergencies

If a person's safety is in immediate jeopardy, call 911. Be sure to identify the case as a suspected case of slavery and human trafficking.

To report a suspected case of trafficking, or for referral to help you get help for a victim or survivor, a federal trafficking hotline is available at 1-888-373-7888. Calls can be made anonymously, operators speak English and Spanish, and professional interpretation is available for other languages.[3]

Many emergency services haven't been properly trained to handle human trafficking, so if the danger isn't immediate it's best to contact the federal trafficking hotline and let them handle the initial contact with police. If you must call police first, call the hotline afterwards–their help increases the chance that the police response will be appropriate.

You can also report trafficking via your state Attorney General's victim/witness coordinator or your local FBI.

For Countries Outside the United States:

1. Call the national or local trafficking hotline, if applicable.

2. If the suspected victim is foreign, contact his or her embassy.

3. If local law enforcement is reliable, contact local police.

---

[3]See http://www.acf.hhs.gov/trafficking/hotline/index.html

Sources and Resources

Sources confirming information presented throughout *River of Innocents* are available in the bibliography and at

<u>http://www.riverofinnocents.com</u>

There you will also find:

- An up-to-date guide on how to identify suspected victims of trafficking and where to go for help.

- Tools for introducing people to the concept of modern slavery, including sample letters and talking points, conversation-starters, templates for weblog posts and profile content, internet memes, email tools, fact sheets, flyers, etc...

- Ideas for how we can fight slavery.

- A place to ask the author questions about *River of Innocents*.

- Reading Group Prompts for those who want to discuss the book's structure or themes.

- News on the state of modern-day slavery, and connections to institutions that combat it.

Bibliography

[1] Pino Arlacchi, Director-General, UN Office at Vienna; Director, UN Office on Drugs and Crime. As quoted in *Refugee Reports*. US Committee for Refugees, Summer, 2000.

[2] BBC. I was sold for 2,000 euros. *BBC News*, October 3rd, 2007.

[3] Robert Elsie. *A Dictionary of Albanian Religion, Mythology, and Folk Culture*. New York University Press, 2001.

[4] Farley et al. Prostitution and Trafficking in Nine Countries: An Update on Violence and Posttraumatic Stress Disorder. *Prostitution, Trafficking, and Traumatic Stress*, 2003.

[5] Katherine Farr. *Sex Trafficking: The Global Market in Women and Children*. Worth Publishers, 2005.

[6] Laura Fraser. Italy's Sex Slaves. *Salon.com*, July 3, 2003.

[7] Carmen Galiana. *Working Paper: Trafficking in Women*. The European Parliament, 2000.

[8] Sophie Goodchild and Jonathan Thompson. 5,000 Child Sex Slaves in UK. *The Independent*, October 12th, 2007.

[9] Anabel Hernández. Prostituyen menores en campos agrícolas de San Diego. *El Universal, Mexico City*, January 11, 2003.

[10] Gilbert King. *Woman, Child for Sale*. Chamberlain Bros., 2004.

[11] Hetq Online. *Desert Nights*. Investigative Journalists of Armenia, 2005.

[12] Peter Landesman. The Girls Next Door. *The New York Times Magazine*, January 25th, 2004.

[13] Dorchen Leidholdt. Prostitution and Trafficking in Women: An Intimate Relationship. *Prostitution, Trafficking, and Traumatic Stress*, 2003.

[14] Victor Malarek. *The Natashas*. Arcade Publishing, Inc., First U.S. Edition, 2004.

[15] Meredith May, Deanne Fitzmaurice. Diary of a Sex Slave. *SF-Gate.com*, 2006.

[16] Meredith May. Sex Trafficking: San Francisco Is A Major Center For International Crime Networks That Smuggle And Enslave. *SFGate.com*, 2006.

[17] Piro Misha. Invention of a Nationalism: Myth and Amnesia. *Albanian Identities: Myth and History*, 2005.

[18] Ms. Julia Ormond, Goodwill Ambassador for the Abolition of Slavery and Human Trafficking, UN Office on Drugs and Crime. *Testimony before Subcommittee on Africa, Global Human Rights, and International Operations*. United States House of Representatives, International Relations Committee, June 14th, 2006.

[19] Janice Raymond, Donna Hughes, Carol Gomez. Sex Trafficking of Women in the United States. *Coalition Against Trafficking in Women, funding from the National Institute of Justice*, 2001.

[20] Janice Raymond, Jean D'Cunha, Siti Ruhaini Dzuhayatin, H. Patricia Hynes, Zoraida Ramirez Rodriguez, Aida Santos. A Comparative Study of Women Trafficked in the Migration Process. *Coalition Against Trafficking in Women, with support from the Ford Foundation*, 2002.

[21] United States Attorney's Office, Southern District of New York. 31 Korean Nationals Arrested Throughout the Northeastern United States in Federal Human Trafficking Case. August 16th, 2006.

[22] United States Department of State. *Human Rights Report, Albania*. US State Department, 2005.

[23] United States Department of State. *Human Rights Report, Italy*. US State Department, 1999.

[24] United States Department of State. *Human Rights Report, Italy.*
     US State Department, 2006.

[25] United States Department of State. *Trafficking in Persons Report.*
     US State Department, 2006.

[26] United States Department of State. *Trafficking in Persons Report.*
     US State Department, 2007.

[27] Henry David Thoreau. *Civil Disobedience.* 1849.

This bibliography is not meant to be an exhaustive list of the research materials used in the writing of this book, but rather to demonstrate support for various facts presented throughout. For more reading on the subject of sex trafficking, go to http://www.riverofinnocents.com/more/

www.ingramcontent.com/pod-product-compliance
Lightning Source LLC
Chambersburg PA
CBHW031340170626
46807CB00002B/775